Shuyani

(Hope)

by Leslie Curtis Davis

I Street Press

Copyright © 2013 by Cherie Goodenow O'Boyle

Printed in the United States of America

I Street Press

828 I Street

Sacramento, CA 95814

****

Davis, Leslie C. 1877-1969

   Shuyani (Hope)/ written by Leslie C. Davis

   Transcribed and edited by Cherie G. O'Boyle

   ISBN 978-0-9889839-7-7

LCCN 2013914175

Cover Design by Cherie G. O'Boyle

Dedicated to:

The technical field workers,

the greatest of all explorers,

to whom thrilling adventure is all in a day's work --

but seldom told.

Introduction

Sometime shortly after May 7, 1924, my maternal grandfather, Leslie Curtis Davis went to Peru, South America, to travel and work driving locomotives. He left behind my mother, Colette Germain (Blanche) Davis, 7 months-old at the time, and his wife. He did not return to his home in Oregon until September 8, 1928. During this time, he traveled the length of the Amazon River, returning to the United States from the state of Pará, Brazil, at the mouth of the river. Shuyani is a novel written by Les Davis in 1929, after his return from South America.

My brother, Donald Leslie Goodenow, and I do not know much about these years spent in the jungle. There were artifacts around our grandparents's house as we were growing up: some small spears, a blow gun, and the dried skin of an Anaconda snake. There is a small photograph album, under separate cover, with several intriguing pictures, but there are precious few details. About the only information we have is a letter composed by our grandmother. I have copied that letter here to provide context for the story.

Les' Trip to South America

He was just being graduated from the Oregon State College at Corvallis. He was now a horticulturist and I presume could have gotten a good job on some fruit farm. Just at that time he got a letter from Bill. Bill was a guy he met while they were both driving engines for supply trains in France during World War I.

Bill told about this job he had just got in South Am. and that they were short of help and why didn't Les go.

Of course for anybody who loved to travel as much as Les did that was a must and there was no stopping him.

So we all went to Michigan and you and I stayed with Mother while he went on and got started at the work.

They told him the air was too thin for babies but I guess if they were born there they got used to it. Anyway Les hadn't been there long when he drove this train to the top of a hill and suddenly saw a woman and baby that he thought must have been just about your age. He couldn't stop in time and the baby was killed. I don't remember whether the mother was killed too or not.

Well Les went completely to pieces and got so hysterical that his co-workers took him to his room and poured all the liquor down that they could until he was so drunk he went to sleep and I have forgotten how many hours or days he slept but when he awoke he remembered what had happened but it seemed so long ago that it didn't bother.

After a while he got tired of that job I guess or I don't know what happened but anyway he quit and got the job with the Standard Oil. That didn't last long so he came home.

By that time he had forgotten all he learned about raising fruit - or he thought he had so he didn't have confidence in himself to get a job in that altho he did raise beautiful fruit here on this place.

That's all I can remember about the trip but he did pick up a lot of information and history about the country, and wrote several articles for magazines.

Did you ever read his book-length manuscript called Shuyani? There are several copies around here. You were too young to read it while we were working on it and by the time we quit I presume I was so tired of it that I just put it away and forgot it. But it seems as if you must have read it.

Clara Janet MacDougall Davis

Shuyani is an exciting adventure tale of pure fiction. The story is based on many of Grandpa's experiences living and traveling in Peru and in the jungles of the Amazon River in the 1920s. After resting peacefully in dusty attics for 84 years, the book you hold represents Grandpa's publishing dreams finally brought to fruition. That's him on the cover, and in the window of the locomotive on the Dedication page.

Submitted respectfully to the family,
Cherie Goodenow O'Boyle

CONTENTS

CHAPTER ONE

Pampa Diablo

Superintendent Dillard regarded Rand with a look of astonishment.

"What! After all these years of laboriously cutting trails through the jungle, now when you can go direct to Molendo and take a comfortable steamer for New York you want to spend months more of monotonous traveling going down the Madeira and Amazon before you reach civilization. The postman who took a walk on holidays has nothing on you."

"That's it," admitted Rand. "I want to take my time and enjoy the trip. No reports to make, stop when and where I please, to be free and easy as life should be, not always forced to push on like I have to when someone is paying me to make surveys."

"Forget that free and easy idea. That's the wrong way to go back to the United States. They step high and move along there now; there is no time for free and easy tropical life."

"So I understand, " Rand answered. "That is one of the reasons I choose to go leisurely down the Madeira and Amazon instead of rushing back by the first available steamer."

Randolph Morley, familiarly called, "Rand" among his friends, had almost completed his second "hitch", as he called it, in South America.

Upon his graduation from a well known university in the United States with a B. S. degree in geology, he had come to the West coast of South America under contract to do general reconnaissance work for a North American Company interested in the development of any mining prospect that suggested possibilities worthy of promoting.

This work carried him into the remote Andean regions and into the jungle lands to the east of the mountains. Quite often his expedition consisted wholly of Indians and the nature of the environment forced him to pick up the Quichua Indian language, the language of the Incas -- the original inhabitants of the country -- the language of most Indians living in the interior mountain regions today, with the exception of the jungle where each tribe has its own dialect.

Rand had long been a student of Inca history and his contact with Quicha enabled him to learn many things which he would otherwise never have learned. Having been raised in the southern part of the United States, his acquaintance with the Negroes enabled him to get along with the Indians.

At the expiration of his contract with the prospecting company Rand had made a leisurely return to the United States, he had found himself, like most North Americans who are outside the country for a few years, completely out of step with conditions. The Rio Blanco Mining Company of New York had offered him a position at their mine in Northern Bolivia; thus he had come to the Rio Blanco mine.

To the north of Rio Blanco lies the jungle -- undeveloped, unsurveyed, unknown. White man has navigated the big rivers, but back in the brush the land is as unexplored today as it was before the days of Columbus, and the savages lead a life just as primitive.

There are always fantastic rumors about this region to be heard either in Bolivia, Peru, or Brazil. The inhabitants living on the border of this unknown region will tell stories of fabulous mines of which they have heard, some who claim to have absolute proof of the existence of such, and of savage Indians there to be dealt with. These are such tales of riches and superhuman men, or demons, as belong in Greek Mythology. What is true and what is not, no one knows. The jungles are there, white man goes in and is swallowed up for a time, or forever, or he staggers out, glad to escape with his life.

Scientific expeditions go in with elaborate equipment and come out some place, but they have only marked a line across this thousands of square miles of jungles. What did they learn of the inhabitants? Comparatively little! Perhaps they came upon some deserted homes, but even these were seldom seen, for the savage knows how to conceal his abode.

While working at Rio Blanco, Rand learned of a place called Pampa Diablo. This was a mesa or table-like formation standing some two thousand feet above the surrounding jungle, reported to have a rock escarpment surrounding it, unclimbable, inhabited by savages at league with the devil -- hence its name.

Certainly no one had ever been known to climb the perpendicular ledges, although glimpses of the inhabitants were sometimes reported, and raids were sometimes made on the more friendly Indians living towards the Urubamba, or Purus river.

When the unfortunate natives below were raided by these imps of Satan from his domain on the Pampa, they made no effort to resist, but fled panic stricken, for how could people combat the devil, or those in league with him.

3

Rand listened to all the fantastic rumors about Pampa Diablo, at first giving them little thought, as he knew there were usually a dozen idle rumors for each fact. At first he did not even credit the existence of such a place.

However, when his first vacation came instead of going to La Paz, like most of the gringos do who work the mines, he plunged deeper into the jungle. With an Indian carguero, he made his way along Indian trails as far as he could proceed into the unknown, considering he must return inside of four weeks.

All the Indians he met would tell him more of Pampa Diablo. One day he struggled to the summit of a high point overlooking the Purus valley. Far beyond in the blue haze of the distance, standing out alone, was a flat mesa-like formation. A powerful pair of binoculars enabled Rand to trace the outlines, and he could even see the blue grey scarp. Of course he could not trace the scarp around the mesa, but he could see that part, at least, of the stories about Pampa Diablo were based upon facts. Such a place did exist!

Rand spent hours studying the environments of the Pampa. He had his carguero cut some brush on the hillside to enable him to view the land in front. Then climbing a tree and cutting the branches that interfered, he was able to get a good view of the country in front of him. Beyond the Pampa Diablo which would be the north of it, was the grey-white horizon of the Amazon basin, while between him and the Pampa, and to the right and left, was all one vast sea of tropical jungle. From this point this looked flat, but close observation of the part of the foreground showed the topography not to be level, but to be composed of many small and steep haystack-like hills which Rand knew from experience it would be extremely difficult to cross. Cargueros could go only a short distance a

4

day over such terrain, for it was a grueling task for man alone to climb up and down the steep hills. To do so with a heavy load would tax the cargueros to the limit of their endurance. Rand could see there was no way of reaching Pampa Diablo except by days of toiling through the jungle barrier.

Long after he had retired that night, he pondered over the problem. It would be out of the question to attempt carrying food for such a trip. Could one live off of the jungle? Of course the question of meat would be simple, especially if intervening forests had few inhabitants, for there would be an abundance of game. But man could not live on meat alone for any length of time. The factor that would contribute to the meat supply -- the absence of human habitation, hence no hunting -- would eliminate the chances of supplying yucca and plantains -- bananas -- the bread of the jungle.

Inquiries among the Indians as to the possibility of reaching Pampa Diablo, always met with the same response. It could not be done! No one would for a moment think of going near the place. Rand understood all that. He knew the jungle Indians' antipathy to going beyond the boundaries of his country.

"But perhaps," he would suggest, "further on there may be others who would go a little way, and by relays the place could be reached."

"No, no!" they would always reply. "There is no one living near Pampa Diablo. How could people live near such a place?"

Upon his return to Rio Blanco, Rand's desire to visit Pampa Diablo was overwhelming. Knowing now the existence of such a mysterious place, the difficulties of reaching it only whetted his desire to do so. He pondered over the problem for days. One idea after another flitted through his mind, only to be discarded as not feasible. The difficulties were too well understood by Rand for him to go into the matter in a haphazard fashion.

Before any definite plans had presented themselves, the Montaña Linea Aereo announced the extension of their service to Baña, a point near Rio Blanco. This line was to carry government mail and passengers into Baña.

One of the pilots assigned to Baña, Alberto Vargas, was a native Bolivian, and also an old friend of Rand's. They had worked together in reconnaissance work, before Alberto took up aviation. When Rand learned of the air line to be established, he at once conceived the plan of getting Alberto to fly over Pampa Diablo where he, Rand, could jump off with a parachute.

How simple it all was now. But of course the air line official would not approve of such a procedure. It would have to be done in secret.

With this plan completed, he began active preparation. He ordered a parachute from the States and stowed it away, unknown to anyone. When his time was up he would take passage with Alberto in a plane, ostensively for La Paz, but when out of sight of Baña, they would swing around and fly over Pampa Diablo where Rand would drop off. Alberto would return to one of the emergency landing fields, then back to Baña, report engine trouble and say his passenger had gone on by some other means.

Shortly before the expiration of his contract, Rand approached Alberto with his plans. Although Alberto had known Rand intimately for a long time and had known him to engage in several reckless escapades, he was almost dumfounded at this absurd plan.

"Dios mio! No, no, my friend, I could never think of letting you jump to what I'm sure would be horrible torture, far worse than being killed by a parachute leap, if you attempt to jump out over the pampa."

"But listen, Alberto, you can't believe all this bunk about the Pampa Diablo. It's just Indian superstition concerning a place they know nothing about."

"Know nothing about!" exclaimed Alberto, so astonished that he permitted the cigarette he had just lighted to drop from his mouth unnoticed. "Carambo! All the world knows a Christian could never go near Pampa Diablo! Did not the devils kills four of my Uncle Enrique's peons, and carry off two of the girls, disappearing through the woods like spirits, leaving no tracks to be followed?"

"If they had left tracks like a herd of elephants, I doubt if the peons would have followed them," Rand replied. "It's just Indian ways, true to life. How many times do the Campas raid the Piros, or vice versa?"

"But all Campas are not infideles. Some of them are Christians, while theres is not a Christian within a hundred miles of Pampa Diablo," was Alberto's rejoinder. "No, my friend, " he continued, somewhat less agitated, as he patted Rand on the back, forget all about your crazy gringo idea of going where man was never intended to go."

Alberto could not have been more astonished had Rand suggested that he be permitted to drop into the authentic abode of the devil instead of this reputed one.

Rand was not in his usual jovial mood that night, and his room-mate, Jerry Long, noted the preoccupied state of his mind.

"What's the matter, Rand, getting cold feet over the proposed Madeira trip?"

A vicious kick at a shoe was Rand's only response.

"I thought you would return to the States like a man should," was Jerry's continued comment. "Gosh, I wish it was my time to go back. They say everybody has a car in the States now."

"Yes, and a lot of pleasure they get out of them," replied Rand, "going forty miles an hour to God knows where. But they are in a hurry to get there before they change their minds and think of some other place they want to go. Too busy driving to see anything but a road full of cars."

"So that's it? Ah! South America has got you like it gets 'em all. You will be looking for another contract back into the jungles before you get by New York. One hitch in the jungle is enough for me."

"Yes, that's what they all say," was Rand's reply, "but wait until you get back into the States and see."

Next morning Rand was up and whistling when Jerry awoke. Whatever problem Rand was worrying over the night before had evidently been solved.

"That's the spirit, old timer," Jerry said. "Forget the jungle stuff and begin to think of Broadway. They say the talkies have taken the town."

"They must be good," was Randolph's absent-minded comment as he started towards the mess hall.

One Sunday shortly after this Rand took the trail for Baña -- the jungle end of the air line.

"There are going to be some fine cocks in the pit today," was Alberto's greeting to Rand. "Jose Munzon has his Blue Devil here. Jose never loses a fight."

"Well, it's about time, I think," said Rand, "I feel lucky."

"Me too," replied Alberto, and then in a more melancholy mood, "but there will be no money to be made since they will all want to bet on the Blue Devil. I don't suppose I can get a boliviano on the fight."

"Oh, yes you can. I hate to take your money, but I should strip you for turning me down on that Pampa Diablo trip."

"No, you don't get any money from me on Blue Devil," said Alberto. "That bird never loses."

"Tell you what I'll do, Alberto. I'll bet you one hundred bolivianos against that trip."

"But -- " began Alberto.

"No buts to it. I've got one hundred bolivianos I don't need and you say you can't lose. Come, take them. Don't back down on your judgment."

Seeing Alberto hesitate, Rand began to tell him he did not know a fighting cock when he saw one.

"Well," said Alberto, "I hate to rob you but you gringoes have plenty of money, so I'll take you up. But it's just like -- what do you say in your country, "take baby from candy?'"

"Yes, that's it," said Rand, "so come on, baby, put down the candy."

Late that afternoon the Blue Devil turned up his toes and his trembling head settled to the ground. He had fought his last fight! Alberto was trembling also. With blanched face he turned to Rand.

"Cheer up, it's my funeral, old pal," Rand said. "Come over here and I'll tell you how we pull it."

"But where did that scrubby cock come from? He looked terrible, but he -- he --"

"Yes, he looked terrible and fought in the same manner, " said Rand, laughing. "Listen, pal, that was Gallo -- cock -- Diablo from Pampa Diablo. I'll send you a dozen from there after I've had time to pick out some good ones. This Gallo was a runt that got chased off the Pampa because he could not fight."

Alberto turned and starred at Rand in silence. What was the use of trying to reason with one who made a joke of everything, and who would not listen to reason. "Muy bien," was all he could say. "When do we start?"

You leave Baña Friday morning at seven o'clock. I'll leave Rio Blanco the day before and will be awaiting you at the Cerro Verda field alone. As soon as you alight, I'll jump in and we will be on our way. We had better not talk too much or someone will suspect a coalition."

Rand did not want to give Alberto a chance to argue the matter. Now that he had his promise he knew it would be kept; therefore the best thing to do was to treat the matter as a closed incident.

"What did you take off your friend, Alberto, at the cock fight today, Rand?" one of the boys asked in the mess hall that night. "He looked like he wagered his best girl and lost her, along with his month's wages."

"He still has his girl and most of his wages," Rand replied with a grin, "as far as I know. His dejection was, no doubt, due to the fact he had made a bad guess -- a question of pride, you know."

"Where did that scrubby looking cock come from that cleaned Blue Devil? No one but you seems to be in on it. Why didn't you let a few of your friends in on the secret so we could have a chance at a little easy money without having to slave in the mines for everything we get?"

"Slave for what you get, eh?" Rand chuckled. "All I ever saw any of you do was to stand around and advise a bunch of peons how to do a job. Giving advice is considered recreation, not work. Look how many people do it for sheer joy. You see

10

that cock cost real money in La Paz; not having his keeper on the trip, he didn't look so well, but he was in good shape otherwise."

CHAPTER 2

Meeting the Savages

The following Thursday Rand left over the trail presumably for Requeña, the first lap of the road for the Madeira route to the Amazon. Since the most likely way of getting away from Pampa Diablo would be by following some stream down to the Amazon, and since he knew he would be fortunate if he did not lose even his clothing on such a trip, he planned to take no money; therefore, in order to have funds when he should get out, just before starting he had sent five hundred dollars to the American consul Manaos, Brazil, with instructions to pay it to one Randolph Morley, North American citizen, upon his appearance in person.

Rand had all of his belongings in a compact kit which he himself could carry. However, the superintendent at the mines insisted that he should take one of the company mules to carry his kit, and he was to leave the mule at Requeña to be returned by the next party coming in.

Rand traveled most of the day along a good trail over undulating foothills. Mid afternoon, he met a party going into the mines. Writing a note that he was in a hurry and had no time to be bothered with a mule, Rand turned the note and mule over to the in-bound party, took his kit on his back and continued on his way.

Late afternoon he took a side trail that led up a hill to the right; about half a mile brought him to the top of the hill where there had recently been cleared several acres of the flat hilltop. A small shack with a Montaña Linea Aereo lock on the door stood at one edge of the clearing. This contained gasoline and the place was called Cerro Verda, one of the emergency landing fields of the newly established air line. After eating a cold lunch he made himself comfortable for the night.

At daylight he ate a cold breakfast of canned goods as he did not want to build a fire for fear of attracting the attentions of some nearby Indians who would give the secret away. He then packed everything and awaited Alberto.

About seven-fifteen he heard the drone of a motor overhead and soon a plane shifted west to head into the wind. Skipping the treetops at the west, it settled in the opening. Rand hurried out and crawled aboard. Alberto taxied back to the west end again to head into the wind, and they were off.

Swinging far out to the west in order to double back out of sight of Baña, they headed then to the northwest towards where they knew Pampa Diablo lay. In about an hour they could see Pampa Diablo rising out of the jungle surrounding it, like the enchanted mesa it was meant to be. It began to enlarge before them.

First they flew directly over the Pampa. There were the brown-grey specks that showed the characteristic palm-thatched huts of the jungle; toward the north they were larger, more numerous, and symmetrically arranged as would be a village.

As they circled the entire Pampa, Rand could see scarp breaking down towards the south. There were green streaks breaking through the grey, showing where drainage had broken through and vegetation set in.

Why the Pampa had a far greater population than the surrounding jungle, was now quite apparent. Obviously its approximately two thousand feet of elevation above the neighboring lands gave it a theoretic temperature of six below the other land; then, the air drainage would contribute towards making it a more agreeable climate. No doubt there was good soil drainage also, which would mean few mosquitoes. These factors would explain why it was a more desirable place in which to live than the adjoining land. Its physical features made it, no doubt, easy to defend.

All these thoughts came to Rand as they circled around over and near the Pampa. He could not tell Alberto what was passing through his mind, of course. Besides, Alberto would not understand; few people seemed to understand Rand's inner thoughts, when he tried to voice them.

"What a wonderful thing is law and order," Rand mused as he gazed down at the Pampa. What was the "law and order" of the Pampa? Was it a cannibalistic monarchy or was it a communal government? Oh well, he would soon find out.

Rand would have liked to explore the place from the air for hours, but it could not be done. There was insufficient fuel for the plane to tarry long. Alberto must start back with a good safe margin.

Over on the southwest, right on the margin of the Pampa they had noted a pajanal, as the open places free of timber, are called. Rand pointed this out to Alberto who nodded and headed over it. The open space was several acres in extent. No huts were near. Rand had two objects in wanting to land away from houses. First it would give him time to form contact with the savages in a less spectacular manner, thus

14

giving them time to get over any panicky reaction that would be caused by too sudden contact; and second -- well, poor Alberto had worried enough about the trip without having to witness the tragic ending -- if tragic it proved to be! Alberto had been a true pal and if another white man was to sacrifice his life in trying to pry into the mysteries of the unknown, Rand preferred to let the drop curtain of the tropical jungle cut off and spare his friend the necessity of witnessing the tragedy.

As they passed over the pajanal, Alberto gave Rand an imploring look and pointed back towards Baña. Tears were in his eyes and Rand could see his lips quiver as if pleading in prayer. Rand shook his head and looked quickly away. He could not bear to contemplate Alberto's dejection. He had his kit bag securely strapped on, also the chute in place, ready for the jump.

Suddenly Alberto decided that since Rand would not listen to reason, he would take matters in his own hands, and he accordingly headed back towards Bana. Rand saw the move and immediately started climbing out. He would jump just where he was and take a chance. When Alberto saw Rand's intention, he quickly swung the plane back. Since there was no way of changing Rand's plans, there was nothing for him to do but go on with the project.

As they passed over the pajanal Rand grasped Alberto's hand in one long, firm grasp. Then placing his finger to his mouth, he wagged it back and forth in front of his face -- the characteristic Spanish sign for secrecy. Then he started again to jump. Alberto pulled him back, at the same time pointing below. They had passed far beyond the pajanal.

Circling again, Rand was ready when they reached the clearing. With a last smile he looked at his companion, then was gone.

Pulling the rip cord, he soon felt the tug and found himself suspended, floating toward the ground. Looking to the east he could see the plane making a wide circle. He waved his hand in a last farewell, then began to look towards the ground which seemed to be coming up to welcome him. There was nothing but tall grass. If he could only make it, but he had jumped too late, he was going into the woods. The weight of the pack in addition to his own weight was a heavy load for the parachute, but he noted with grim satisfaction that it had withstood the shock.

Rand had read that in parachute jumping the passenger crosses his legs to prevent straddling objects. The chute was apparently directly over the edge of the pajanal. A moment later he shot through the canopy of vines in the tree tops. The hole he made in the foliage in passing through forced the cords together, closing the chute with a rush like an umbrella; but the cords had begun to foul in the brush and soon the chute stopped, completely demolished, while Rand dangled below suspended by the cords, some few feet from the ground. He climbed onto one of the branches where he freed himself of the wreckage. Dropping his kit to the ground he quickly followed, then hurried into the open pajanal.

After dropping Rand, Alberto had circled and was coming back overhead. He was watching the chute when it reached the tree top. He had seen chutes drop in the open country, while at training school, but he had never seen, or thought of what would happen to one in the jungle. Therefore imagine his surprise when apparently the chute was swallowed by the earth. He was looking at it when it suddenly was no more. From his position, he could not distinguish the canopy-like,

16

vine-covered, small tree that blended with the surroundings which had swallowed the parachute.

One circle back over the pajanal at a safe distance to look for his friend, revealed nothing, for at the time Rand was under the tree trying to free himself from the wreckage. The leaves overhead completely concealed him.

Seeing nothing of Rand, Alberto swung to the south and left the region of Pampa Diablo as fast as the plane could take him, thoroughly convinced that he had seen his friend disappear into the mouth of hell itself.

When Rand got clear of brush into the open pajanal, the plane was a mere speck in the southern sky. "Strange that Alberto should be in such a hurry," he thought, not understanding how spectacular had been his disappearance as observed from the plane. "Well, anyway, I am on Pampa Diablo," he grinned to himself. "Now for getting acquainted."

Looking over the situation Rand decided his landing place was as good as any for a camp. He knew civilized man has no chance with a jungle Indian in the brush. The Indians' eyes and ears are sharp, they see and hear everything, while civilized man sees nothing. The romantic tales of whites fighting against great odds on the North American plains are all very good -- there a white man's weapons give him the advantage. But the close proximity of a jungle fight makes weapons almost equal, while the acute jungle knowledge of the savage gives him an advantage against which the white man is helpless.

The more he looked over the site the more pleased he was with it. Here was an open space of several acres, near the center a big boulder suggested some protection from ambush. Taking his pack he went to this boulder and decided it was an ideal place for his purpose. It was still early in the day. They had flown over a great deal of Pampa Diablo and the Indians had certainly seen the airplane. Of course they would keep it in sight as much as possible. No doubt some of them had seen the dark speck fall from the plane, then spread its beautiful odd-shaped wings and settle to the earth at the pajanal. Curiosity would do the rest! What Rand wanted to do -- what he <u>must</u> do -- was to form contact with the Indians as soon as possible, while they were still excited over seeing the monster in the sky overhead. If he could form contact at once while they were still under the spell of the mystery, his chances were much better. They saw him flying to them, why could he not fly away, if he so chose? Above all, he must not go into the brush!

Following this line of reasoning, Rand's first move was to start a fire. Some broken branches near the clearing made this simple on this clear, dry day. After he had a good fire, he cut some green branches and placed them on the fire, leaves and all, smothering the blaze. He soon had a column of smoke that he reasoned must be visible for miles. After getting his fire signal going he then removed from his kit some trinkets, -- a small mirror, a pair of scissors, and a mouthorgan. He placed them on a near-by rock, all the time keeping a close watch on the borders of the pajanal, especially towards the east where he knew the nearest huts to be.

His next move was to get upon a boulder, where he knew he would be visible from all sides, then placing his hands to his mouth he hallowed as loudly as he could, at the same time facing various directions. He repeated this at intervals. Nothing but silence met these efforts. But Rand only smiled -- and waited.

Nothing happened until well into the afternoon, after he had been sending out his signals for hours. But at last he heard a distinct reply, far off to the west. Rand knew enough about Indians to feel quite sure that this reply to his shouts did not come from an approaching party. He knew very well that they had been looking him over from ambush for sometime before deciding to reply to his calls. He knew that at that very moment he was under surveillance and that all his actions would be observed; he knew that his reception -- perhaps his very life -- depended upon the way in which he responded to the challenge from the brush. Under no circumstances must he leave the open and seek shelter or prepare for attack!

With hands open and above his head, that all might see he had nothing in the way of weapons, he replied to this call. Complete silence was his only answer; but Rand realized that the next few moments held his destiny.

Outwardly calm, but with a pounding heart, he waited. At last he started turning slowly, with hands still elevated, and began facing each point of the pajanal in turn. When he had completed but half the turn and was facing east, a lone savage arose from behind a boulder, well out into the pajanal and stood with arms folded on his breast.

Rand nodded his head in the most sophisticated gringo style, waved his hand, then again assumed the same pose as before. With an upward wave of the hand from the savage, a score of men stepped into the opening on all sides. Not a sound had been made. All were armed with chunta -- palm -- lance-like spears, or bows and arrows, all of the same material. They were all dressed in cuzmas, the long flowing robe worn by many of the savages in this region. They were barefooted, as are all jungle inhabitants.

Realizing that the fellow who showed himself first was the chief, or curaca as an Indian chief is called in this part of the world, Rand continued to face him and paid no attention to the others. He motioned the curaca to approach, but the latter remained as he was.

Rand sensed some action behind and glanced over his shoulder. The whole pajanal behind him contained a circle of savages, with either bows or lances drawn, and they were advancing towards him. The crisis was approaching.

Rand was naturally unemotional and usually had complete control of himself under any pressure, but his knees began to tremble and he felt himself weakening as the tenseness in the air increased. Mustering all his courage, he slowly but firmly, turned his back on the advancing warriors and faced the curaca as before. He could still sense the steady advance of the savages in the rear, but he did not dare turn to look at them. It seemed hours that he stood there, bravely trying to conceal all evidence of emotion which wrecks the human body when it is faced with destruction. When he knew they must be within a few yards of him, he saw the curaca raise his open palm. The savages halted. Then the curaca began advancing towards Rand.

As he came closer, Rand gazed at him in open-mouthed wonder, completely forgetting his own danger in his astonishment. The savage was not an Indian at all, but a white man -- and with red hair!

The astonishment at seeing white men instead of Indians, as he had been expecting, completely upset Rand's line of reasoning; and momentarily forgetting the strained relations, he stepped down off the boulder and started towards the curaca with outstretched hand. It was almost like recognizing a friend in some stranger. In fact, Rand was almost at the

point of saying, "Why, I thought you people were savages."
But he did not get that far!

The curaca sprang back, crouched, thrust forward his
lance, and stood poised for a lunge. A rattle and grunt told
Rand very plainly that every other man of them had assumed
the same attitude. It was quite evident that, although white
they had appeared to be, they knew nothing of white man's
custom of the friendly handshake. What was to be done now?
He had evidently violated their code of ethics and he must
retrieve the lost assurance of friendship.

Remembering the pose with arms on chest, Rand assumed
this position with a very slight nod toward the leader. Slowly
the lance was lowered and with the relaxation in the tension,
Rand began to smile as he always did after being confronted
with a situation that taxed his ability to the limit. With a wave
of his hand towards his fire and kit, he motioned the curaca a
welcome and sat down upon the boulder he was standing by.

As the sullen attitude of the savages gave way to the
overpowering trait of human nature -- curiosity -- glances
went from the strange garb of their visitor to the brown kit
bag.

Looking over his host, Rand noted that several of the
Indians had the reed whistle, queña, or musical instruments,
which are common with the South American savage. These
are made by binding a bunch of canes of varied lengths
together. The savage blows into the end of this bunch of canes
alternately producing a sort of doleful sound.

Pointing to one of these whistles, Rand put his fingers to
his mouth and blew. The native grunted a "yes" and Rand
then pointed to the harmonica on the rock nearby and made a
sign to denote that its purpose was similar.

This information was received with great interest and Rand was able to pick up the mouth organ without arousing their suspicion. Had he reached for it before its use had been explained, he knew he would have been run through with a dozen lances before he had moved a step. As it was he was permitted to pick up the musical instrument and start demonstrating its use.

Rand was not an accomplished artist with the harmonica but he could, at least, get several different tones out of it, and this music was received with delight by the astonished natives.

They immediately forgot all about their arms. All looks of hostility had now disappeared and only curiosity and interest were manifest. From the mouth organ they turned their attention to Rand himself. They pulled at his garments, feeling of them curiously. They made signs and jabbered about his hair and eyes. Rand had light hair and blue eyes and he noticed that while some of them had the black hair and dark complexion of the Indian, most of them had rather fair complexions and reddish hair, but there were no blue eyes. All of their eyes were velvety brown, and they were decidedly of the white race.

But what interested these natives the most of all was Rand's shoes. They pointed at them, felt of them, and all talked at once. In fact, they seemed to consider the shoes quite a joke. The curaca maintained all the dignity his curiosity would permit, but he too, was plainly interested in this strange visitor.

Since night was coming, Rand was anxious to reach some kind of understanding before it became dark. Turning to the curaca he rubbed his stomach and pointed to his mouth, to suggest hunger. They all understood and began to jabber among themselves, not a word of which Rand could distinguish, although he was familiar with several different Indian dialects. At last the curaca pointed to the east and turned in an inquiring manner to Rand.

"Sure, old boy, I'll go home with you, " he replied.

Whether for politeness of for other reasons, the curaca had one of the younger men carry Rand's kit and they struck out east through the jungle. There were no trails, but the savages made their way with ease and maintained a speed which required all of Rand's jungle craft to keep the pace. Most of the savages had gone on out of sight while Rand kept beside the curaca. After about a mile, they came to a trail which went up a gentle slope for a way and then was level again. Looking back from this trial, Rand could see all of the pajanal; even the faint smoke from his signal fire was still visible. He knew that he had been watched from this point long before he had been approached.

Along the trail which they followed were plantains, yucca, corn and many other plants common to the jungle and familiar to Rand. Presently the beating of the trocan told of some message being broadcast by those loudspeakers of the jungle. These trocans are logs hollowed out in the center and are used by the Indians to send warnings. They do this by pounding on the logs, drum fashion.

Shortly before sundown they reached the village where several women and children were standing around at the entrance of a large muloco -- house. The houses were built large, circular in shape with palm thatched roofs. They had an entrance at each side of the circle directly opposite each other. There were no partitions dividing the interior, but each family had space assigned to them. In the case of the curaca, who apparently had several wives, occasionally a wife seemed to have a place assigned to her alone, while in other cases two wives might share a space between them.

Each apartment had its own fire for cooking. The fires consisted simply of bonfires built on the ground and were usually built toward the center, of in front of the apartment.

The curaca moved freely among his various wives' apartments, sampling the foods offered by each as he did so. One of the wives seemed to have something extra, as the curaca favored her culinary efforts with the most of his grace. She offered a large earthenware pot containing a generous amount of what appeared to be a savory stew. As a special guest, Rand was invited to partake of this stew. He was furnished with a half of a big gourd, which is what is used among all the jungle inhabitants for bowls. This bowl was filled with the steaming stew. The curaca then gave him a half of a large bivalve, the shell of the freshwater mussel, to use for a spoon.

Not having eaten all day with the exception of the cold lunch which he had for breakfast, Rand had a good appetite. The stew showed a lack of civilized man's seasoning, but otherwise it was very palatable. "It has the making of a good clam chowder, or oyster stew," Rand thought, "if only it had a little salt, butter and milk." It was too dark by this time to see what the stew looked like, but he good distinguish besides the meat, the taste of of yucca, a starchy tuber which is a very good substitute for potato.

A tropical thunderstorm came up soon after dark, driving everyone indoors. As Rand did not understand their language, all communication had to be done by signs and signs could not, of course, be seen in the dark. Therefore, Rand retired to the apartment which had been assigned to him and, reclining on the ground with his shoulders on his pack, watched the strange figures by the flickering light of the various cook fires. What a strange world it all was! Here he had apparently dropped down out of the sky among what was reputed to be one of the most savage tribes left in the world, and they had received him as a matter of course. What would Alberto think if he could see him now! "Poor Alberto," he mused. "It was too bad to do him the way I did, but how else could I have got here?"

While thinking of these things Rand fell asleep and although he awoke at intervals throughout the night, as all outdoor sleepers will do, he felt as secure as when he was in the quarters at Rio Blanco.

CHAPTER 3

The Interpreter

At daylight all were astir. Rand went out and walked around the yard looking at the other houses. There were five big houses in all and Rand estimated each house must hold about ten families.

Now he could see the women and children better and he marveled still more as to why these people were white. He had never had much faith in the sensational reports of tribes of white Indians in South or Central America, but what else could one call these?

Soon the curaca joined him and the sign language began again. While they were strolling about the place they came upon two girls with ollas, big earthenware jars, bringing water from the spring. The curaca stopped and began to talk to them, evidently giving some instructions.

One of the girls had the fair complexion and red hair of these people. But the other girl was of a distinctly different type. She had the blue-black hair and liquid black eyes of the Indian. She was dressed just as were the other women, in the typical cuzma robe of rich mahogany brown, and at the first glance looked like any ordinary Indian girl. But as Rand watched her, he was impressed with the intelligent expression in her face, unlike the blank look of an Indian.

"This is no ordinary Indian woman," Rand thought as he watched her.

The girl had noticed his interest in her and began digging her big toe into the ground in an embarrassed manner. To relieve her confusion, Rand started to look away, but as he did so he caught a glance from those deep black eyes -- a glance that somehow compelled his eyes -- though just why he could not say.

As the girls were about to pass on, Rand made a gesture to the curaca, pointing to the black head of the one and to the reddish brown of the other. The curaca understood and pointing to the girl with red hair he placed his hand on his own breast; then he pointed to the other girl, then off to the southwest towards the Urubamba River.

So that was it! One girl was the curaca's own daughter, while the other, the black-haired one, had been captured by some raiding party.

This gave Rand an idea. Addressing the black-haired girl he pointed to the olla of water and asked, "Yacu?" This is the Quichua word for water.

"Ari," -- "Yes" -- replied the girl in the same language.

Just as he had thought, the girl was from the Quichua country and could speak a language with which he was familiar. Now he could have an interpreter. What luck.

"What is your name?" he asked the girl.

"Shuyani."

Shuyani, the Quichua word for "hope". Although Rand knew the name was common among the Quichuas, he was struck by the appropriateness of the name just now.

The curaca too, was elated over learning that Rand could talk with Shuyani. He immediately flooded her with questions in such rapid succession that none of them could be translated.

Realizing that he was making no progress, the curaca stopped and began all over again. Where was Rand from? Why did he come? Could he fly away as he had come?

Rand answered all the questions as best he could. The curaca was surprised that the bird could not alight on a tree, but if not, surely it could light upon the big rocks in the pajanal? No? The curaca pondered. Suddenly he asked, "Were you alone on that bird?"

"A friend was with me who went back."

The curaca shook his head in meditation.

After breakfast Shuyani was taken from her regular work and told to accompany Rand and the curaca around the grounds. There were some splendid gardens with abundance of fruits and vegetables of all kinds. These included all the indigenous economic plants as well as some that were not indigenous, and there were some plants unknown to Rand.

Everyone about the village seemed to be assigned to some particular task. A group of girls under the direction of two old women were working under a shed making earthenware utensils of all kinds. Another old lady had charge of the weaving department where cotton was spun and woven into cloth. Rand had seen the jungle Indians weaving and knew there was nothing complicated about the simple looms the jungle Indians use. Many times small girls would be operating them. Why, then was there so much supervision here?

As he drew nearer he was surprised by the beauty of the cloth they were making. Instead of the coarse cloth, almost burlap in texture, the savage usually makes, this was almost like silk. In fact, there was silk in it, he saw upon closer examination.

"Where did this silk come from?" he asked.

"That," said Shuyani, "is huimba as it grows here."

Huimba is the silky cotton that grows on trees common throughout the jungle.

Rand picked up some of the lint and was astonished to find that it was at least a three inch staple. He knew that huimba grew to only about one-half inch, as a rule, which of course was too short to spin; but this was so long that it could be spun into a soft, silky skein. There was evidence of expert selection and plant breeding to produce this type of lint.

He saw as he continued through the gardens, the same expert supervision everywhere manifest. An old man, the curaca told him, went through the plantain each morning and marked stalks whose stems were to be cut for the day's food. No one could cut a stem which did not have his check. Expert judgement was used on everything.

Returning towards the village, the curaca led Rand towards another large shed. Here there were stacks of bamboo and chunta (palms). Inside were men and boys converting this material into knives. There were rows of flat sandstones of all textures. After the knives had been shaped out in the rough, they were ground into shape on the coarse stones, then a razor edge was ground on the finer stones. The chunta was made into heavy daggers, and into javelin tips; the daggers were used for butchering meat animals. The short bamboo knives were made for all general purposes. They were cut with one edge bevel, always ground on the inner-side. This grinding formed a razor-like edge of the hard epidermis tissue of the bamboo which held a long time if used correctly. These artisans always cut with a drawing motion which prevents the grain of the knife blade from splintering.

Later Rand saw one of the women skinning a deer with all of the ease of one equipped with a hunting knife. Not only was the animal skinned, but it was also cut up with this instrument. Of course the operator never cut directly against a bone. A joint was bared and a twist given to expose the ligaments which were then severed with a surgeons' expedition.

"These knives are called chichica," Shuyani explained. "That is a word from the Pano dialect. There are many Pano and Quichua words used here, But perhaps you do not notice them," she continued.

"I do not know Pano, " Rand replied, "but I do notice some Quichua now, since I know what to expect. At first I could never get a word they were saying."

Shuyani told Rand that the Pampa was called Purac and that the Ruler's name was Chinawa. The ruler lived in the northern part of the Pampa -- which was much better developed than the southern part -- at the capital which was called Churic. She said a runner had been dispatched to inform Chinawa the particulars of Rand's arrival, the trocan not being able to transmit details.

CHAPTER 4

Camachicushca -- The Law of Puca Uma

It was near noon when they returned to the village. The foragers were coming in with the day's food and preparations were underway for the mid-day meal. Noticing a basket of large white grubs, Rand asked Shuyani, "What in the world are those doing in here?"

"They are found in rotten palm trees," the girl replied looking at him wonderingly.

"But what are they going to do with them?"

"Eat them, of course."

"Eat them?" Rand exclaimed. "Well, don't give me any."

She looked surprised.

"You ate plenty of them last night."

Rand starred in amazement, then a light began to gleam in his eyes. "So that's how they make clam chowder," he said slowly. "Well, I'm not dead, and I don't even feel sick. Shuyani," he continued with a quizzical smile, "don't call me until the meals are ready. I want to eat my food and not look at it too closely."

While the villagers were at lunch a runner arrived from the North bringing a message from Chinawa. There was quite a commotion at the news the messenger brought. The curaca

31

seemed agitated. He told Shuyani they must leave for the North at once. She was to go on as interpreter and a carrier was to take Rand's kit.

Rand was told that he was to be taken before Chinawa. He did not understand the apparent agitation of the others -- to him it was just a continuation of the escapade.

He walked around, watching the hurried preparations. He was much interested in watching the working of the trocan. The operator picked up the small maul-like club with which the trocan is operated and began pounding. The drumming is done by thumping with the end of the club instead of hitting hammer fashion. It was like a soldier pounding upon a log with the butt of his gun. Each station, or village, has one of these logs, and none of the logs corresponds in size, length, or thickness with any other; therefore, each has a slightly different tone and thus enables the operator to tell which station he is listening to.

The operator would pound a tattoo of single, double, and triple blows, together with all shades of pounding. Then he would await the response from the next instrument farther on. If everything was going right, the operator would nod his head in approval. Once he frowned furiously and pounded a terrific fanfare of raps on the trocan for an instant, then broke into the rhythm of singles, doubles and triples again.

"Well," said Rand to himself, "they even "break" when the guy down the line does not get it right."

While Rand was watching the operator at the trocan, the curaca came up with Shuyani and she said, "We are ready."

"So am I, " Rand replied cheerfully, and the party started north.

It was not ten minutes from the time the messenger arrived until the party was on the road. It was a big party, too, as most of the important people of the village seemed to be going. "What a contrast to the usual methods of doing business in the tropics, " thought Rand. No preparations had been made. None were encumbered with bundles. In fact the only delay was by way of a hurried counsel between the curaca and some of the head men. Rand had no idea of the nature of this consultation, and no one gave Shuyani any message to convey to him. However, he noted that she seemed somewhat excited over the news from the north -- as did all the others -- and he often saw her big black eyes upon him.

The party traveled over a good wide trail, through an open forest, most of the underbrush having been cleared away. There were small villages at frequent intervals and it was evident the Pampa supported a fairly dense population.

A striking feature of the place was that in every village there were not only fruit trees, but also nuts of all kinds. The savage of the tropics is not given to putting forth effort for which it will require years to reap the benefits. He will plant plantains and other quick-growing crops, but trees that require years of growth before fruit will develop do not fit into his plans. But what a difference here. Castaña (Brazilnuts) were growing along the roadside -- monstrous trees that evidently had been planted centuries before.

At each village through which the party passed, big ollas of chicha -- a slightly fermented drink made from ground corn -- were sitting out under the trees and the marchers refreshed themselves from these.

Mid-afternoon a village was reached where a bounteous lunch had been prepared and here they stopped to eat and to take a short rest. Evidently one of the messages which the trocan had sent ahead was to have this food prepared.

Most of the party, after finishing the lunch, sprawled on the ground and relaxed. After they had rested they took up the march again. No particular formation was maintained by the lines of marchers; they walked in groups, or singly, as suited their fancy. At first Shuyani walked with half a dozen other girls somewhat behind, but at Rand's request she was asked to walk near him in order to interpret. At each village there were additions to the expedition.

Soon after they resumed the march, they met a woman coming from the direction they were going. This woman was decidedly not of the Pampa type, but was dark and had Indian features. She stopped and conversed with the curaca in an undertone for a moment, then turned and fell into step with the crowd. She kept near Shuyani and Rand, but said nothing to either, although she occasionally joined in the general conversation.

Many of the men had taken their queñas, or musical instruments, and both in front and in the rear, Rand could hear the doleful cadence of Quichua music. He had heard this music many times before. It is all very much the same, both in the jungle and on the borderland. Even in the mountains where there are no reeds, they have their music for they use bones in place of reeds.

Rand wondered why there was so much of the Quichua art here -- if art it could be called. Certainly there was nothing of the Quichua type about these people. Perhaps it was because their only outside contact came from that source.

Rand became tired of his own thoughts and of listening to the monotonous music. He turned to Shuyani.

"How long have you been here?" he asked.

"Three years."

Her answer was short, but she replied pleasantly, and Rand persisted with his questions, trying to draw her out.

"Where was your home?" he asked.

"I was born on the Rio Apurimac," she replied after a moment's hesitation. "Then my father moved to Urubamba." She hesitated again and seemed to be considering whether she should go on, then continued slowly and with a sad note in her voice. "He was trading and had to make a trip to the Rio Madre de Dios. I pleaded with him to take me with him and he finally consented. But we were attacked by the Mayorounas. Our party was broken up and they brought me here."

Suddenly turning to Rand, she addressed him in Spanish:

"Mas tarde diere todos, Señor. Hablo Castellano. Pero no, podemos hablo Castellano ahora." "Later I shall tell you all, sir. I speak Spanish, but we cannot talk Spanish now."

Rand naturally was surprised, but he nodded his head in assent, and Shuyani continued hurriedly, in Spanish:

"The woman we met a while ago was sent to listen to our conversation. She understands Quichua, but not Spanish. You are in very great danger, sir."

"Muy bien comprendo," "Very well, I understand," Rand replied quickly.

But he felt as if he understood only a part of these queer happenings. This was evidently why Shuyani had hesitated in telling her story; she knew the woman was listening to everything they said and she had wished to discontinue the conversation. She had said, "I shall tell you all later." What did she mean, that she would finish her own story, or would tell all about this woman, or what? And why had they sent this woman to listen, didn't they trust Shuyani?

Thinking it safer to talk to the curaca, Rand had Shuyani ask him how they came to plant the fruit and nut trees along the road and expressed his admiration at the plan.

"They were planted long, long ago, " was the curaca's response. "Not only along the road, but every part of Purac has plantings the same. No matter where one goes there are all the produce of the Pampa at his disposal."

"That's great," said Rand, "but who attends to them?"

Clearly the curaca was astonished. "Why, we do -- everybody. Don't they belong to us?"

"Yes," Rand replied smiling, and he was reminded of the Incas. How else could one account for this apple-seed Johnnie stunt?

The sun was now getting low and they were approaching a village where many of the party who were ahead had stopped at various houses and were visiting among their friends. Big pots were steaming under a shed. It was evident that the party was to spend the night here and that food was being prepared for all. Now Rand understood how a party of this size could get off at a moment's notice. There was nothing to prepare for the trip.

"Rather tough on the host," he thought, "but still this is Incaic again." For this was the Inca plan of travel, having supply stations along the route to take care of the wayfarer. Didn't the Incas move an army of 50,000 men and care for it en route from Quito to Cuzco, 1,500 miles, five hundred years ago, in a much shorter time than the same number of men can be moved between these points today?

There were several curacas in the party now, for one had joined at each village. Sometimes there would be three or four, evidently from villages off the main road. Large stacks of calabash bowls, or gourds, were stacked in a rack. Each guest

-- standing in line, military fashion -- took one, also a mussel shell for a spoon, and had his bowl filled from the pots.

At the finish of the meal the dishes were stacked for someone to clean before placing them back in the rack. A big bumper of tobacco was placed conveniently by, where everyone could have a helping if he desired.

The type of buildings had changed now. The large round communal houses were replaced by individual houses. Rand learned later that the big houses were in reality houses of the first line of Purac defense and were used mostly for soldiers. He was here assigned a room in one of the houses, which he was to share with two of the curacas.

He was weary after his long march and sat down in his room to rest. He thought of Shuyani and of the story she had promised to tell him later. He wondered what it was and why she was afraid to talk! Was it for her own safety or his? She had said he was in great danger. Ah! That expression, "great danger". Why could people never use the word danger, without the adjective? Here he had come among these people and they had offered no violence whatever. He could see that they were not the bloodthirsty savages they were reputed to be. They evidently had a civilization far superior to any found elsewhere in the jungle. The struggle for existence did not drive them to raiding their neighbors, as was reported, yet they did raid. The presence of Shuyani proved that.

There were many puzzling factors which Rand pondered over, but what interested him most was who these people were and how they happened to be so much different from other tribes of Indians in the jungles. His own fate among them did not concern him much, his fun-loving disposition refused to accept the seriousness which the savages seemed to be experiencing. At last he retired and, in spite of the strange conditions, he enjoyed a good night's rest.

The following morning everyone arose at daylight, as usual. The regular schedule of twelve hours of daylight and the same of darkness in the tropics is rather conducive to regular hours in the rural districts, among either the savages or civilized people.

Rand was glad to find these people were given to something more substantial than "drinking breakfast", as they call it in many places in the Montaña, for he had a good appetite. A good helping of boiled corn was served for breakfast, then the party moved off with dispatch.

Rand had Shuyani ask the curaca when they would reach their destination and in reply the curaca pointed to slightly east of the meridian. Just before noon. The savage always points out in the sky where the sun will be when he wants to designate a certain hour.

All along the route they were joined by others, among whom Rand could see were the leading men of Purac. Apparently some question of grave importance to the state was to be settled. Houses were more numerous now: in fact, there was almost a continuous line along each side of the road. The trocan boomed out messages at intervals.

Rand did not make any effort to talk with Shuyani but on the contrary, always directed his questions through her to the curaca, even when he knew she could answer them. The woman spy, whose name Rand had learned was Nucui, paid particular attention to everything that was said, but never for a moment pretended to be able to understand. She talked with the others in the Puracian dialect and was apparently interested, only in a general way, about the trip. Rand felt sure she, too, must be one of the victims of a raid. She had the Piros features, no doubt she was a Piros.

The road ascended for a short distance after the day's start, then the land was level. Here they left the forest behind. There were plenty of trees and vegetation, but they were all growing under control like a country estate. The wild vegetation gave way completely to plantings of useful trees.

There was a slowing down now of those in front as one group after another stopped to visit and talk with friends standing beside the road. Of course the inhabitants of all the villages they had passed since the start had lined the roadside, but now there seemed to be more general excitement. There was much jabbering and head shaking.

The party was approaching Churic. Ahead Rand could see the trees come to an end; over yonder must be the escarpment, for beyond the trees was the gray horizon.

The streets were lined with soldiers who were armed with chunta spears, or javelins. There were few bows and Rand wondered why, because he knew this was the most deadly weapon of the jungle. From a concealed position the swift silent flight of its arrow deals death to its victim in a gruesome manner.

Another thing Rand observed was the apparent classification of the army units. There would be a detachment armed with spears, festooned in the gay feathers of that regal bird of the Amazon, the hyacinth macaw; another detachment was decorated with the plumage of the scarlet macaw; others had selected the green parrot. It was like the division insignias in the World War, such as Sunset and Rainbow. How did these people get this idea? Certainly Purac did not have any official military observers in the World War.

The curaca and Rand marched between these lines of soldiers drawn up at what no doubt was "attention", directly towards a large building that occupied the center of the plaza. The building consisted of roof only, the eaves being some twenty feet above the ground. The roof was of thatched palm leaves. Upon entering this building Rand saw in the center a dais. Seated on this was an elderly man of rather small stature. He was of the Purac type, but certainly not of such a dominating physique as is associated with primitive rulers. Looking into his eyes, Rand could see that he was not an ordinary person. Rand's preconceived notions of what he would find were upset, since ruling brain instead of over-ruling brawn is the distinct achievement of civilization.

The ruler was dressed in a rich brown cuzma of silky lustre. Over his right shoulder hung a sash made of teeth and claws -- apparently every known animal was represented. And how significant this was -- insignias of utility instead of a dazzling show.

Marching directly to the dais, the curaca saluted, then with a glance at Shuyani, he addressed Rand in his native tongue.

Shuyani translated: "He says, you stand in the presence of Chinawa, the great curaca of Purac."

Rand nodded to the chief and, standing very erect, replied, "Sir, I am glad to be a visitor from the world outside, to visit your beautiful Purac. I consider it a great honor."

Without a change of expression Chinawa asked, "Why do you come to Purac?"

"Because Purac, unknown to the outside world is a great place of mystery to-day. It was the call of the unknown."

"What do you intend to do here?"

"Visit among your people, then go back to the land from which I came."

40

"You do not cared to live with us and be one of us?"

"For a time, yes, but I fear it would not do for me to live here always."

"Why?"

Rand hesitated. How could he explain to this savage that the world he knew was far different from anything these people could imagine? Could he explain the advantages of civilization, if any, to this man who knew only Purac and the savage tribes immediately surrounding? Certainly anyone who ever came to Purac -- the poor Indian women for instance, victims of raids -- would consider it a paradise to what they were accustomed to in the jungle. His hesitation seemed to agitate his host.

"What is your business?" was the next question.

Rand's reply that he was a geologist conveyed no meaning whatever to Chinawa. Floundering for words that would convey the meaning, he said it was the business of looking for minerals in the ground. When Shuyani had translated this to Chinawa, Rand noted that an alert wave swept over the listening crowd.

"So," hissed Chinawa. "You are looking for curi -- gold."

The words were spoken softly but their softness did not conceal the contempt in his voice.

Shuyani began to tremble with the tension, but like womenkind among the primitive, she held her tongue.

Chinawa continued, "What would you do if you should find curi here? Bring your countrymen to eat up all our food while you made us take the curi out of the ground for you?"

"I am not looking for curi," Rand said.

"How do we know you are not?"

"I shall live with you and be one of you as long as I stay," Rand replied.

"As long as you stay? You surely do not understand our laws. We know nothing of the world you speak about. We know that all around Purac there are lands not as good as ours. It is hot and people die in the forest below us. Therefore, peoples in those lands want our Purac, but they can never take it. They can never come and eat our food and make us work for them. Every man, woman, and child in Purac will fight as long as they can stand, before they can make slaves of us. And I, as the head of the people of Purac, will keep Camachicushca Puca Uma."

When the chief had made this dramatic statement a murmur of assent swept over the crowd. What attracted Rand's attention, however, was the fact that this word "Camachicushca" was Quichua. Now he began to understand. Since the word was Quichua for law, perhaps the law itself was of Quichua origin. It struck back to the Inca regime.

"What is the Camachicushca?" Rand asked.

"Do you want to know? Yes, we must tell you."

"Long years ago the trees you see now were small, even before that Purac was inhabited by people like those in the forest below, today," said Chinawa. "One day a stranger stood in their door. He was tall, Puca Uma, red headed, as we are today.

"All the people on Purac were not friends then. There was much warfare among them. Puca Uma said, "I have come a long way. All my companions are dead in the brush. I alone am left. I can never go back for the road is long and I do not care to return. I will live with you and teach you many things and you will be a great people. No one can take your lands because I shall teach you how to defend them from those who seek gold and are cruel beyond your knowledge.'

42

"Long was the reign of Puma Uma and the people all became like him, as you see us today; and so shall we always be, if we keep the Camachicushca of Puma Uma. But if we forget this law, cruel men will come and take our women and we shall be slaves, not daring to look them in the face, unworthy of the name Purac. The law of Puma Uma is never to permit anyone who visits Purac to leave. If they do not care to become one of us, to --"

Here Shuyani, translating, hesitated and hung her head, unable to continue.

Rand looked at her trembling form and wondered. Woman though she was, still she was Indian trained and not given to any display of emotion.

"That's all right, don't take it so hard, Shuyani. What is it?"

"The law of Puma Uma is that all who come to Purac shall remain forever -- if they try to escape the penalty is -- death."

Chinawa considered for a long time, then continued:

"We saw the big bird pass over that my people tell me you came on. Have your people many such birds?"

"They are not birds," said Rand. "It was a machine my people have just learned how to make. It is new to us. Had the machine been in use long, no doubt there would have been many of them passing over Purac before now."

This interested Chinawa immensely. What? Not birds? Well, how did they make them go? Can they come here?

Rand explained the airplane, in its present state, was not adapted to jungle travel; that it must have a big field or a body of water in which to alight. That at present it would be impossible for a plane to land at Purac because of these reasons. And that at present jungle flying was dangerous. This seemed to please Chinawa. They could not come to Purac then?

"Not now," Rand explained, "but perhaps next year they will have planes that can light in the plaza here at Churic."

"How many people can they carry?"

"Oh, a dozen now. Perhaps in a year -- certainly in five years -- they will be able to carry hundreds."

This information profoundly impressed Chinawa. It was a matter which would require deliberation to handle. Right there Rand began to see why Chinawa was on the job.

"If it is not a bird, how did you get off it?" was the next question.

Rand tried to explain the parachute. Chinawa turned and said something to one of his attendants who produced a bag which he placed before Chinawa. The latter spoke again and the attendant opened the bag and drew out the torn and tattered parachute.

"Well," said Rand to himself, "the detective force seems to have been on the job."

Rand explained as best he could the working of the parachute, but it was almost as difficult as trying to explain the airplane. But why, he wondered, did they attach so much importance to the animal theory of the plane and parachute? It seemed as though the fact that they were not animals could not fit into their minds.

Chinawa and several of the curacas examined the parachute, minutely. They could understand the cords, for they were huashca -- rope -- but the silk cloth! It was not millma -- feathers -- surely it was some sort of huimba -- the silky cotton. It had to be feathers to fly, if it was a bird.

Rand thought of how he could demonstrate. Taking a handkerchief, he tied a string to the four corners, then fastened a small stone at the end of the strings. Taking the handkerchief by the center he slung it high into the air

44

overhead, as he had often done when a boy. As the handkerchief started down, the air was trapped within its dome and it floated slowly to the ground.

A shout of approval went up from many in the crowd. That was just as they had seen Rand settle to the ground from the plane. Instantly there was a change in the attitude of the crowd; where before there had been only frowning looks, of skepticism, now there were many friendly faces in the crowd.

Such is the temperament of the primitive mind. It has but a few yardsticks to measure by. Not being accustomed to all gradations of fellowman, it has but a few groups, usually only two, either good or bad. If you are not one you must be the other. Rand thought of how he had often come in contact with Indians who gave him a cold welcome. Ignoring the scowling glances of the adults, he would pick up a fretful baby and, jouncing it on his knee, begin singing any silly ditty that came into his mind. The child would at first look at him in wide-eyed wonder, then it would smile. Like a bright ray of sunlight breaking through a murky sky, the mother would immediately beam approval upon him and the mood would be absorbed by the other onlookers. Instantly he would be on easy footing with them all.

After Rand had several times demonstrated the workings of the parachute by means of the handkerchief, Chinawa wanted to know if it were possible for him to jump off the edge of the cliff with it. Rand tried to explain the wrecked condition of the chute, but it was evident they did not understand. Pointing to the torn places, he then took his pocket knife and made similar splits in the handkerchief. The throwing it into the air it dropped to the ground like a plummet. The crowd was convinced, therefore, he could be classified as good.

45

Chinawa conferred with several of the curacas then turned to Rand and said: "We admit you to Purac, but it will be necessary to keep you under surveillance until we know more about you."

"Well, that's that!" thought Rand to himself. But little did he dream what was in store for him on the morrow.

CHAPTER 5

The Red Heads

The assembly broke up, all moving in the general direction of the shed where lunch was to be served. Chinawa walked beside Rand and Shuyani, surrounded by a group of the councilors, or curacas. The meal was served in the big gourd bowls as usual. Most of the food had been cooked together, Indian style. However, there were several acceptable roasted agoutis -- that delicious rabbit-like animal of the South American jungle -- done to a nice brown. There was corn on the cob which was in season the year round at Purac. Although there was such an abundance of fruit growing everywhere, none was served with the meal. Fruit was so common and so accessible that it was not considered part of a meal, especially was this true with fruits that were in season the year round, such as the papaya -- sometimes called tropical canteloupe -- and guinas, the eating bananas (not the cooking variety which is called plantains.)

A large olla of fine tobacco was nearby for the convenience of those who cared to smoke. Rand was not surprised to see most of the elderly women smoke. The men smoked big elaborately carved wooden pipes, while the women in most cases, seemed to prefer light clay pipes, the stems of which were made from small hollow palm roots. The clay pipes, of course were not a surprise as these people were obviously far advanced in pottery.

As the party filed out towards the plaza again, Chinawa touched Rand's shoulder and smiling pointed down the village street. A small boy had a square of cloth tied at the corners with stones attached and was demonstrating the parachute. Within a short time this pastime had spread all over the town.

There were stately rows of the mango tree, that king of the tropics -- or of any part of the world for that matter, when it comes to artistic symmetrical growth. Rand stopped to admire the beauty. Then the question arose in his mind, "Where did those trees come from?" The mango is not supposed to be indigenous to South America, certainly not this fruit bearing variety.

"Where do all these fruits come from?" he asked Shuyani.

"They are all grown here," she replied.

"Yes, but where did they come from originally?" he persisted. "Someone must have brought these trees here to begin with."

Shuyani translated the inquiry to Chinawa.

"They came from everywhere," he replied with a wide swing of his arm indicating the horizon which circled the Pampa.

"My people go far. They visit all the chacara -- gardens -- in the pacha -- world -- and when they find some new plant we do not have, they bring it here and we grow it in the chacara here at Purac."

"And do you bring women the same way?"

"No, we do not need any more women," Chinawa replied. "Sometimes we are forced to raid people who come too close to Purac, but that is to frighten them off. We exist because we are feared, one of the provisions made by the wise Puca Uma. We do not want the chuncha -- wild women of the pacha. We are a proud people and take only women we know will not reduce our racial standard."

"So that is why you took Shuyani. But how do you tell good women when at war?" -- Rand hesitated at saying "raid", war sounded more dignified -- "according to civilized standards?"

"We do not always get women as good as Shuyani. When we get women of a low type, we keep them but they are never allowed to marry. We do not want children of such women. But we cannot return them on account of the Camchicushca Puca Uma."

This remark caused Rand to wonder why Shuyani was not married -- or was she?

The houses of the town were mostly of stone, but there were also houses of adobe. Some of the latter had thick walls and were made by the use of moulds, flattened logs with wooden clamps being used for this purpose. However, many of the houses in the suburbs were of canabravo, the bamboo-like canes. These canes were tied to the frame work with small vines very much as lath is used in the United States today, while for plaster they used a tenacious mud. This made a very comfortable dwelling. Almost every house had a supplementary roof, constructed over it similar to a rain fly, but with two or more feet between the two roofs and the top roof extending far beyond the limits of the building. This top roof was built in hinged sections which could be propped open when it was desirable to let in more light overhead. "What a wonderful adaptation for the tropics," thought Rand. The timbers of the houses were both enduring and of a gum species that was repellent to ants which are so destructive to house timbers in the tropics. Rand learned later that this timber was planted and grown especially for this purpose.

Chinawa occupied a large stone house, as his needs would require. It was the president's mansion, so to speak; and since the rulers were given to large families the housing problem was no small matter.

There was a long frontage with rooms on each side. Behind was an open court, or patio, well fitted with small plantings. The wings of this building extending back on each side of the patio were used for servants' quarters and for the domestic needs, such as cooking and other household requirements. In the rear was an extension of the patio with well laid out grounds, all enclosed in a stonewall. This area covered some two or three acres. Flagstone walks meandered here and there. Several of Chinawa's daughters, as much alike as a bevy of quails, were loitering about.

Chinawa seated his guests on richly carved log seats under one of the trees and requested the servant to bring chicha for them. Shuyani did not sit with the party, but strolled on some distance beyond. Immediately she was surrounded by the young ladies of the household and the questions she was asked were all that romantic maidenhood could suggest. Shuyani could see that until Rand was able to converse in Puracian language she was going to be a very popular young lady. And so she was. When she was not busy translating between Rand and the Puracians, she was plied with questions by the Purac maidens.

Huipuco, the curaca who first met Rand in the pajanal and had conducted him before Chinawa, was also in the spot light. The delay in not bringing Rand (when first found) before Chinawa had irritated the latter considerably; that a visitor

50

from the sky was not to be treated as a common pick-up by a raiding party had been conveyed to Huipuco by the runner whose arrival had started the march to Churic at noon the day before. But all this protest was now forgotten.

Huipuco, who had not accompanied Rand and Chinawa to the latter's house, was now sitting under a tree in the plaza explaining to an eager group of listeners how he had vigilantly watched the bird soar overhead, then drop Rand down to the Pampa. He told how astonished he had been at seeing a man hanging below the parachute. Huipuco even described the boots (as though he had seen them a mile away) in order to impress upon his listeners the fact that he had known he had no common man to deal with. He told of how he threw out his warriors, surrounding Rand, and sent the decoy who answered the call from the brush behind. None of Uipuco's valor in the defense of Purac was omitted in his vivid description.

Chinawa and the party had finished their chicha and the councilors were in the doldrums because the young ladies were still plying Shuyani with questions so she could not get back to translate. There was a hilarious shout from towards the house. Looking around, the party saw one of Chinawa's small sons climb out on the housetop with a wriggling puppy with an improvised parachute attached, in his arms. He threw the puppy into the air and it floated to the ground, not a very slow fall, but a somewhat successful parachute drop, nevertheless. Everyone laughed at the demonstration. Purac youths were coming on.

Chinawa, seeing that flaming youth would never take life seriously, called to Shuyani. Matters of state must take precedence over maiden's gossip. They must look about the place. Rand must be assigned quarters and told what was expected of him. Of course this must all be decided by the council. There was an animated conversation while this point was being discussed. Rand looked at Shuyani and caught for a fleeting moment her eyes upon him, through her long eye lashes, then she looked down. The conversation continued, but Shuyani did not look up; she stood digging into the ground with her big toe. Rand could see the color surge through her olive-tinted cheeks.

At last the council reached an agreement and gave Shuyani the decision. Still she dug into the ground. Then she said, hesitatingly, "They say that since you are here and must be one of us that you should marry --"

A loud scream, followed by wails and calls, came from the edge of the cliff. Everyone ran towards that point. People could be seen at the brink looking down. Rand got separated from Shuyani in the confusion. Looking over the edge he could see nothing, nor could he imagine what was wrong.

Searching he found Shuyani and she told him that a youth had tired of the small parachutes they were throwing up with stones and that he had constructed a large one and had jumped off the cliff. Rand could not help shuddering at what he knew lay upon the rough talus at the base below. Another martyr offered up on the altar of science.

Rand and Shuyani walked slowly back towards the town. Chinawa had paused only for a moment at the ledge. When he learned what had happened, he began giving orders and a carrier was dispatched to the southwest. It was miles to where there was a canyon breaking down off the Pampa where someone could get below to go around to the base of the ledge at Churic. Almost before the runner was on his way, the trocan was carrying its message ahead of him. It was now near nightfall and a fire was started in the plaza. Groups began to collect and the small children, innocent of the recent tragedy, were running here and there between the crowds, just as youngsters are prone to do.

Fatigued with the events of the day, Rand sat back and watched the scene. Individuals passing would smile at him with a look of recognition, but who they were he had no idea; perhaps it was some of the councilors whom he should have recognized since he had drunk chicha with them in the afternoon, but he could not tell, for they were just like so many peas to him. Perhaps he would, in time, be able to distinguish individuals of Purac, but just now it was hopeless.

Someone started up a song, or chant; what the words were Rand could not tell, but it was the same melancholy rhythm of the Indian music. "As advanced as the Puracians seem to be in other things," thought Rand, "their music is still primitive."

Chinawa came for him, somewhat exasperated. He had sent two messengers for Rand, but neither of them had succeeded in getting him, because Shuyani was not around to translate. Chinawa would see about this -- and he did. He found two of his wives and he never knew just how many of his own daughters, in the group surrounding Shuyani. Chinawa threw up his hands in surrender. Then as the group began to disperse he said to Shuyani, "If you will tell our guest to follow me I shall see that he is given quarters. You certainly cannot be spared just now."

When Shuyani had given Rand the message he accompanied Chinawa into the house. A small boy with a torch of the same material accompanied them to Rand's room. Here the boy lighted an oil lamp, setting it on a projecting stone in the wall at about the height of five feet. Chinawa bade Rand good night, or at least that was what Rand took it to be, and returned, accompanied by the boy.

53

The lamp consisted of a large snail shell. One would hold almost a pint. This was filled with some variety of vegetable oil. The wick was made of loosely braided cotton.

The large, thick gloomy walls of the room were almost monastical in appearance. The floor was of flagstone, worn smooth with time. Palm leaf mats lay about to keep bare feet from the cold floor.

A niche in the wall with a built-up extension from the floor formed a roomy bed. This was upholstered with a bag of huimba for a mattress and covers were of cotton. A canopy, or curtain, of the same material drooped from above and covered the whole bed.

Rand looked at the bed. Where did that niche idea come from? Was it Icaic or European? It could be either.

He retired early, but he did not sleep. He pondered long over the strange events with which he had met. From where and who was Puca Uma? He evidently knew all about the cruel conquest of Peru by Pizarro for had he not warned these simple Indians against just such characters who might be looking for gold? Who could Puca Uma have had in mind but the conquistadores, when he warned them against men who would come and eat their food and take their women while they made the men mine the gold from the ground?

Yes, it must be Inca tradition handed down to these people. Then there was Machu Picchu, the last Inca refuge recently discovered by Bingham. It was not a great distance south of here. Rand had about convinced himself that he had solved the mystery when he recalled Puca Uma. There certainly were no red heads among the Incas. But wait, there were red heads among Alonso de Alvardo's colony which settled Moyobamba, Peru four hundred years ago. And there were still red heads in Moyobamba, Rand had seen them not

54

only in Moyobamba but other places nearby. A red head in the Montaña is pointed out as a Moyobambiano. That must be the answer to Purac, but still, why were they now <u>all</u> red headed? One red head doesn't make a nation. Pondering over the matter, he dropped off into a fretful sleep.

CHAPTER 6

The Terrible Weapon

Rand was awake at dawn. With the first streaks of light shining through the cracks of his window, he arose, dressed, and stole softly from the house. Early as it was, there were many of the Puracians up and about their day's work. Strolling off to the east where he could get a glimpse of the sunrise from the eastern scarp, he passed through a park-like grove. With the coming of daylight the denizens of the forest were busy with the daily food supply. Empty crops had to be filled; the trees were filled with songs and chirps.

Rand stopped and admired a pair of scarlet macaws who were feeding on some flower buds not twenty feet overhead. They gazed at him for a moment, then continued feeding as they carried on a conversation between themselves in subdued squawks and guttural sounds, awkwardly pulling themselves about with their beaks. The sheen of their feathers in the first rays of the morning was brilliant. "If those who admire the gorgeous plumage of tropical birds when seen in cages at zoos could only see these," Rand breathed, half aloud.

No where had he ever seen such a wealth of bird life. "It must be protected here," he thought. This he found later to be true. All Purac was a refuge, for no bird, except game food birds, was molested.

At the eastern rim of the scarp, he gazed across to the east where the sun was rising. The southeast trade wind seemed to be riding the sunbeams to fan the tree tops. Among all this beauty and tranquility in the early morning light , Rand little dreamed that a dark and hideous monster was hovering over him like the shadow of death itself -- that moloch gobbling its victims year by year, old and young -- superstition!

Reluctantly he retraced his step towards the town. He must not go off on strange trips until they had more confidence in him.

Shuyani met him with a troubled look. The boy who had jumped off the cliff the evening before, it seemed, was the son of Nucui, the woman who had been sent to listen to their conversation en route to Churic. She had told Shuyani that Rand was the cause of her son's death. Not only that, but a baby had been found dead that morning, a baby who was as well as could be yesterday. The mother had held it up to see Rand when he passed, he had looked at the child -- the woman saw him look at it -- and now it was dead.

The situation began to look serious. Rand feared ignorant superstition more than anything else. He knew it was the most difficult to control when it got started. It hits blindly, without rule or reason, and woe unto those it falls upon. Shuyani understood, perhaps better than Rand, how serious was the situation. She knew that their talking together alone would fan the flame of suspicion, therefore they must get Chinawa at once.

Together they passed through the hallway into the patio. Here at last was refuge from prying eyes. Chinawa soon joined them. It was evident that someone had already told him of the accusation against Rand. His troubled face betrayed his emotion. Of course the boy was foolish to jump off the cliff. But the baby dying -- that was another matter. Everyone knew there were evil eyes that could bewitch or kill. Hadn't it been done time and again?

Too late Rand realized that he had made a mistake in considering these people too civilized to be swayed by silly superstition. He should not have taken that early morning walk alone, for every moment they could not see him would be used as evidence that he was off at league with evil spirits.

Chinawa had fried plantains and chocolate served for breakfast, the latter so bitter that Rand could not drink it. Several of the curacas had dropped in. Realizing that the sooner he found out all there was to be told about Puca Uma, the better it would be for him, as it might give him an insight as to their beliefs, Rand asked Chinawa to tell the story of his race and location. As some of the important councilors had not yet arrived, Chinawa was willing to narrate while waiting for them.

"Soon after Puca Uma came, " he began, "he called the curaca and all of the people together and said, "I can never return to my country, so I shall stay here and become one of you and shall teach you how to protect yourselves from the people around Purac.'

"Then he set all the men to making bows, the like of which they had never before seen, for this man had seen many things and was very wise. He also showed the people how to plant crops and raise plenty of food which had always been scarce before he came because the people planted little, always living on what they could find, sometimes being forced to war upon neighbors for food.

"The people with whom the stranger made his home soon prospered and became a very powerful people, the most powerful tribe on all Purac. When asked who he was the stranger would say, 'I am Puca Uma,' and point to his red head. The people did not know the meaning of 'Puca Uma'; but sometimes when people from far off came they called him Puca Uma, even before they heard his name. The people wanted to make Puca Uma curaca, but he said, 'No, I do not want to be curaca of this tribe; I shall be curaca of all Purac and let each curaca be as he is.'

"This did not suit some of the tribes and there was much warfare, but soon all the tribes on Purac came under the rule of the wise Puca Uma. There were many more women than men, the men having been killed in warfare. Puca Uma had many wives and soon there were many children, most of them being big and with red hair like their father.

"Then came a great war with people from the Pacha and many of the men of Purac were killed. This war lasted a long time and Puca Uma always was in the fight, sometimes slaying great numbers with a sharp stick he had that never broke, no matter how hard he smote with it. It is told that he could cut a head off at one stroke with this sharp stick. His name became a terror among the enemy and the cry 'Puca Uma' was enough to set them to flight.

"When Puca Uma first came, Purac was not as it is now. He put many men to work and soon had the Pampa so fortified that no one could get upon it. He made the walls surrounding it high and steep so no one could pass them. Where there were no walls Puca Uma planted bad vines that not even the Zachavaca (Tapor) could pass.

"When Puca Uma became old, there were but few people in the lowlands arounds Purac. Those who were there never interfered with us. Then Puca Uma gave the Camachicushca of Puca Uma; calling the curacas and others together he said:

"My children, I am getting old; I will soon pass on and you will have to rule Purac. I know many things of which you never dreamed. Some things will happen to you that I cannot foretell. There are other things of which I can warn you. The world you know is little, but the real world is large. There are lands so far apart that it takes moons to go from one to another. I have come such a way myself. Others will perhaps follow me. Some will be good, others will be bad. No one can tell which will come first. Therefore, always be on your guard. Should strangers come among you, by all means resist them with all your power if they show force. If they do not show force, conduct them to a council of the rulers of Purac and there inquire into their reasons for coming. If they come as I, to be one of you, receive them as such, but if they are interested only in what you have, beware. Above all, beware of any seekers of gold for such will take your gold, make slaves of you and of your women.

" 'If one comes among you as a friend whom you receive as such, keep watch of him until you know he has no evil designs towards you. If any of you should fall into the power of such a stranger do not hesitate to fight until the last man of you be slain, for worse than death would be your fate if you submitted.

" 'Strange men with strange weapons may appear, but do not fear strange weapons. Always remember no matter how terrible the weapon, more terrible is the fate of him who falls into the hands of the enemy; so fight to the last man. And remember always, <u>remember</u> <u>always</u>, the most mysterious stranger with his magic weapons dies just the same as a chunco if wounded the same. None have magic lives!' "

60

As Rand listened to this he recalled the coming of the conquistadores and their cruel treatment of the Incas. Had Atahualpa himself risen from the grave, he would no doubt have given his people this same advice. What a striking similarity to the fate of the poor Incas was forecast for Purac if she did not resist to the last man the invasion of the gold seekers.

The fate of the Incas was certainly known to Puca Uma and he was warning his children in the hope such a fate would not be theirs. Now Rand began to understand. Still how could there be a nation of red heads now?

"That," said Chinawa, "is the Camachicushca of Puca Uma who before he died showed the people how to make the walls that guard Purac so that no one could climb them. He also made many rulings that our people have kept. It was he who sent out parties into the land of the Chuncho and beyond for many of the seeds and plants we have today. Each year a party goes miles in search of plants and animals for Purac. Our people are accustomed to the brush and go many places unknown to the people of Pacha."

Chinawa paused and looked off into the distance -- or was it far into the past? All was quiet, perhaps out of respect for Puca Uma. Rand could understand much of what had happened now. Of course Puca Uma did not make the perpendicular walls of Purac. He perhaps blocked trails to a certain extent. Mythological stories from the hazy past were interwoven with historic facts.

Again Chinawa took up the narrative:

"There were many women and few men. Puca Uma gave each of his sons two wives. If a son was also a Puca Uma, which most of them were, he gave them more. Others could have only one wife. We live by this rule even today, but now we are all sons of Puca Uma; so we let all the Puca Uma have as many wives as they can get; but those not of the features of Puca Uma can have only one wife. For many years all who showed physical or mental weakness were put to death. Never were they allowed to marry."

With a bound, Rand jumped to his feet. "Now I know how it all came about," he all but shouted.

The assembly looked startled and asked him what he was talking about. Realizing that it would be impossible to explain to these children of the forest that Puca Uma had produced in Purac a race that geneticists call "pure line", Rand only said, "I know now what a wonderful man Puca Uma was." And he meant it.

Rand was so elated over his discovery that he wanted to start at once to tell the world of what he had found. But -- getting out was another question. Besides, even a more serious matter confronted him just now.

When Chinawa had completed his narrative, he sat long in thought. Rand watched expressions of care and apprehension that were written upon his face. No doubt Chinawa was burdened with the responsibility of the welfare of Purac. He could imagine how the warning of Puca Uma to beware of strangers who would ravish his land as the conquistadores did the land of the Incas, was the responsibility now troubling him. There was one ray of hope for Rand: Puca Uma had said, 'Some will be good and others bad.' It was necessary that he convince them that he had no selfish designs upon Purac.

All respected Chinawa's meditations and there was a long silence. Rand realizing that it would be more ethical for him to give Chinawa an opportunity for discussing the matter with the councilors, told Shuyani that he would walk in the garden while they conferred. She conveyed the statement to Chinawa who nodded his approval.

Wrapped in deep thought, Rand wandered among the flowers. He was too preoccupied to appreciate their beauty. What a contrast was his mood now to what it had been as he watched the sun coming up in all its glory a short time before.

As he strolled along he came upon a beautiful girl, evidently one of Chinawa's daughters, collecting a handful of jasmines. Their fragrance recalled to Rand memories of springtime in Dixie.

The girl was startled at meeting him face to face and was on the verge of flight when she was assured by Rand's smile. It was a sad smile, for Rand felt the hopelessness of his position. Slowly the startled look in the girl's face was changed to a smile of welcome. Pointing to the flowers Rand said, "Zumac", the Quichua word for beautiful. The girl nodded her head in agreement. Yes, she understood the word, whether it was Quichua adaptation to their dialect or that she had studied the Quichua, he did not know. How he wished he could tell her that those flowers grew in his yard at home, far far away. How he could close his eyes and see his mother coming in with a bunch of them, fresh with the morning dew.

Pointing to himself he said, "Rand."

"Rohnd," she repeated after him, though unable to accent the name as he spoke it. Then pointing to herself she said, "Maiboya."

Not caring to get too familiar with one of Chinawa's daughters while under suspicion, Rand again turned his attention to the flowers. Seeing a beautiful bud just opening into a flower, he plucked it and handed it to Maiboya who placed it with the others. Had he been looking he would have seen that it was held separate from the others by one finger.

He touched various flowers and bushes in turn and Maiboya would tell the Purac name which he would try to repeat after her.

They were soon joined by two other girls who grew bold at seeing Maiboya trying to talk to Rand. Although the young ladies did not seem to fear Rand, it was not so with the smaller children. One of the children while playing in the yard, caught a glimpse of him and ran screaming towards the house. This commotion caused Rand to retreat to where he could be seen by Chinawa and his group, in order to let them know that he was not trying to murder the boy.

Chinawa had Shuyani call Rand to their conference where he learned that they had agreed to take no action at this time, but to await developments. He was to be assigned to a house by himself with a boy to care for his needs. His bag would be sent there at once.

The party was breaking up when Rand turned to Shuyani and said that he would like to make a talk to the people. Permission for this was granted and he began by saying that he was very sorry the boy had been killed, but that he was no more responsible for his death than he would have been had the puppy been killed the same way by Chinawa's son. The case of the pup differed only in results from what had happened to the boy. He was responsible for neither act.

To this most of them agreed by nods of their heads; but they at once began talking among themselves. Of course Rand could not understand their talk, but he could readily guess what it was like. "The baby -- what about that? How could he explain its death? It had been perfectly well yesterday, and now it was dead. Surely it was bewitched."

As he watched the crowd, Rand knew he could make no impression by trying to reason with them. He suggested that if he might see the baby, perhaps he could appease the mother's resentment. They were surprised at Rand's request, but after a discussion conceded it. The party left for the house where the body lay.

The mother objected strenuously to Rand's coming in. Had he not caused her grief enough? She had more children whom she did not want exposed to the evil eye. Chinawa had to be firm with the woman. She could send the other children elsewhere if she liked, but they were coming in.

The dead child was lying on a big flat log that served as a bench, beside the wall, nude. A bunch of flowers was in its wax-like hand. It was a little boy about two years old.

Rand looked over the body. He could see no marks upon it. One after another he felt each limb, then he felt the stomach. It was well nourished and nothing to indicate the cause of its death. It had been dead only a short time and rigor mortis had not set in. Placing his hand under the head he started gently to raise the body and was surprised to notice that it was flexible. Then placing his fingers at a wide range of angles at the top of the head, he moved it at various angles. There was no doubt -- the neck was broken.

He stepped back to think. What should he do, tell what he had found, or ponder over it first? He decided he would not tell just now. Looking around, he was about to say, "Let's go," when his eyes met those of Shuyani. There was such a depth of feeling in her eyes that he wanted to talk the discovery over with her. But at the same time he saw Nucui standing beside the dead child's mother, with a look of hatred in her eyes. He dared not try to communicate with Shuyani now, the situation was too strained. Still -- Shuyani understood Spanish.

Placing his hand again on the child's head he said one Spanish word, "roto" -- "broken" -- as he twisted the head ever so slightly, sadly shaking his own head as he did so. The word meant nothing to anyone in the assembly except Shuyani. It had been spoken as if it were a word of pity. As he stepped back, Shuyani came close and viewed the body and then started to turn away, but she turned back and folded the little hand firmly upon the flowers which had become disarrayed, and gently placed her hand under the head as Rand had done. So gentle was her action that no one, except Rand who was watching for it, saw any movement of the head.

Without a word the party left the room. "Well," thought Rand, "Shuyani knows what I know." But he had no chance for a word with her.

Heartsick with the injustice, Rand could feel already the demon, superstition, gripping at his throat. He asked the party to go with him to his quarters. In the rock seat that extended along the front of the house was his bag. He remembered that some half dozen cigars were in the bag. He longed to smoke a real cigar, he wanted to get as far away from Purac in mind as possible. Different articles were laid aside in his search for the cigars. These things, of course, were very mysterious to the Puracians.

First he took out a small camera which he did not try to explain. A pair of clippers came next. He always carried a pair of clippers in the jungle; they were used in place of a razor as well as for the head. He demonstrated the use of the clippers and told them that later he would give them all a hair cut like his own if they wanted it.

"Have you any weapons?" asked Chinawa.

"Yes," said Rand, holding up a small 32 caliber revolver.

"Does it roar like thunder when you use it?" Chinawa asked.

A hush fell over the assembly.

66

"No, it does not roar like thunder, but it makes some noise," Rand replied.

"How far can you kill with it?" was the next question.

Rand hesitated as he tried to estimate the distance the weapon was effective. The delay in answering increased their suspicion. Not waiting for a reply Chinawa turned and began an animated conversation with his people which Shuyani made no effort to translate.

A boy was dispatched on some errand and the assembly stood around in silence until the boy returned, accompanied by an old Indian woman, evidently a victim of one of the punitive expeditions the Puracians had made on some of the neighboring tribes of the lowland.

Chinawa pointed to the revolver which Rand had placed beside his kit. When the old woman saw the weapon she threw up her hands and ran screaming as though pursued by a legion of demons. Her panic-stricken retreat was followed by all the children in the neighborhood and some of the men. Chinawa and his councilors stepped back, but did not run away.

The old woman who had fled at the sight of the gun dodged behind a nearby house and began to tell in a loud voice something of the terrible effectiveness of the weapon. Nothing could persuade her to get where the thing could see her for it would kill her on sight. She called down all manner of curses on those who had exposed her to such danger. Why, the thing could kill everyone in the village with one blast of its breathe! No tree was big enough to stop it.

Rand stood thunderstruck at the turn of events, and then he recalled the Camachicushca of Puca Uma:

"Strange men with strange weapons may appear, but do not fear strange weapons. Always remember no matter how terrible the weapon, more terrible is the fate of him who falls into the hands of the enemy; so fight to the last man, remembering always that the most mysterious stranger with his magic weapons dies just the same as a chuncho if wounded the same!"

Rand could imagine they saw him as Atahualpa would see Pizarro today if they were both alive. He represented Pizarro to those people, but Pizarro alone. Then his mind went back to the early history of the United States. He saw his own forefathers dancing jeeringly around a poor defense-less woman, calling her a witch and shouting in righteous glee as she was hanged. His forefathers had had far more chance to know right from wrong than these poor people. He could see that none of the men were panic stricken now. There was nothing but grim determination to face the unknown, whatever it might be. To fight to the last man!

Although none of them had weapons of warfare, they all had the bamboo lance-like daggers which they carried and used as everyday knives. Every man among them was ready to sacrifice himself for what he thought was the good of Purac. He knew he could grab the revolver and kill perhaps one or two, but he would be torn limb from limb almost instantly. They knew he could be killed and that he was not protected by the magic life the Incas had feared in the Spaniards. He realized that he was face to face with a situation beyond his control.

Looking at Chinawa Rand saw a pained look upon his face, a look that he would expect to see on the face of a general who had made a blunder in military tactics and the lives of his men were being sacrificed by his error. He would err no longer! All he asked now was to be the first to sacrifice himself to protect Purac.

Everything was quiet except the ravings of the old woman behind the house. Her ravings about the calamity that was about to befall Purac was to Rand's ears like the chanting of a priest administering the last sacrament to a condemned man on the scaffold. He could fight anything tangible, but what could be done against blind superstition.

He saw Chinawa's jaws set and hand clinch as he stepped forward! At the same moment Shuyani took a step forward with one hand raised. There was a suggestion of a smile on the girl's lips.

"Why do you let an hysterical old woman get you so excited?" she asked. "Surely the descendant of the great Puca Uma whose very name caused the Chuncho to tremble, isn't going to pay any attention to the fears of such as she?"

"We know she is a Chuncho," said Chinawa, "but she has seen such weapons before she came to Purac. She has seen many things that we know nothing about."

"I, too, have seen many things before I came to Purac and I know she is an old woman who recalls the past with a child's exaggerated mind," replied Shuyani.

"We do not fear for ourselves, but do you hear what she says the weapon can do to our people? Did not Puca Uma warn us of just such weapons as she describes? We must spare nothing to save Purac."

"Yes, I know Puca Uma said many things. He said men would come, some good and some bad, and that the wise curaca must look out for the good as well as destroy the bad. If this strange weapon is so terrible, why does not the stranger use it to protect himself? If one blast of it is so terrible as to kill all in Purac, could all of Purac prevail against it? Surely it has no such power."

"True, we do not know how terrible the weapon is, but no matter how terrible it is we must not consider ourselves, but Purac. But if this is not a terrible weapon, why does he bring it here if he did not have evil intentions towards us?"

At this question Shuyani dropped her sarcastic smile and her eyes opened wide in apparent amazement. She looked long at Chinawa as if unable to believe that he could ask such a question.

"Why does he carry a weapon? Do not all men carry weapons? That is the weapon of his people just as the bow is the weapon of the people of Purac. Doesn't the bow supply you with food when you go on a long trip? How long could you live in the woods without your bow? Don't you carry it when you go to see distant friends, and do they think you and enemy because you carry a bow to feed yourself? The stranger carries a weapon because he is a man and not a woman."

All this conversation had been carried on in the Purac language. Rand could not understand a word of it, but not a shade of its meaning escaped him. Spellbound they all stood without a move. Shuyani, knowing that any break might upset the mood and that she must carry them on while she could, turned quickly and picking up the revolver, fired point blank at a nearby tree.

Not a move followed the shot. Everyone stood still for a moment. Pointing to a small bullet hole in the tree Shuyani said, "There, see what the terrible weapon which had you all in a panic will do? Did it pass through the tree? I think you could do better than that with your bow, Chinawa, the weapon is like the old woman, all fuss."

A long wail was heard from behind the house where the chuncho woman had been predicting the total destruction of

70

Purac by one blast of the terrible weapon. At the top of her voice she was now declaring that she had been killed.

The comedy of the situation was too much for even the dignified Chinawa. He broke out into a laugh in which the whole assembly joined, with the exception of Rand. He, not being able to understand the old woman, missed the point.

Rand was looking at Shuyani with complete astonishment. How could the jungle produce a woman like that. "My God! And I thought she was a little savage," he said to himself.

"Th--ank you, Shuyani." It was all he could say.

CHAPTER 7

Jasmines

Chinawa and the councilors collected around the tree to examine the hole made by the bullet. They poked with sticks and located the depth the missile had penetrated. One of their flechas -- arrows -- would, as Shuyani had said, do better than that. The hysteria of the crowd was over and they began to form in small groups and to talk in a rational manner. But Rand realized the question was still not settled. The most trivial incident could upset the passive state of their feelings.

Sitting beside his bag, the cigars now forgotten, he looked with a blank stare at the scene before him. At last he called to Shuyani and told her he wanted to talk with Chinawa. When he had secured the latter's attention he said, "I cannot speak your language. I must learn it at once. Also, in order that you know all my movements it will be necessary for someone to be with me all the time. Therefore, I ask you to select a Puracian youth who will be my constant companion. A youth whom you can trust and who is to help me learn the Purac language."

They approved of this. Whom did he want? "That," said Rand, "I shall leave to you. I will not select one myself for if I do, someone may suspect him."

This point, too, appealed to their sense of fair play. There was much discussion of the matter. Many names seemed to be suggested, but no decision was reached. There seemed various plans suggested. Rand spoke again.

"Why not tell all the youths and let those who want the place appear before you? Then you can select the applicant."

The suggestion was approved; they would spread the news and those who wanted the place were to appear before the assembly when the sun was low in the west.

All agreed and a feeling of restored confidence seemed to obtain. Pointing to the revolver, Rand said, "I do not need this. There are no animals here to shoot. Perhaps you will take this weapon, Chinawa, and keep it."

But Chinawa shook his head emphatically. He would never think of such a breach of ethics as to take a friend's weapon. Of course they had no enemies on Purac; in warfare they took weapons from the enemy, but this was always in the zacha -- woods -- off the Pampa; only the council had authority to take weapons from one on the Pampa. Such was their civic law.

"Very well," said Rand, "I request the council to take charge of this weapon. I ask it as a favor."

This was agreed to and an attendant was requested to take charge of the revolver and convey it to the depository. It was now near mid-day and they began a movement towards individual homes. Most of the crowd which had collected was retiring to the various homes in the village.

Chinawa told Rand he was to eat at the civic table as was the custom with visitors from outside. Shuyani had disappeared and while waiting for the meal to be served, Rand pointed to various articles and indicated that some member of the group give its Puracian name which he would try to memorize.

When they had finished eating, there was a movement towards the mango trees in the plaza. Several members of the council had begun to yawn and it was evident the mid-day nap had been neglected long enough in their excitement created by the visitor from the sky.

A commotion down the street attracted attention and Rand heard Shuyani's name mentioned. Looking in that direction he saw Shuyani approaching accompanied by another woman. He could not make any great event out of this and wondered at the interest manifested by the crowd. Shuyani and the woman marched directly to Chinawa and when they stood before him, Shuyani began talking while this woman stood with eyes downcast. Almost with Shuyani's first words the crowd was alert with interest, and as she proceeded it increased as did the apparent embarrassment of the woman who was with her.

Rand could only gaze in wonder at the scene before him. Shuyani had not looked at him since she came up, evidently what she had to say was for Chinawa. Her speech was very rapid and Rand, of course, could understand none of it.

She paused. Chinawa hissed something at the woman who was now sobbing hysterically. Chinawa was visibly disturbed. He looked around, pulled his hair in a nervous fashion and then stepped up to the woman and shaking a finger in her face, grew eloquent in expressing his views.

Being as he considered an innocent onlooker, Rand was in a mood to enjoy watching the affair from the sidelines. Purac would be a politician's delight, he thought. No trouble to get an issue here, one or two crises almost any day instead of every four years. Chinawa choked twice with rage before he finally relieved himself of his emotions. Throwing both palms outward, with a shrug of both shoulders, he relaxed and then gazed around as if saying, "What next?"

Rand was truly sorry for the woman. It was evident she had done something which had upset Chinawa very much. Rand tried to attract Shuyani's attention, but she was standing with eyes downcast.

"What is it, Shuyani?" he asked, drawing nearer.

The woman, upon hearing Rand speak, turned to him dropped upon her knees in front of him, and with hands up, pleaded with him in her native tongue.

Unable to understand why she was appealing to him, Rand again asked Shuyani the reason.

"Don't you know her?" Shuyani asked.

"How could I know her? Isn't she just like all the rest of the Purac type? I can't tell one from another."

"That," said Shuyani, now beginning to understand Rand's bewilderment, "is Yamariqui, mother of the child who died. She now admits that it fell out of a hammock and broke its neck."

"Oh, I see," was Rand's reply. "Just how --"

He started to say, "Just how did she happen to confess," but he knew she did not "just happen" to; Shuyani, he could see, was back of it all. Twice in one day she had saved the situation. Of course this last event was not so dramatic from Rand's standpoint, but he knew it was just as important.

"What are they going to do with her?" he asked, moved to pity by her dejected appearance.

"That will be for the council to decide," Shuyani answered.

Chinawa, with the council, started for the council hall, the place where Chinawa had received Rand upon his arrival. A police acting with military precision took charge of the situation. The councilors followed Chinawa into the building.

The trocan sent out a tattoo, presumably notifying the people that court was in session and to stand by. Two guards escorted Yamariqui into the building. Shuyani was instructed to follow. Rand was evidently not considered necessary to the procedure and he was left standing under the trees. Seating himself upon a log he watched various persons go and come.

Sometimes a messenger would come from the building and go directly to some place, shortly to return with another person. Other times there would be criers sent out. When such a cry was sent it would be taken up by persons in other parts of the city. Then the individual called would appear on a trot.

Rand saw Nucui escorted into the building. She, like the others who were called in, stayed only a short time. Rand wondered why Nucui was called. It was true he had seen her at the house where the dead child lay. She also had accused Rand of being the cause of the death of her son who had jumped from the cliff in the improvised parachute.

Shortly after Nucui came out two guards appeared with the accused woman. She was half dragged between them towards the heavy stone building that proved to be a jail. Soon after Chinawa and the crowd came out also. Rand arose and hurried toward them. Chinawa said something to Shuyani as Rand came up.

"She is to be sent to the Ushcu," -- hole -- Shuyani said.

"What is that?" Rand asked.

"It's a big hole over here," she replied pointing to the south. "She goes tomorrow."

"How long must she stay? asked Rand.

"One never comes back from Ushcu," Shuyani replied.

"Oh, I understand now. Isn't the sentence too severe? Of course I don't understand the case, Shuyani, but I want to ask the council not to be so severe."

Shuyani translated Rand's request.

They were surprised. They never reprieved a criminal in Purac. The accused had a fair hearing and was found guilty.

Rand considered for a moment. The sentence would not be carried out until tomorrow. He would get Shuyani to tell him the particulars.

One of the councilors said something and Chinawa suddenly discovered it was long past chicha time, which was to the Puracians what tea is to the English.

Chinawa led the way to his house and conducted the party to the shade of the garden. As soon as each member of the party was supplied with a gourd of chicha, Rand made his way to where Shuyani was seated at the outside of the circle. She looked up with a smile, as he approached, and made room for him. When seated he said, "Tell me all about how you managed it."

"It was not difficult," she replied. "You see there was the question of the boy for your companion, that was to be explained to the youths. So I went to the houses near where the baby had died. At each house I told of what a good chance it was for some youth to learn much from the stranger who had been in many lands. Most of them were afraid to expose their sons to such danger. They all mentioned the dead child and several mentioned Nucui's son.

"By this I was able to learn that Nucui had visited the house early in the morning as soon as she heard the child was dead. Then I decided that Nucui was at the bottom of it.

"Going to Yamriqui I told her that I knew Nucui had poisoned her mind against the stranger and asked her why she had listened. At first she denied everything, but then I decided to work upon her superstition myself. Looking into a mirror I pretended to see the baby falling and told her that soon I would know all. She then pleaded with me and admitted that the child had fallen from the hammock, that she had awakened when it fell, had gathered it up and nursed it until daylight. Yamariqui was almost distracted; then came Nucui and asked her if the stranger had looked at the baby the day before. Yamariqui said he had. 'Then,' said Nucui, 'he bewitched it.'"

Yamariqui had told no one what had really happened, so Nucui went out and spread the report with the results which from there on were quite vivid in Rand's memory.

After Rand had listened to Shuyani's explanation, he understood that Yamariqui was not to blame, altogether, for the situation. He again appealed to Chinawa and the council to release her. But they would not consent. The discussion became heated. Hadn't the woman falsely accused another with a crime so serious that it might have resulted in the innocent party being put to death? She must suffer for the crime. It was in vain that Rand pointed out that Yamariqui was excited and not accountable for her acts.

Chinawa was obstinate; she had caused him to suspect an innocent friend, a guest who had come among them.

"But," said Rand, "she did not know, she only allowed the suggestion of Nucui to arouse her into an irrational state."

"That is true, but one must not let the hysteria of others influence them to crime," Chinawa said.

Rand wanted to ask him how near he had come to being swept away by the same hysteria a few hours before, but he did not dare to suggest that. He was heartsick at their actions.

It was now growing late and the crowd had begun to collect on the plaza where the youth Rand was to have for a companion was to be selected. There had developed a changed attitude towards Rand since Yamariqui's confession. Chinawa asked all who wanted the position to step out in a line. There was a big line and almost at once the elimination began. Walking up and down the line looking them over, he asked on after another to fall out.

Only ten candidates remained in line. The council, realizing Shuyani was more familiar with what was needed than they, asked her to select the final one. This Shuyani did not wish to do. But she agreed to select three applicants from whom someone else was to make final choice. Then she questioned one after another. She motioned three youths to step out in front. This accomplished, she stepped back for someone else to make the final selection.

Telling each applicant to select a small stone and put his mark on it so as to be identified, Rand had the three stones placed in a gourd. He then had Shuyani bring a little girl with her. Chinawa held the gourd above the girl's head, he requested her to reach in and select one stone. This she did, thus inaugurating the first drawing recorded in Purac. All seemed well pleased with the selection.

Jitibi was the youth's name. Rand told him he was sure they would be good friends. Jitibi, Rand learned, was the son of one of the councilors who had charge of agriculture. It seemed that each industry was represented in the council and Jitibi's father was secretary of agriculture, so to speak.

The selection over, Rand told Shuyani he wanted her and Jitibi to see what they could do to get the council to release Yamariqui.

This they talked over together and then appealed to the council. Jitibi got his father, who was named Zarapacha, to agree; and after this one after another of the councilors consented to the liberation of the condemned woman.

The crowd stood silent as Yamariqui came out of the jail. This was an unusual occurrence for Purac. Yamariqui seemed scarcely able to believe she was to go free. Silently and with no display of felling whatever, she walked to her home.

Chinawa, perhaps feeling some remorse at the suspicion he had held in the morning, told Rand he had better stay at the executive mansion until permanent quarters could be arranged for him and Jitibi. Since Jitibi was to be his companion, it would be necessary to furnish more room.

Rand decided it would be best for him to have a talk with Shuyani, now, while conditions were favorable. She had said, while they were en-route to Churic, that sometime she would tell him her story; and since she had saved situations in which he was so completely helpless, he was anxious to learn more about her; she was becoming almost as much of a mystery as was Puca Uma. As they neared Chinawa's house he asked her if he could see her later. With a nod of her head, she said in Spanish, "Se Puis," -- "of course" -- as she skipped through the doorway and joined the Chinawa girls, as Rand called them.

After the evening meal, Rand was strolling in the garden behind the patio. Evening freshness was in the air and the soft tropical twilight was fading fast. Fragrance of the flowers hovered around him. Rand stopped deeply to inhale. Of blossoms there were myriads of varieties. Suddenly he detected the perfume of his old friend, the jasmine, which Maiyoba was gathering when he came upon her. Strange that jasmine was not here, yet its fragrance was distinctly noticeable.

"Aqui hay algunos flores que creo a Vd le gustan, Señor," --
"Here are some flowers I think you like, sir," said a voice in
Spanish, and a large bunch of jasmines was placed under his
nose. It took Rand but a moment to discover that it was
Shuyani who was offering the flowers from behind a tree
where she had concealed herself. She was laughing happily
and Rand laughed too, as he accepted the flowers.

"Yes, I am very fond of jasmines, Shuyani. They are my
favorite flower. But we have them for only one month at
home."

"You will like Purac then, for they are here the year round.
Perhaps you would like to have someone gather some for you
each day," she added with a peculiar note in her voice.

Rand glanced at her suspiciously, but her eyes, black as
night, blended with the dusk and told him nothing. Who had
told her about Maiboya and what had been told?

Strolling on, they came to one of the rock seats and sat
down. Presently Rand reminded her of the promise to tell him
of her coming to Purac.

CHAPTER 8

Shuyani's Story

Shuyani told her story quietly in Spanish, using many of the Indian terms of local adaptation.

"When we moved to the Rio Urubamba father had a trading post there. As you probably know there are but few white people on the Urubamba. To the west of us were the Campas and to the east lived the Piros. We were friends with both tribes, but the Piros and Campas never got along well together. After we had been on the Urubamba two years my Mother died, leaving Father and I alone." Shuyani's voice trembled slightly and she paused as if to regain her self control; then she continued.

A traveler told Father of the babassu business on the Rio Madre de Dios. He decided to go there to look it over. It was a long trip and would take many days. I pleaded with him to take me along. At first he would not listen. He said it would be difficult to carry food for such an expedition and they would perhaps have to live upon what they could find. I told him I could live on what he could, and he finally consented.

"There were besides Father and me, ten peons. We started in two canoes, going up a small river that flowed into the Urubamba from the east. We traveled this way for seven days, then the river became so small there was not enough water for the canoes, and we started over land. For two days we had a good trocha -- trail. Then it became difficult and by another day there was no trocha. We had taken the wrong route. One of the men said if we went north we could come to the Rio Purus down which we could navigate and cross over south to the Madre de Dios. We traveled north for three days, then came to a river. The men said it was the Purus. Father had the men cut some balsa trees and make two balsas -- rafts. Father and five of the men got on one balsa and I, with the remaining five, got on the other. The river was muy peligroso -- very dangerous.

"Father always went ahead with his balsa in order to watch for malos pasos -- dangerous rapids -- and would signal us in the rear the best course to follow. If he saw a mal paso ahead he would stop, and signal us to do the same. He would then make his way along the edge of the stream to look the channel over and pick out the most favorable passages to navigate. If the passage looked very dangerous he would if possible have us carry the cargo which was now very light, along the river's edge, to below the rapids by land and let the balsas go through alone to be caught below, where we would load and continue our way.

"To our surprise the stream swung northwest instead of northeast as the Purus should flow. We were evidently going to the Rio Ucayali into which the Urubamba flows. Therefore we would have to return home again before we could make the trip to the Madre de Dios. This was unfortunate, but it could not be helped, for our supplies were getting low and we must get out as soon as possible.

"One morning we started early, for father said we must go far each day in order to get out before our food was exhausted.

The balsa which carried my father was about fifty meters ahead of ours. We were being swept along by the current between high rocky banks that flanked each side of the river. I was looking at the beautiful scenery when I heard a terrified cry, 'A tierre, a tierre!' -- "To land, to land!'

"The men paddled our balsa towards the nearest bank, but this was a perpendicular, smooth rocky cliff some forty feet straight up, and we, swept along the smooth bank by the swift current, were unable to arrest the onrush of the balsa. At last one of the men was able to grab a small bush growing out of a crack in the rock wall. It required all his strength to hold the balsa against the swift water.

"I was watching Father's raft ahead. I saw it slide down an incline where the water flowed smooth as oil, then it crashed under a slanting ledge of rock. When the balsa hit this rock I saw it stop with a shock, then the front went down under with the rear at first sticking out of the water; but this too disappeared almost instantly.

"I watched below but could see nothing more of either Father or the men on the balsa; however, the stream swung to the left below and I could not see what came to the surface beyond the curve.

"It required two men to hold our raft against the current and the small bush was likely to be torn out by its roots with the strain that was upon it. The current swept most of our food away as well as the escopeta --shotgun.

"Of course we could not move the balsa upstream against the current. Any attempt to go down would mean being swept into the mal paso. Nor could we hope to cross to the other bank before the balsa would be carried into the mal paso.

84

"There was a tree growing in a crevice some yards below us with a branch drooping almost to the water's edge. If one could reach that branch he could climb to the tree, then get to the top of the ledge above. One of the men slipped into the water and swam along the bank directly under the branch, but he could not catch the over hanging limb and was swept into the mal paso. This was the last we ever saw of him.

"We considered letting the balsa float down under this limb and grabbing it for another anchor; but this move was not possible because it would permit the raft to go too near the mal paso. Nothing could hold a balsa in the current below that tree.

"Then Pedro, who had always been my servant, said he would try. I did not want Pedro to go, but what could we do? If he could hold to the slick rock at the water's edge below the branch perhaps he could reach it, but no one could do that because of the strong current. Then Pedro began to unwind one of the sogas -- vines -- with which the balsa was bound together. When the soga was free, Pedro fastened one end around his waist and he then took to the water.

"I held the soga and let Pedro swim along the rock until he was directly under the branch, and there I held him. By placing one hand on the rock he was able to jump high enough out of the water to grab the branch overhead. Pulling himself up by this, he reached the tree trunk; then climbing this he succeeded in getting over on the top of the cliff above.

"He cut a long soga, letting one end of this over the cliff down to the ledge where one of the other men climbed up the soga to Pedro above. Then we tied our olla and food to the soga and they were drawn up. When the soga was let down again, I climbed it to where they were, the other men following.

"We made our way along the ledge down beside the mal paso and watched its swirling waters for hours, but never saw anyone. All day we waited on the cliff above the pango -- rapids. It rained most of the afternoon. We did not try to build a fire, for we could find no dry wood; nor did we cook, for we were too miserable to be hungry. All night we sat huddled together to keep warm. I could not sleep, though the men slept some.

"When day came at last I wanted to get as far away from that river as I could. The men ate some farina, but how could I eat there at that place? We had only enough farina for one day. We started west hoping eventually to reach the Rio Ucayali. All day we traveled through the monte -- forest -- and we ate all the farina.

"At night the men made a tambo --shelter -- and a nice bed of leaves for me and I slept, for I was very tired. The next day we started without anything to eat, for we had no way of killing game: the men carried only machetes. If we had not lost the escopeta in the river we could have killed some monos -- monkeys -- for they were plentiful.

"Soon after mid-day I was so weak I could hardly proceed. I told the men we must stop, for I could go no farther. They built a fire and cut some chunta -- palm (cabbage palm), and we cooked it. We had nothing else to eat that day.

"When we were ready to start the next morning, one of the peons dropped the olla and broke it. Now we had nothing to cook even chunta in. What should we eat now? We struggled on to the west, up steep hills and down again. Late afternoon we came upon a large charapa -- turtle --. The men built a fire and I roasted the charapa. It made a scant meal for us, but we shared it equally. Somehow I felt better that night, but I did wish I could cook some chunta with the meat.

86

"The next day we kept a lookout for charapas. We found two in the morning and that afternoon came upon a big one which would weigh at least twenty pounds. I had the men build a fire and clean the charapa; then I told them to cut a chunta.

"But señorita, we can't eat chunta raw, it must be boiled," they said.

"However, they went in search of the chunta. When they returned with it, I had the charapa cleaned, and placing the shell bottom up on the fire, I boiled the meat and chunta together. That night we had all the food we could eat, and although we had no salt, I enjoyed it. We carried the shell of the large charapa with us in which to cook chunta, in case we could find no more charapas. We could cook several times in a shell before it would burn through, if we kept plenty of water in it while on a slow fire.

"Some days we could not find enough charapa, but the large snails were used. Also the grazanas -- grubs you ate the first night you came. Do you remember?"

"Yes, indeed, I remember, " Rand replied, "but go on with your story."

"Early one morning as we passed over the crest of one of the steep hills, we were pleased to see what appeared to be a wide flat valley in front of us. What a relief it would be to travel over level ground, we thought. Yet what a nightmare that level ground proved to be.

"Soon after we had started across it, the underbrush and vines which were almost absent on the altura --high land -- began to interfere with our traveling. It was necessary for one of the men to cut the way ahead of us. The farther we went the more difficult progress became.

"First one then another would take up the burden of cutting a trocha; and yet those behind fared little better that the one cutting the trocha for the zancudos -- mosquitoes -- were so numerous it was necessary to fight them off with a bundle of small branches of trees used fan fashion. All day we cut and slashed our way through the tangled brush. The man cutting the trocha would be showered with ants which his cutting had jarred from the brush overhead, while we who were following would be attacked by myriads of them as they tried to avenge the destruction of their nests. Nor did we find anything to eat, for there was so much vegetation we could not even see the ground to find charapas.

"Late in the afternoon we made camp and cooked some chunta. Night fall brought on more zancudos, and they all but drove us into the fire for the protection of the smoke; and yet the sides of our bodies away from the fire would be covered by swarms of them. No one was able to sleep and all night we sat huddled around the fire longing for daylight that we might take up the grueling task of going ahead.

As soon as it was light enough to see, we started on. We had eaten the last of the chunta long before, so we had nothing to wait for. As the morning wore on we began to despair, because of our weakened condition. We had no idea how far we had progressed because there was the wall of foliage ahead and behind. We could only occasionally see the sky overhead through the leaves. Pedro climbed a tall tree so that he could see the horizon and obtain some idea of how far away the hills were. He said we were near the center of the flat. This meant halfway. Could we endure another day and a half of that torture, and what should we eat?

"The valley stretched on for miles and we must pass it, some way; so we decided to go on, and on we went all the weary afternoon. When night came we were in a marsh where there was not even any chunta to be found. But I had found two sapos -- frogs -- in the afternoon. These we roasted, though there was but a mouthful for each of us. We were completely exhausted and at the mercy of the zancudos; we had no strength to fight them off.

"With heads and bodies wrapped in clothing we placed our feet as near the fire as we could endure it, covering them with small branches and leaves. By keeping the fire going, we managed to get some sleep. But what did the morrow promise? No food, yet a tiresome day's toil. We could not hope to find food, for the noise made in cutting the trail would give even the slow moving charapa time to escape our sight, even where there was enough opening in the brush to see the ground.

"From the time we had come upon the flat there had been small strips of water -- stagnant, dark, with decayed vegetable matter. Now there were pools which we had to wade, sometimes up to our waist. We wondered if we should come upon a cocha -- lake -- which we could not pass, and then what should we do? We came upon a large alligator, but we had no means of killing it. It would be impossible to kill such an animal in the brush with a machete.

"Later one of the men saw a small one sticking its head up out of the water near a rotten log. He made his way along this log, but as he approached, the alligator's head sank beneath the water. The man stood ready to strike with the machete; regardless of the zancudos that settled upon him in a swarm he kept quiet until the head of the alligator arose again. With a stroke he split the head open. When the struggle ceased the body was raked up with a stick.

"We were not far from our campfire of the night before, and we returned there to roast the animal. It was a small one and we picked its bones as we continued on our way. Soon after we started again the man who was cutting trocha ahead was bitten by a large surucucu -- bushmaster -- which, as you probably know, is the most deadly snake in the jungle.

"We could do nothing but help him along, but he finally became insane with the pain and tore away from us, rushing into the brush. We could hear him for a while as he cried with the pain, but soon his cries ceased."

Here Shuyani paused and shivered with her memory of the incident. Rand patted her on the shoulder and said softly, "Yes, I know what it was."

After a moment Shuyani continued.

"There was more water, sometimes open places where we could see the sky, and shortly after mid-day we saw the hills a short way ahead. Still there were deep pools of water we could not wade, and it was slow cutting through the brush. Sometimes we would climb from bush to bush over the water. But just before it became dark, we reached the altura and never was I so glad to see clean land, free of the ooze we had been traveling over for the past three days. You know the jungle marsh, Señor?" Shuyani asked.

"Yes, I know it," Rand replied. "A few days is a lifetime there."

"When we got on the altura we almost ran from that marsh, exhausted as we were. We camped on the hill where there were but few zancudos.

"Three days later we stopped in the afternoon beside a large quebrado -- creek. The next morning I went up the quebrado and found two large snails. Returning I heard screams and rushing towards camp saw a party of

Mayourunas slay all the men before my eyes. The poor fellows had no weapons, so what could they do? Pedro saw me coming and called to me to run, as he attacked his assailant with this machete, but he died with the call on his lips, run through with a lance. Horrified at the sight, I turned and ran, but soon a hand from behind grabbed me and I was overpowered.

"I did not know who the Indians were who had captured me, but I thought from the tattooed faces they were Mayourunas -- which proved to be true. There were seven in the party, all nude. They seemed to be in a great hurry and we started through the woods. However, we had not gone ten steps when the leader dropped dead with a flecha -- arrow piercing his body.

"The rest of the party stood still for an instant, then started to run up the quebrado, but two more fell. The remaining four jumped into the swift flowing water of the quebrado and swam, bobbing and diving along with the current. Once I saw a swish in the water near one and then there was red in the water; after that there were only three heads that would come up for air. All this time I never saw anyone in the brush.

"After all was quiet I heard what I took to be a guacamayo -- macaw -- squawking near by, as they do when feeding; and then another began squawking, in a different direction.

"I did not move, for what was the use? Then I looked at the flecha in one of the bodies. I had never seen a flecha like that. It was at least eight feet long and had passed through the body, the point extending far beyond. After a long wait a youth appeared before me and addressed me in a dialect I did not understand. I looked at him in amazement for he was red headed and of a fairer complexion than I. He looked at me in pity and said, 'Yarcani?' -- Quichua for, 'Are you hungry?'

I was more astonished than ever and said, 'Oh, why did you not come sooner and save my poor Pedro and the others?' He shook his head and I could see he did not understand what I said.

"Several others came up and the youth repeated, 'Yarcani?' Sadly I shook my head.

"They looked over the bodies of the Mayourunas and took what they wanted, then threw the bodies into the quebrado, where the current swept them away. I went to where poor Pedro lay and folded his arms over his breast, but I could not leave him so; I took the machete which he had been trying to use in my defense when he died, and started to dig a grave. When they saw what I was doing, they took the machete, dug a grave and placed Pedro in it and covered the body. The other two were also buried while I gathered some wild flowers and placed them on Pedro's grave. Then taking the machete, I cut two sticks, split one and made a cross. When this was placed at his head, I turned to the Puracians, for this is what they were.

"They talked together, then started northeast and motioned me to follow. This I did. Some would walk ahead of me, others behind. At no time were they rude.

"Soon as we started, one advanced rapidly ahead and was soon lost in the distance. Another dropped behind while two others went to the right and to the left. They called to each other in the voice of birds: usually on the march they mimicked the paucar which, as you know, is very common in the forest. Later I learned that this call meant, 'All is clear'.

"We never stopped until mid-afternoon when we reached a tambo where there were several others. They had plenty of food and it seemed to be a regular camp.

"There was a youth here at this camp who was delirious with fever. He was rolling and tossing so pitifully that I took an olla of water and sponged his head and kept a damp cloth on his brow. I did this for hours until he fell asleep. In the morning he was better and it was decided to bring him to Purac.

"I walked beside the ones who carried him and had them lay him down at intervals for rest periods. The second day we reached the ledge below Purac. A soga was let down and the sick man was drawn upon the ledge above. Then I was drawn up in the same manner. Then the others came up. So here I am."

"What became of your patient?" Rand asked, "Did he get well?"

"Yes, he soon recovered when he was brought to the Pampa. His name was Pushca; he was a son of Huipuco at whose house you found me."

Shuyani hesitated, then continued:

"Although I was not of Purac, and sons of caracas seldom marry any but Puracians, Pushca wanted to marry me."

She paused again and Rand said nothing, thinking it best to let her tell the story in her own way.

Continuing she said, "Pushca had more time to serve in the woods, so he went back before we were married. The soga broke when he was coming up one time and he fell and was killed. Now I am a widow. It is the Purac custom that when one's fiance dies, she must go into mourning for three years."

For a long time neither spoke, each thinking of the past -- perhaps of the future, too.

"You were probably fortunate in falling into the hands of the Puracians," Rand said, breaking the silence.

"When I could talk to the Puracians I learned many things. The party who attacked the Mayourunas had been following us for two days. They saw the smoke of one of our camp fires from one of their lookouts and came to investigate. They could tell we were lost and trying to get out, so they did not molest us.

"The Mayourunas came from the other direction and there was only one Puracian on guard who saw them. He summoned the others by the calls they use, but before they could arrive our men were all killed. The Puracians who captured me were the Zachas -- woods guards -- organized by Puca Uma. They roam the woods surrounding Purac. They speak some of the key words of Quichua, and other Indian dialects, thus they asked me 'Yarcani', was I hungry."

"They are no doubt much better to you than the Mayourunas would have been. Still, you might have escaped the Mayourunas and reached the Rio Ucayali."

"Oh, no. You do not know the Mayourunas if you think I could have escaped from them. They always tattoo a girl's face so she is ashamed to go among other people. When the Mayourunas get you it's forever. It makes me shudder to think of those terrible tattoos all over the face. I would rather be dead."

The sky had become overcast while they talked and dark clouds were rolling up from the northeast. The roll of thunder was frequent as were the flashes of lightening which showed them face to face for an instant, then obliterated every vestige until the flash came again. Large raindrops began to fall. They started towards the house, hurrying through the intermittent light and stygian darkness. When they arrived under the shed of the executive mansion Rand's arm was thrown protectingly about her shoulders.

94

Shuyani went towards the girls' end of the building while a boy took Rand and escorted him to the same room he had occupied the night before, lit the oil lamp, and departed without a word. How familiar the room looked. He had slept in this bed ages ago -- so it seemed.

Then he began musing. It had not yet been a week since he had set out from Rio Blanco. It did not seem possible. How much had happened in the interval. Since then, there had been almost a lifetime of events stamped vividly on his memory.

His thoughts went back to Shuyani. Why had he done just as he always did -- arranged for a very important interview and after it was over, he had been left to think of what he had missed his chance to say.

"Well, that's my type," he thought regretfully. "It's why I trudge through life doing chores for the chap who thinks of what he wants to say at the time, instead of the next day. What I wanted to know about Shuyani concerned the time before she came to the Rio Urubamba as well as afterwards. She had said she was born on the Rio Apurmic where most of her life was spent. Perhaps she has attended missions there Didn't she place a cross upon Pedro's grave? Why did I not ask about her father and mother? That was what I wanted to know."

Instead, he had lived with her the horror of her trip through the jungle. He had been through just such trips himself and understood its perils. He could even hear the mosquitos that swarmed about them in the marsh and feel the ants that he knew crawled over their bodies as they sat huddled together at night. And the days spent shooting the rapids on those frail balsas. Hadn't he been through just such rapids by day until he could see the angry swirling water all night?

And the Puracians instead of being the blood-thirsty savages they were supposed to be were by nature docile; all their dealing with the outside was to protect themselves, nothing more. They had, no doubt, fostered the idea that they were very hostile as a protective measure. They seemed more like the Incas every day. These were his thoughts as he went to sleep listening to the rain beat against the buildings.

CHAPTER 9

Puca Uma's History

In the morning the storm had passed and there was the freshness that only a rain can produce.

"I feel rather secure, but perhaps I had better go into the garden until I get the day's communique," Rand said to himself. "I don't want another day like yesterday."

Some of the Chinawa girls were in the garden ahead of him, but he only nodded and smiled a greeting and remained aloof. Shortly afterwards he was joined by Jitibi. The greetings over, Rand began to indicate various things and Jitibi would give the Purac name. Rand had a notebook and pencil and he would write down the names as they were given him phonetically. Jitibi was interested in the paper. It was of hoja leaves, almost like plantains; the pencil interested him but little.

While they were thus engaged, Shuyani came up.

"You will soon not need me for an interpreter, and I shall be forgotten," she said sadly.

"Indeed, Shuyani, I'll <u>never</u> forget what you did for me yesterday, not for one minute, do you understand? But say, why can't you -- " He stopped suddenly. He was going to say, "Why can't you write out the names of articles in Purac and then either in Quichua, or Spanish," but how was Shuyani to write? He did not want to hurt her feelings so he said no more.

Looking at the paper Shuyani said, "I'll write your whole lesson today and you can sit up tonight and study it."

Rand opened his mouth three different times before he finally said anything!

"Bueno," -- "good" -- he managed at last.

Chinawa came out and breakfast was served. The men ate alone, as is the custom among the people in this part of the world. Rand wondered if this custom had been introduced by Puca Uma, or had the later arrivals told the Puracians that women did not eat with the men in the best society.

After the meal Shuyani came and Rand asked Chinawa if he could tell him more of the history of Purac. Did he know just when Puca Uma came?

"Yes," Chinawa replied, "the record is accurately kept. We know just how many years it has been."

"Who keeps the records?" Rand asked, very much excited at the news as to tangible facts.

"There is a building where all the records are kept," Chinawa said. "Do you care to see them?"

Did he care to see them? He was more interested in them than all the treasures to be found!

Chinawa looked at him appraisingly. Just why should a stranger be so interested in Puca Uma? "We can go to the house and you may count them yourself, " he said, "if you care to."

Rand could not conceal his eagerness to see the records. How were they kept, he wondered. Perhaps they had the quipus, that bundle of multi-colored strings with which the Inca records were kept by the aid of knots. There was so much of the Incaic tradition.

"How are the records kept?" Rand asked. "Like this?" He picked up a leaf and tied a knot in the stem.

Chinawa nodded his head. "Yes, it is like that."

"All the luck that missed me yesterday is just falling into my hands today," Rand thought.

He must see those quipus at once. Perhaps he could really establish the date of Puca Uma's arrival by them; but of course, outside of the date he would be unable to learn much. Chinawa did not seem inclined to act hastily in the matter. He said he would await the arrival of the other members of the council.

Rand had not yet learned just how Purac was governed. Chinawa seemed to be the presiding member, but not disposed to act alone. But just now Rand was not so much interested in the present government of Purac as he was in the past history. He was evidently on the threshold of reliable information, and he was impatient for it.

After what seemed a long delay, most of the councilors had arrived and the party started in the direction of the "house of records."

It stood back alone -- a small square stone building, apparently with a thatched roof, such as all the houses of Purac had. But close inspection showed a roof of stone under this roof of thatched palm. Rand called attention to this.

"Yes," Chinawa said, "there is a thick setting of stone underneath. This is to protect the interior of the building in case of fire."

"Fire proof building," thought Rand. "It certainly stimulates interest."

At the eaves, just under the ridge directly over the door was a large hornet's nest. These hornets, Rand was told, were the sacred guardians of the records.

A square stone was used as a door. There was also a row of square holes in the walls higher than one could reach. These too were blocked with snug fitting stones. A man with a pole, notched ladder fashion, was removing these, thus making windows. After these stone stops were removed, two men began to remove the square stone from the doorway. It, too, was snug fitting. In fact, all the stones fitted so accurately that nothing could pass them when they were in place.

When the doorway had been opened, one man after another peeped in. Rand did not want to appear too hasty, but it was difficult to await his turn. At last, when he did look in, instead of seeing bundles of varied colored cords, as he had expected, he saw instead rows of smooth well-made sticks. These, he could see, had small notches marked upon them. He stepped back and meditated. This was not so different from the quipus, after all. If anything, it was more simple. He would no doubt have less trouble in deciphering them than he would have with the quipus with its many colored strands.

No one made a move towards entering the building. Impatiently Rand awaited a move from Chinawa, but Chinawa seemed in no hurry.

"Can one enter?" Rand inquired at last, unable to stand the suspense any longer.

"It is not safe to enter until the spirits have retired, " Chinawa said. "When the light comes in, the spirits retire; but we must not rush them. Once there were two councilors in a hurry and they rushed in searching for a record to settle some argument and both of them were struck dead."

"That's odd," thought Rand. "I wonder where the idea came from."

He peeped in again. Of course the place was almost air tight when the stones were in place; the air inside should be good, though, with nothing but the stone walls for contact.

When it was decided the spirits had had ample time to vacate the record vault, one of the workmen who had assisted in opening the building crawled through the narrow doorway, which was about twenty-two inches wide and thirty-four inches long.

Since the man inside was not molested by the spirits, the rest began to file inside. Rand followed Jitibi. A line had been formed and all stood in solemn contemplation of the records. There were rows of sticks, some standing on the floor, leaning against the wall, others placed in a row in niches in the wall. Blocks of wood of varied length were setting about for use in reaching the higher niches.

At the rear of the building was a deep counter-sink in the wall padded by a silk upholstering of huimba. In this row were twenty-three sticks. All sticks were made of mueano, a wood with a very pungent camphor odor. This was to prevent them from being eaten by termites. The sticks were square and the four corners were utilized for cutting the notches which were the records.

"Where are Puca Uma's records?" Rand asked.

"There with the hanac curacas -- the great chiefs."

Chinawa indicated the stick on the extreme right of the line. Then going to the left of the line, Chinawa chose a stick and handed it to Rand, pointing to himself.

"He says that is his records," Shuyani said.

Rand looked at the stick and asked Shuyani to draw an explanation from Chinawa as to its meaning.

One corner of the stick was beveled off at the lower end. Above this bevel there were notches for each year until thirty-seven was reached. Here there was a space with a cross, and beyond that there were other notches.

"To here," said Shuyani, pointing to the thirty-seven notches, "is Chinawa's life before he was chief of the council; from this sign where Chinawa was made chief of the council are twenty-four notches. These are the years Chinawa has been chief of council. This makes Chinawa sixty-one now." Turning the stick to the left she continued, "These notches represent his wives. They are placed directly opposite the notch which represents his age when the wife was taken. The right hand corner is to record sons, while the left one represents daughters. Each wife is represented by a stick with three corners; on this she records her age and the years also of her sons and daughters."

Rand stood back and admired the orderly row of sticks set in the niche. Now, for the counting: he had it all worked out. There were twenty-three sticks in the row. Rand counted them particularly. Twenty-three rulers including Puca Uma.

There were on the beveled notched corner where age and length of reign was recorded three sets of notches, the first before the reign began, then the number of years of the reign, and last the years lived after he had resigned.

"Then the reign is not for life?" Rand asked.

"No, when the chief of the council gets old, he resigns."

Looking over the record Rand saw that some of the rulers had died while in office, but most had resigned. Those who had died while rulers were always the younger men, - no doubt fellows who died before they began to feel the cares of state pall upon them.

Taking the record of Puca Uma, Rand saw that he had assumed office at the age of 38, had ruled for 37 years, and had lived eight years after he resigned. This made him 83 years old when he died. Puca Uma had had seven wives, 18 sons, and 21 daughters. No wonder Purac had become a nation of red heads.

After Rand had checked this record over, he then took each in turn and put down in his note book the number of years of the reign of the whole twenty-three chief counselors, adding the figures he secured a grand total of 551 years! Surely there was some mistake. He went over his figures again. No, that was right, the mistake was in taking the records off the sticks. Carefully he checked over the sticks again, while the councilors looked at each other in wonder. Rand checked them backward and forward. Then he asked Shuyani to compute the number. What he needed was an adding machine, the spirits had addled his brain.

"Five hundred and fifty-one, " said Shuyani, when she had finished.

Rand was too dazed to trust himself to figure any further.

"And that from 1929 is what?" he asked her, thinking it best to let someone else do the calculating.

"1378," she said.

"Well, Puca Uma," Rand muttered to himself, "you certainly have trumped Christopher Columbus's trick, as well as punctured my hypothesis. I wonder if the vikings lost any of their crew while picking grapes in New England. They, too, were red headed. Red heads are always reputed to be trying to start something and they certainly have got one Randolph Morley guessing."

Too dazed for coherent thinking, Rand told Shuyani that he was going outside. He had to get into fresh air. Maybe the spirits were there after all. He was almost ready to believe anything! Before he went out he gave Shuyani the note book and pencil and asked her to go over the 23 records again, carefully, and to get Chinawa to verify the numbers on each stick that represented the total of years each ruler had reigned. Then to turn the leaf and do it all over in some other place, add up both sets for a check and see if they were the same.

After he had cautioned Shuyani for the third time to be sure she made no mistake, he motioned to Jitibi to follow and they left the chamber. He was pale and trembling.

Chinawa noted Rand's condition and wanted to follow him out, but the latter had Shuyani tell him he would rather he, Chinawa, would help get those records correct.

"The spirits have been offended," the people in the village said when they saw Rand's agitated face. Rand took Jitibi by the arm and started off into the open forest east of the village. But Jitibi was soon forgotten, for Rand's thoughts were too muddled to think of him. What Rand really wanted was to be alone.

He had convinced himself so thoroughly that Puca Uma was one of the Conquistadores who had lived among the Incas! He had pictured him as pushing into the wilderness in search of riches and struggling along through hardships and provocations until he reached Purac, where he had met some kindly Indians with whom he had decided to spend the rest of his life, instead of facing the ordeal of a return to the point on the west coast whence he had come. Now he had found that Puca Uma arrived at Purac in the prime of life where a man would never admit that he had grown tired of pushing on; and that, by the records, long before the Conquistadores of Peru were born. Rand's feelings were similar to those of one who has been traveling all night thinking he is going west only to have the sun rise before his face at daylight. He would have to revise all his preconceived ideas and start all over again.

Then he thought of Colonel Fawcett who came into the jungle from the east for what he believed was a site of higher civilization hidden some place in the jungles south of the Amazon. What started all those rumors which had sent investigators into this part of the world? Perhaps Purac was the source of these rumors. Any jungle Indian who had seen Purac would consider it a wonderful place and spread the report of it far and wide. Rumors that would excite the anthropologist into action; and no doubt at some time there were Indians who had seen Purac. Then too some Puracian might have been captured in some war by outsiders and have told of it in the jungle lands round about.

"Now," thought Rand, "I know how Bingham felt when he discovered Machu Piccha.

"Well, I'd better not build up another hypothesis until I get more facts," he decided as he turned his attention to Jitibi.

As they turned towards the village they could see the house of records as again closed. Attendants were putting the last rock shutters into place in the windows; so Rand and Jitibi proceeded to Chinawa's house.

Passing through the hallway into the patio beyond, Rand saw the executive group seated under the trees, drinking chicha. Shuyani was seated as usual at the outskirts of the group with Rand's note book and pencil in her hand. He approached her to inquire how the check-up had been.

"Quinientos cincuenta uno," -- "five hundred and fifty-one," she said, unconsciously relapsing into Spanish, the language of her mental training.

"Both counts?" Rand asked.

"Si, Señor."

Rand considered a moment then asked:

"Shuyani, do you know what Christopher Columbus did, or was credited with doing?" he added as the humor of the situation began to dawn upon him.

"Se puis, they taught us all that in the convent," she replied.

In the convent! So she had been in a convent! Well, that surprise would have to wait. He did not have any wonder left in his reasoning power now. If Chinawa had told him that Puca Uma had come over in a private galley and that Puracians spoke better Greek than Aristotle he would not have been surprised -- maybe they did speak Greek for all he knew!

"Well," Rand drawled, with his characteristic grin, "if you will help me get these records before the National Historical Society, or whoever it is that referees these matches, we shall see something interesting."

Shuyani stared at him with a puzzled look, but said nothing.

Chinawa was rather impatient at Rand's interest in the records. What he wanted was to have Rand tell Puracians of the wonderful world outside, about which Shuyani had been telling them.

So Shuyani had been telling of some of the wonders of civilization, it seemed!

Chinawa had planned an inspection trip for the afternoon, so Rand could see more of the village. Jitibi said he wanted to go home to look after some affairs and would return in time for the trip. Rand went with him to the street and waved his hand as they parted, Rand walking towards the cliff at the north of town. He still wanted to consider and check over matters, and he could always reason better if he were walking alone.

For sometime he strolled around, seeing nothing, mentally particularizing on what the records had revealed. Had he eliminated all possible points of error? Of course he could not prove the records had been kept accurately. There are fakes turning up every day over the world, but a reason for deception is usually found in the desire for notoriety through the outside world. These people had no possible reason to be deceitful. They did not even know the world, let alone know how to deceive it.

"1378," he kept repeating, "551 years ago!" What was the world doing then? Of course the Inca empire was well established. If it were not for the Caucasian features, he could still fall back upon the Inca origin. Just what Europeans were doing at that time he could not recall from his superficial study of history. He had no ready reference in which to look up current events about 1378, nor any newspaper files to tell who had failed to return to his bed and board among the red headed citizens at that date.

Suddenly Rand stopped. Now here was one factor he had overlooked! What was a year in Purac? It was located at about nine degrees south latitude. The sun would pass over it twice each year. That was it -- each passage of the sun was a year, therefore a year was but six months! This would place the coming of Puca Uma after 1600. How careless not to have thought of this before!

Rand whistled as he strode back. He always whistled when he had solved a perplexing problem. As he passed through the hall into the patio, he fond Chinawa and two of the counselors. Shuyani was not in sight. Rand spoke her name inquiringly to Chinawa who looked around and dispatched a servant for her.

When she came Rand said, "How long are the years in Purac, Shuyani? That, I am sure, is where we made our mistake in the estimate."

She looked at him in surprise. Why, the years here are the same as they are everywhere. How could there be a difference in the years?"

Possibly Shuyani began to suspect, like the others, that the spirits had affected Rand.

"What I mean is this," he said, somewhat vexed that she did not understand. "If the sun comes up and we call it a day, then when the moon comes up we call that a day, we get two days count for every day, don't we? Well, if they count a year when the sun goes south of them, then when it goes north of them another year, they get two years in one."

"Oh, but they do not do that, -- at least I don't think they do," said Shuyani, somewhat bewildered.

"Well, when did they have a new year? This is now August. You should know how long ago the New Year has been," he said.

"There was a new year two or three moons ago," she replied, still uncertain of herself.

"There, see what I told you! It has been many moons since there was a new year. Every year in Purac is counted twice; that is, they have a new year every six months."

"No, I am sure they do not," she paused. "Let me ask Chinawa."

"Yes, go ahead and ask him. I think you will find that what I am telling you is true. How else do you account for a new year at mid year if it is not counted twice?"

"Very well, let's ask Chinawa," she said.

Chinawa said, "Yes, it has been two moons since the new year."

"How long before another new year?" Rand asked.

"A long time; the sun goes south and then back north again," said Chinawa tracing over head its course with his finger.

"What's that?" inquired Rand somewhat mystified.

"You want to see how we keep time?" Chinawa asked. "Very good, come."

He led the way back to the house of records. Going to the south of the building he indicated a stone buried in the ground, several feet south, where the shadow would reach the spot only when the sun was furthest north.

"When the shadow is on this stone, that is a new year," Chinawa said. "We then make a notch in the records."

"And at the north of the building when the shadow is there?" Rand asked.

"That we know is half of a year, but it is not a year as we keep records. Only when the shadow is on this stone is it a new year."

There was nothing more to say about the matter. Of course when the sun was in the north and the long shadow would be south, they had their new year. The fact that the year was computed from June instead of January had no effect upon the length of the year.

"The 'no' side of the question has it as usual," Rand mused. "Come to think of it, the pre-Incan calendar dated from September third, the planting season. That is what comes of being so cock-sure of everything. I get to following a theory and overlook the small matters that count. It's going to take a real anthropologist to decipher the history of this place. It's too complicated for me. Yet how could such an individual get to Purac? It has been resting secure for five hundred and fifty-one years, and so far as I can see now it may continue so indefinitely."

After the length of the Puracian year had been settled, Chinawa led the way back to the retreat, the mongo tree in the patio of the executive mansion.

Rand considered this an ideal time to get Chinawa to tell him more of the history of Purac. When there were many present, as was usually the case, there were always some to grow impatient with the delay, thereby much detail would be missed.

"Tell me of the Zachas, were they really organized by Puca Uma?" Rand asked.

"Yes," Chinawa replied. "What do you want to know about them?"

"How do they work?" Rand asked.

Chinawa deliberated over the matter before beginning.

"It is not customary," he said at length, "to inform people who come to Purac about the Zachas; but since you came by way of the sky, of course you did not come in contact with them.

"The Zachas are organized to protect Purac. Puca Uma knew the best protection for Purac was in keeping others ignorant of it; therefore the law that no one who came here could leave. However, the Zachas are expected to see not only that no one leaves Purac, but also to prohibit the settlement of lands nearby.

"At all the high observation points on the rim of the Pampa are located lookouts from which the Zachas scan the forest for miles below. At any time smoke is seen that indicates a camp fire (there are no other kinds of fires in a tropical rain forest) a message is sounded by the trocan at the lookout station. The Zachas in the forest below go and investigate. There are posts throughout the forest and also lookouts from high hill tops, even miles from Purac. Nothing can take place that the Zachas do not know."

"How are the Zachas selected?" Rand asked.

"They are selected from among the youths who are most proficient," Chinawa replied. "Those who from childhood train for the work. They begin by mimicking birds and beasts. Contests are conducted to select the most adept. Also those who are the best marksmen with the bow. It is a great honor to be chosen for the Zacha, and those who serve four years can retire: they are made councilors. All who have rendered outstanding service in the Zacha are councilors here at Churic. However, there are men in the Zacha who spend all their lives in the service. They are those who are especially skilled in woodcraft and have charge of the work. The Zachas have a call of recognition that changes from time to time. Anyone going into the woods who does not respond to the call is shot without question. I could not go into the woods myself, if not accompanied by a Zacha, without being shot."

"Is the crime that serious?" Rand asked. "You do not bring them here to Purac for trial?"

"Why should there be a trial?" Chinawa replied. "The fact that they were in forbidden territory was proof enough. It is the rule of the Zacha. Besides, no one can even get off Purac alone. There are but five places where the Zachas let people down, and some one is on duty there all the time. There are no other means of leaving Purac, except by the south that is always guarded also; besides the cocha -- lake -- beyond cannot be passed. That, too, is guarded by the sacred mama yacu, mother of the water -- the Indian name for the anaconda, the big water snake. The houses near the cocha are of combustible material so they can be burned down if an enemy should ever attack from that direction. But no one can reach Purac from that side. Perhaps we had as well build stone houses there now, what do you think about it?" Chinawa asked Rand.

"No doubt we should," the latter replied gravely. He wanted Chinawa to understand that he considered himself a part of Purac now. Why not, wasn't he? He could not get out even if he tried. Besides, Rand could never watch events from the sideline: he had to have a part in affairs no matter what they were. Already plans for improvement had begun to take form in his mind.

First he planned to look to sanitation. Then he would take up other matters. Carried away with his optimistic plans for the advancement of Purac, Rand had forgotten how science in the civilized world, where people have every opportunity for knowing and partaking of its advantages, has to fight ignorance and superstition at every step.

After lunch was served, Chinawa went to his room for his midday rest. A habit of a lifetime could not be interrupted many days by the coming of a stranger. It was well along in the afternoon before the councilors again assembled at the point of rendezvous. Shuyani and Rand were the first to arrive. Seeing the girl's troubled eyes upon him, Rand asked what she was worrying about.

"Is it really true, as you said, that an airplane cannot come here to Purac and take you away?" she asked.

"Oh yes, that is quite true, Shuyani. An airplane must have a clear space, either open ground or water, to land upon. They can't as yet come straight down. Some day they will, of course."

"Could they not land on the athletic field?" she asked.

"Perhaps, if some of the trees were cut," Rand replied. "But planes are not likely to come near Purac, and if they did, they would not dare alight, for you know the reputation Pampa Diablo has.

"No, there isn't a chance, Shuyani. We can't get out by land nor can we be picked up by air. So let us not entertain hopes there are no chances of realizing. We must make the best of it. Man and maid shipwrecked on a jungle island with not a wing in the sky! How is that for a setting of modern romance?" he asked laughingly.

Shuyani smiled faintly at Rand's refusal to be alarmed at the situation. She understood better than he the dangers he was facing and knew that no one could always win in a game of chance. History tells the fate of a pitcher that went to the well once too often.

The arrival of Jitibi interrupted the talk. Almost simultaneously Maiboya and one of her sisters came from the house. Maiboya was spinning by hand, a fine skein of huimba.

"That reminds me, Shuyani," Rand said, "I must get me a cuzma, and lay this garb away. They won't last always and I'd as well get used to going barefooted, which is going to be somewhat painful on these sharp granite pebbles, although I used to enjoy it when a youngster."

When they were informed of the decision, the other girls eagerly volunteered to help Shuyani make Rand a cuzma, and at once the three of them began to estimate how much longer his garment should be compared with the regulation Purac hand-me-downs. About the width of one hand longer, was the conclusion reached.

"I'm not so sure of that," Rand said. "I don't want the thing too long. But have it your way," he added as he thought to himself there would be discussions enough without bringing in the lengths of skirts so fruitful of argument in the civilized world.

"I shall not be able to tell you from a Puracian when you put on a cuzma," Shuyani said, "until I can see your eyes."

"Oh, yes you can. I shall always have a hat on as long as this old lid holds together. I can go barefooted, but not bareheaded in the tropical sun," Rand replied as he rubbed his close cropped head.

This directed attention towards Rand's hair which still failed to show evidence of the Puracian shade. Then attention was centered upon Shuyani. The other girls were disappointed in Shuyani. She had been in Purac three years and her hair still held the blue black luster it had had when she first appeared. Of course chunchas' hair never changed, but they were people of low caste; they did not and could not become Puracians. But everyone who lived in Purac became the same.

When this was explained to Rand he was amused, but not surprised. "All they have to do now is add the story of taking a drink out of Purac's chief water supply and it will be a typical booster club slogan," he thought.

The Chinawa girls induced Shuyani to ask Rand how they danced in his country. When he had explained that in his land dance steps were quite different, he was sure, from Purac dancing, they were very eager for him to demonstrate. Shuyani who knew the Purac dances, also tried to explain that they were different from those of the world outside. This excited the interest of the young people, and Jitibi suggested they have a party that night. Perhaps Shuyani and Rand would introduce some new steps. The idea "went over big," to employ the vernacular. The Puracian dialect was used in arranging the details and Rand was left to his own thoughts.

CHAPTER 10

The Sunset

Some of the councilors began to arrive. Then Chinawa came out and the conference opened in due form. Rand at once plunged into the plans he hoped to work out. First he would rid Purac of the mosquitoes. They were not only annoying, he explained, but a detriment to health. He asked if they had malaria and learned that there was some: it was more common over in the center of Purac. Upon inquiry Rand learned there was a cocha there.

Rand had seen several cases of elephantiasis, and although he did not know how this disease was transmitted, he thought it advisable to get rid of all the mosquitoes and every other blood sucking insect it was possible to destroy on the Pampa, for he had no means of knowing what they were responsible for. Even those that were not biological carriers of disease could be mechanical carriers; so they must all be eliminated.

How was he to get rid of the mosquitoes? Chinawa asked. It was a fine idea, but could it be done?

Rand saw at once that he must devise some means of mosquito control which the people could understand. Purac was a land of specialists. Why not have an entomologist? That was the idea!

116

"Who has charge of poultry?" he asked.

"Pacha Bata," he was told.

He must see Pacha Bata. That individual was expected any moment now; he was one of the councilors, Rand was told.

When Pacha Bata arrived he was amused that he had been selected to take charge of mosquito control: how could he control mosquitoes? You could neither herd them nor fence them in. Pacha Bata considered the idea a joke until he found the councilors were serious about the matter. Then he became irritated. Any man of his standing who had worked all his life with poultry, holding an important position in the economic life of Purac, devoting his time to mosquitoes! The idea was ridiculous. Heretofore the only control of mosquitoes he knew anything about was in the hands of small children who fanned them off some dignitary while that individual enjoyed a nap. Certainly the control of mosquitoes did not require the skill of a councilor.

Rand assured him that the control of insects required the very best skill to be found on Purac; that it took a mind which could reason beyond what could be seen with the naked eye. One must also use special mental faculties beyond what would be required to handle poultry properly.

Then Rand went into a rough sketch of the morphology of the mosquito. "First they lay eggs in water, just as chickens lay eggs in nests," he told Pacha Bata. Then they hatch out and live in the water like birds in a nest until they grow wings and feathers, like birds. Then they can fly away.

It was evident that Pacha Bata was getting enthused. This talk seemed reasonable.

At the eaves of most of the houses there were bamboo eave troughs which carried the rain water into large ollas. These

117

Rand noted were alive with wiggle tails, the larva stage of the mosquito. He asked Pacha Bata to get three gourds. When these were brought they went to one of the ollas of water where Rand pointed to the wigglers and said, "Baby mosquitoes."

Pacha Bata was somewhat skeptical.

Rand quietly looked until he located the pupa, or tumbler stage. He placed five specimens manifesting this stage into one of the gourds which was partially filled with water. Then he placed five more in another gourd. Into the third gourd he placed several large wiggle tails which he knew were almost ready to pupate. He then asked Pacha Bata to count the insects. There were five pupas in the first two gourds and seven large wigglers in the third. Pointing to the enlarged bump on the thorax of the pupa, Rand said, "Wings, tomorrow." Of the larva he said, "Baby today, boy tomorrow."

He then had a cloth cover tied over the three gourds, so nothing could escape, and Chinawa in turn had them placed in a room with orders that no one should molest them. Then Rand saw that a cloth was placed over the large olla of water after Pach Bata had examined it and said there were no mosquitoes in it, only the wigglers.

Rand knew it would be difficult to interest all the old people of Purac in mosquito control. He would have to appeal to the youth, for their minds would more readily take up new ideas. He must enlist the youths in a sort of boy scout organization. He told Pacha Bata that he would need all the boys to help. But to explain this need, he must go back to something tangible.

"Where do chickens come from?" Rand asked Pacha Bata.

"They come from eggs, of course."

"Where do the hens lay eggs?" he asked.

"We have nests for them."

"What if you destroy the nests?"

"Then the hens would have no place to lay. Eggs would be laid any place and the dogs would eat them."

"Mosquitoes come from eggs, too, Rand told him.

Pacha Bata had never thought of that. He had never seen any mosquito eggs. Rand asked him if he thought he could see hens' eggs if the hens were the size of mosquitoes.

"The mosquitoes," Rand explained, "lay their eggs in water. If they have no water to lay in, there will be no more mosquitoes."

Pacha Bata understood that; but was water really the nest for baby mosquitoes?

"That we shall know tomorrow," Rand replied, "but it will take many sharp eyes to find the small nests of the mosquitoes. Therefore you will need all the youths to help you. Get ten of the most intelligent boys to work with you tomorrow."

With sanitation measures under way, the council was ready to take up other matters. Going to the rear of his house, Chinawa led Rand into a room where two men were seated on the floor occupying themselves with a balance. The balance was made of a beam of hardwood about five feet long, with a hole in the center for suspension, while from a notch at each end was suspended a cord. The lower ends of these cords were attached to small, coarse, heavy cloth bags in one of which was a stone which Rand estimated to weigh about five pounds. A man was scooping up something from the floor and placing it in the other bag.

Rand gazed at the scene in astonishment, for he saw what the man was scooping from the floor, as though so many beans, was gold.

119

"Great Caesar!" he exclaimed. "Where in the world --"

"Cuidado," -- "be careful" -- rang out Shuyani's voice in Spanish. Although she was not looking at him, Rand knew the warning was for him.

It was about the gold of course. He had been informed often enough that the Puracians feared the gold seekers, the fear instilled in them by Puca Uma. He must not let his interest arouse suspicion. He pretended he was interested in the crude scale balance.

When there was enough gold in the bag to balance with the stone on the other end, the men would empty the gold bag into another coarse pouch lined with crude rubber; then one man would pick up a bean from a handy pile and place it in a small dish. When there were ten beans in the dish one of the men would take a stick that was used to keep tally and using a sharp edge of a piece of sand stone would file a notch in the tally sheet.

Once when the stone and gold balanced, Rand had the men reverse the weight to the opposite ends. The balance was the same; so Rand knew each bag represented about five pounds of gold, and that the records were correct.

After a minute inspection of the weighing apparatus and the system of keeping count, Rand pointed to the metal and inquired, in a matter-of-fact tone of voice, "Curi?" -- "Gold?"

"Yes," Chinawa replied. "You are now one of us, so there is no longer any need of keeping the secret from you. Besides, you are here alone and can never get out, so what can you do?"

Yes, that was it! What could he do? Nothing!

Rand laughed at the situation and with a shrug of his shoulders indicated agreement with Chinawa's logic.

"What do you do with this? I have seen none of it in use here," Rand asked.

"No, you have seen none of it in use because we do not use it," Chinawa replied. "Puca Uma warned us to shun curi above all things, never to make use of it, or allow it to accumulate, for it would bring a curse upon Purac if we did. It is the servant of Yushin -- the devil -- and we collect it, each moon it is taken to Ushca, the hole, and dumped back into Uca Pacha -- hell where it came from."

"You take it each moon?" Rand asked, looking at the fortune in gold lying at his feet.

"Yes, each moon. We would not think of letting this tool of the devil remain here in Purac."

"Each moon! Oh, boy!" Rand ejaculated in spite of himself. Then he tried to estimate thirteen moons each year for 551 years. The amount must be staggering. It could not be! Such a quantity of free gold could not be found on the Pampa. It was impossible.

Of course no streams could produce gold in this quantity over that length of time. The free gold would be cleaned off the surface within a few years.

"But it would be impossible to collect this amount of gold each month," Rand insisted.

"Yes, that is true," Chinawa admitted. "There was a land slide in the hills lately and this gold was uncovered and the Zachas brought it."

"Where does it come from?" he asked at last.

"Over there," Chinawa said with a sweep of the hand to the north. The Zachas bring it."

"The Zachas bring it!" That was different. Perhaps there were gold deposits near. They must be enormous to produce so much. It did not seem possible, yet where did the Inca gold come from? Pizarro and his followers, took many millions in gold from the Incas, yet historians say most of the Inca gold was concealed from the Conquistadores. Where did the Incas find their gold? All the torture inflicted upon them failed to make them reveal the source of their gold, and it remains a secret today.

Assuredly the Inca gold did not come from the coast or the barren Andes. Those regions have been gone over time and again, until most people consider the source of the Inca gold hidden some place on the eastern slope of the Andes, where rank tropical vegetation has concealed all trace of it.

Rand considered these points in rapid succession. Had he really stumbled upon the source of the famed "Riches of Peru", which has been the elusive hope of man for the past four hundred years? The gilded siren which has beckoned man deeper and deeper into the jungle only to mock his efforts to escape, and where the jungle Indians, to be rid of an unwelcome guest, would say, "Yes, the gold is over there." And white man would go on and on, or fall by the wayside. The search for the source of the Incas' gold had taken its toll as if in reprisal for the injustice of the white men's treatment of the Incas.

While he was thus reflecting the rest of the party were growing impatient with the delay. Apparently the only concern the Puracians had for the gold was to get it out of the way. The men placed ten stones' weight of gold in a bag as they took a light cargo, about fifty pounds, for one man to carry to the Ushcu, where it could be dumped back into hell where it belonged.

As they were starting to leave, Chinawa picked up an olla and said, "Yushin buero," -- "devil's eyes, these go too."

122

Rand at first glance thought the olla contained small quartz gravel. A second glance showed it to hold diamonds just as they were picked from the stream beds.

"Great guns," said Rand in an undertone. "Puca Uma, whoever you were, King Solomon had you beat in the number of wives, nothing more."

Now he was sure the diamonds were not found on Purac. There was no diamond-bearing soil on the Pampa. There were plenty of diamonds in eastern Brazil, but that was over a thousand miles from Purac.

"What are those?" Rand asked, as though he had no idea what they were and was merely curious.

Chinawa shrugged his shoulder in a non-committal way. Some one had called them Yushin buero, that was all he knew. They just did not want them around.

Rand dug into the olla and let the rough stones filter through his fingers. He had to pinch himself to make sure he was not lost in a dream. No, he was not dreaming he could feel the pain! He was going to feel another pain, too, when he saw all that wealth dumped into the bottomless pit.

Going outside, Chinawa led the way to the rim of the ledge overlooking the forest below. With a sweep of his arm to the north, he said, "It comes from there."

"How nicely it would all fit in," Rand thought, "if Puca Uma had come two hundred years later. But that's where I go off in a tangent and lose the facts. No doubt there were plenty of tyrants before Pizarro. Probably King Solomon himself wasn't a very good slave master; not many are."

It was late in the day and the sun was setting low. Standing on the point of the cliff, they could look down upon the tree tops two thousand feet below. The humid tropical air, chilled with the approach of nightfall, was forming into banks of clouds that the varied currents of air were moulding into grotesque shapes, ever changing before the eyes. The setting sun illuminated the whole, blending into all the colors of the spectrum.

Wonderful scene! Rand gazed, enthralled. No place in the world surpasses an Amazon river sunset, and from this point its sublimity was beyond description!

Rand's thoughts wandered off to the civilized world, where man is pitted against man in the mad struggle for existence. Where man, with all his skill, could only produce a crude caricature on a stage or canvas of what filled the whole heaven from where he stood among those simple contented people. It was all he could do to control his emotions. Turning around he said, "Shuyani --"

But what could he say? How could he express his feelings in the limited Quichua language, and she translate it?

Chinawa saw his emotion and slowly nodded his head. Yes, he understood.

With a sweep of his hand, Rand said, although it seemed most inadequate: "Shuyani, tell him this is worth more than all the curi in the world."

The party began to disperse, each going his way homeward. For the Puracians, this was a common sight. Just another sunset. They supposed all places had sunsets like that.

CHAPTER 11

The Tantiti-nete

Chinawa went off, called upon for advice about some matter. Shuyani, Rand, and Jitibi walked together towards the Chinawa house.

"What are you going to wear to the party tonight, Shuyani?" Rand laughingly inquired.

"What can I wear?" she responded. "I have been long in Purac. Besides, I was in rags when I came here. I did not arrive in Purac -- in -- a very, very nice condition -- "

"Go ahead and say it. You did not step out of the sky as I did. I know, I am a duffer to bring it up. You worked your way through toil and hardships to get here, while I just dropped down.

"Never mind," he said, his hand resting for a moment on her shoulder. "Wait until I have been here for a year or two and see how I look. I presume a shave would help matters right now. That is one place you have the advantage of me. No matter how long you stay here, you won't be bothered with a beard; but just look at what would happen to me if I were to break my clippers."

She smiled at his banter and passed into the girls' quarters while Rand and Jitibi continued on into the patio where they enjoyed a light dinner. No one seemed to consider much food necessary: there would be an abundance of that for the tantiti neti -- fiesta.

The tantiti-neti was being held in a garden set apart for this purpose. The grounds were directly rearwards of Chinawa's house. The park, or garden, instead of being enclosed in the regulation Puracian stone wall, was instead an arena surrounded by stone steps leading up about six feet, the entire center of which was filled in. Mounting the steps, Rand found the top level with plantings, walks and rock seats. A large square in the center was paved with what he first thought was hard packed dirt, but upon inspection and inquiries, he learned it was crude balata -- a species of hard rubber -- which made an ideal floor covering for barefooted primitive dancing.

At intervals there were square stone columns about one foot in diameter and six feet high. A round concave disk stone cap on the top of each column was a receptacle for a wood fire which was burning in each. A vent hole from the side near the top of the column led up to the center of the basin where the fire was placed. This supplied the fire with a draft. From piles of fuel near each column the fires were kept going.

There were flowering vine-covered trellises and flowering trees: it was a typical roof garden effect. Coming upon the scene before the arrival of the guests, with only small boys who had lighted the fire standing by, Rand stopped and gazed on the scene in wonder. Broadway in all its ingenuity could not surpass it, and he could easily imagine seeing a well drilled chorus come dancing out from behind the plantings.

He gazed at the artistic effect of the illumination in the flower-grown surroundings. Apparently not a factor had been overlooked. Even the elevation, with no surrounding walls,

126

permitted the maximum of ventilation necessary in a warm climate.

"I don't see how I am going to improve on Purac," he mused.

As usual with open air gatherings, the youngsters came first. They romped across the grounds and climbed over the seats, and would have wrecked the place before the party began had not the caretakers' watchful eyes restrained them.

The elderly people came next; their preparations for a tantiti-nete were simple. Not so with the younger set: elaborate preparations were made by them and criticisms invited, since mirrors were not available. Even Jitibi had deserted Rand to don his gala dress.

The first of the maidens to appear sought the shadows of the plants and giggled among themselves as the young men collected in groups on the steps surrounding the pavilion.

On a large table built up from the ground with stone, was placed a row of ollas containing some kind of beverages. These proved to be chicha and masato, the latter the fermented pulp of the tuber yucca -- mandioc -- which is mashed then placed in the sun until it has fermented, when it is mixed with water. The taste is similar to sour buttermilk. Both drinks have an alcoholic content. Zapallas -- gourds -- were beside the ollas where anyone feeling the need of a stimulant could supply it.

The musicians were the first to take advantage of the potations for who could blow a whistle if the throat were dry. After the handicap of dry throats was remedied, the musicians made their way to an elevated rock seat and began to test their instruments. No delicate adjustment to assure the correct pitch is necessary with the queña. The crude jungle drums were also used.

The older people led off in the dance. They would choose partners and dance in front of and around each other, never touching. Sometimes two men would favor one woman with their attention, then again two women would perhaps dance in front of one man. After the older people had started the dancing, the younger people began to crowd in to look on. Some sedate married man would reach out and pull a timid maiden into the circle, and automatically she would start off with the squatty, weaving rhythm of the Quichua dance.

The doleful, monotonous wail of the Quichua music was unmistakeable. It was very familiar to Rand, for he had heard it often all up and down the Andes.

However, there was nothing monotonous about the garb of the young ladies. They were all decked with bright colored cuzmas, and many were festooned with feathers from the gorgeous plumage of tropical birds. The young men, too, were adorned in feathers: these always drooped, never stood erect as they do with the North American Indian.

Still Shuyani had not arrived. Rand wondered how she would be dressed. He would have given anything to be able to recall the cruel words he had spoken in the afternoon. He knew his thoughtless question had hurt her keenly.

Jitibi appeared dressed in a brilliant red cuzma, girdled with green parrot feathers. A string of teeth of various kinds circled his neck and a bracelet of monkey teeth embraced his left wrist. Standing beside Rand he touched his elbow and pointed towards something at the far end of the pavilion. Rand caught a glimpse of something white, and then it disappeared behind a bush. Making their way towards the bush, they found Shuyani and Maiboya peeping out from behind it.

128

Maiboya was dressed in a white cuzma, but the upper part of her body was covered with a bodice that, at first glance, Rand thought studded with emeralds. "Good Lord!" he ejaculated, "first it's gold, then diamonds, now it's emeralds!"

Dragging the blushing Maiboya into the light, Rand saw the garb was composed of bright colored beetle wings! Their brilliant luster, reflecting in the light, equaled the brilliancy of court jewels. Nor was this all, for in Maiboya's hair were some half dozen live fire flies, tied here and there. They were not the dim-glowing fireflies of the temperate zone either, but the big, high-powered insects of the tropics which have two lights instead of one, like the headlights of a miniature automobile.

Rand looked at Shuyani. What a contrast to the gaudy barbarian costume of Maiboya! She was dressed in a plain, white cuzma, with no "jewels". She was smiling at him complacently.

I'd give a lot to know what you are thinking," Rand mused. "I wonder if you realize how much your good taste in dress elevates you above the rest. Poor girl, I wonder if you must spend all your life here!"

He glanced casually at Jitibi. But Jitibi was admiring Maiboya. The look in Jitibi's eyes told him that no matter how difficult it would be to tell what would become of Shuyani, he could be reasonably sure of Maiboya's future.

"You have no jewels," Rand said to Shuyani.

"Only these," she said holding up a bunch of jasmines. "Do you want one?"

"I'll take one if you will wear the rest," he replied. "I don't want to see you outdone."

She gave him a bud and then stuck another in her hair. "That's nice, isn't it?" she asked.

In the meantime the dancing had begun to respond to the jovial mood that had grown with visits to the refreshment stand. The mournful Quichua music beat with greater animation. Gyrations became more reckless and the dancers did not avoid each other with the skill displayed in the beginning.

Rand and Shuyani joined the others and all was going smoothly until the heel of Rand's hob nailed high top boots came down on a Puracian toe. War has resulted from less than this among primitive people, and some who are not so primitive. However, the incident was overlooked and good will was drunk at the refreshment table.

The party had progressed to where some of the older people began dropping out, when the younger set happened to remember what the affair had been arranged for in the first place. They immediately asked Shuyani and Rand to show them some of the new dances.

"Now, how are we going to dance to the queña and those drums?" Rand asked Shuyani.

"I'll tell you what we can do," she replied, "Let's take them through a quadrille; they can do that."

"Maybe," Rand replied, "if we can get the funeral march out of the musicians. A few more trips to the refreshment table should help some."

After repeated efforts, the music gave promise of results and the quadrille was arranged. Shuyani and Rand, Maiboya and Jitibi and two other couples were to try it first. Shuyani would, of course, have to do the coaching. All the stragglers who had been yawning and remarking that it was about time to go home, forgot about sleep. With everything ready they started off. Of course there was hopeless confusion and the fact that flying cuzmas looked alike on either male or female

130

added to the confusion. Shuyani finally dropped out, getting another girl to tae her place and by shoving this one here and that one there, she began to get results. Then Rand dropped out to assist Shuyani in directing. He could pull and push the others about. When the original couples had become proficient enough to carry on, other couples were brought in. In a short time the younger set were doing very well.

About midnight a steaming roast fowl, agoutis, and other meats were brought in: all had been roasted in the ground. The only criticism Rand had to make was to the effect that the meats were all cooked just as most jungle people cook. The phrase, "Cook until tender," is not found in jungle cook books. There is always plenty left for the teeth to do after the meal is prepared. This is fortunate, too, for there are no dentists, therefore nature must look after the teeth.

The hearty meal slowed down the party. The musicians demanded rest. Substitutes took their places and no one could tell the difference in the results. More of the older people went home while others of the younger set wanted to be initiated into the new dance. The fire tenders neglected the lighting system and only dull red glows came from the lamp posts. Volunteers heaped bundles of fuel on the glowing fires with such recklessness that fire bands fell, causing bare feet to scurry for safety.

Then, one after another, began to drift towards home. Shuyani and Rand, with several members of the Chinawa household, left together, Shuyani and Rand silent, the others talking among themselves in the Puracian dialect.

The next day some of the members of the council were tardy in assembling. But not so Pacha Bata, who was out early. He had ten young boys with him -- the nucleus of a Puracian Boy Scout organization. Rand strolled in the garden with Jitibi while the crowd gathered. He did not want to go near the mosquitoes until every person of authority had arrived.

He noticed an elderly man with somewhat stooped shoulders dressed in rich garb. Although his garb suggested rank, Rand had never seen him before.

"Jahuete Janeta," -- "What do you call that?" asked Rand, pointing out the new comer, unable to say "who" in Purac.

"Matiyero," said Jitibi with such reverence that Rand knew the new man was of some consequence in Purac.

Chinawa finally emerged, but still Shuyani was absent. Chinawa sent a messenger for her and she came, but with downcast eyes, with nothing like her accustomed fearless open gaze. However, Rand had no time to speculate on Shuyani's moods. Everything was not ready for the field trip to begin.

First Rand had the cover taken off the large olla which had contained so many larvae and pupae. Several mosquitoes flew out. Pacha Bata showed his astonishment and declared that he was sure there were no mosquitoes in the olla yesterday. The three gourds in which the specimens had been placed were then brought and Pacha Bata explained to the crowd what was in each gourd.

Rand then removed the cloth from the gourd which had contained the pupae and two mosquitoes flew out. The gourd that had contained only the larva stage was now opened and of the seven larvae of yesterday, there were only three now and four pupae. Rand assured the interested on-lookers that the other larvae would pupate by the next day. He then took the remaining gourd and shook it violently. When it was opened there were three adult mosquitoes floating on the water and two of the pupae still in that stage.

When the demonstration was over, Rand stood for a moment looking at the doubtful faces before him. Then he explained how easy it would be to experiment for themselves in their own homes; thus they might hope to remove all doubt. Then he asked Pacha Bata to explain mosquitoes to the Puracians just as he would explain chickens to people who knew nothing about them. Pacha Bata did this in a manner which showed clearly why he occupied the chair of poultry husbandry at Purac.

After this discussion was finished Rand had Chinawa and Pacha Bata explain the method more in detail to the ten boys, all of whom had watched the demonstration with the alert eagerness of youth. Then Rand explained his plan of proceeding with the work. Pacha Bata was to have charge of the work and each of the ten boys was to have a team of his own and each team was to have an area assigned to it and was to see that no mosquitoes could find a place to lay eggs.

"All receptacles containing water must be dumped," he finished emphatically.

"But where will we bathe?" asked several at once.

Rand looked his astonishment and it was hurriedly explained that the water he had used for his demonstration was for the family bath. They could not bring enough water from the spring for bathing purposes, so rain water was caught in these ollas. Whenever a person wished to bathe he climbed into the olla and bathed in a squatting position, then left the water as it was for the next bather.

Rand thought a moment then turned to Pacha Bata.

"If you close a nest so a hen can't get in, she can't lay in that nest. The same thing would happen to a mosquito. If the ollas of water were covered with a cloth to prevent the mosquitoes from getting inside they could lay no eggs there, then there

133

would be no baby mosquitoes, for mosquito eggs cannot hatch if they are not laid in water."

Pacha Bata grasped the idea at once, and began planning what they could use for covers. What was needed was a covering that would not be difficult to place. Rand offered a prize for the boy who would design the best cover for the ollas of water. Until this cover was designed, cloth coverings were to be used. In two days the judges would meet and decide which of the boys had designed the best cover. Chinawa, Pacha Bata, and Rand were to be the judges. The prize was to be a small mirror from Rand's kit bag.

After this the boys were taken on a trip through the village to show them how and where to look for breeding places. Most of the councilors made the trip, too, but Rand concentrated all his efforts towards seeing that Pacha Bata and the ten boys understood what they were about.

He showed them the breeding places were not only in containers about the houses, but also in pitcher plants, banana shoots, the hollow of tress, and other places where water could be trapped. The progress the class made was nothing short of marvelous. Born and bred close to nature, as were the people of Purac, they readily understood what Rand explained to them.

As they were returning from the field, Chinawa looked around at the clear sky and remarked that it was going to rain. Others agreed with this prophecy.

"Are you sure of it?" Rand asked, looking in vain for some indication of a cloud.

Yes, they were sure it would rain before the day was over. Perhaps late in the afternoon.

"If it is going to rain, why not get the cloths ready, and when it starts raining dump all the wiggler infested water out

134

of the bath supplies, then screen the <u>ollas</u> so no mosquitoes can lay eggs in there?" asked Rand.

Pacha Bata assented to this suggestion and gave instructions at once for all ollas to be dumped and screened as soon as the rain had begun.

"They certainly take to new fads," Rand mused. "It would not be like this every place."

Rand had started such a vigorous mosquito campaign that he almost eradicated himself along with the mosquitoes, but this he did not know until later.

Matiyero, the new member of the group, followed Rand's every move with his eyes and listened attentively to all Shuyani's translations. Otherwise he ignored Rand completely.

After Matiyero had left the party, on the return trip, Rand asked Shuyani who he was.

"He is head of Auca Ambi, the medicine men of Purac," she replied. "If you make an enemy of him, your days here will be numbered."

There was no time for further talk, as the party was now disbanding. Tomorrow the gold was to be taken to Uschu.

By mid-afternoon, clouds began to roll in the east and the sky became overcast. The ollas of infested water were being dumped and cloth strainers placed over them. Soon the tropical storm broke over Purac and the down pour was heavy for a while, then developed into a slow rain that continued into the night.

CHAPTER 12

An Exciting Day at Ushcu

The village was astir the next morning early. Preparations were being made for returning the moon's accumulation of gold to the sender. Rand understood the event was carried out with elaborate ceremony under the direction of the Auca Ambi. Matiyero himself was to be in charge.

The musicians were out in force with queñas and drums, representing Purac's fife and drum corps. Everyone was dressed in fantastic garb and many were masked to represent some animal. They were to collect at a point southward called Ubini where the procession would be formed and the real ceremony begun. The bags of gold and other consignment to the infernal region was dispatched by cargodores to Ubini.

Rand was disappointed to learn that only the adult male population were eligible to take part in the ceremony. He did not want to miss any of the details and how could he learn anything without Shuyani? He tried to coax Shuyani to ask Chinawa if she could go, but this she refused to do. However, Chinawa asked what the discussion was about and when told, he too, was quite emphatic about the matter. It was not a woman's business and that settled it.

"But since most of you are masked, how is one to tell man from woman?" Rand asked.

Chinawa looked at Shuyani quizzically.

"Of course if a woman were to mask and go I would know nothing about it," he said glancing at Rand with an amused smile.

Rand turned eagerly to Shuyani. "Certainly I do not want you to risk any danger," he said, "but you know this idea of danger is all ignorant superstition. Come on, let's get masks. Get Maiboya to mask, also, and the four of us will go together."

Maiboya and Jitibi were enthusiastic about the plan. Reluctantly Shuyani consented.

The departure for Ubini was in groups of two and three, up to several. Some were masked, but for the greater part most people carried their masks to be donned at Ubini since the masks were warm and it was pleasanter to go without them until the ceremony should begin. Shuyani and Maiboya wore their masks from the start, of course. Rand and Jitibi were to mask at Ubini.

For some distance the route led south over the road Rand had used in coming to Churic, then it branched off to the right, and shortly afterwards the party arrived at a large square building set upon a slight elevation and surrounded by a grove of trees. There were no other houses near, but otherwise the country was like the rest of the pampa: there was no underbrush and each tree was of some useful variety.

There was a reasonably large crowd surrounding the building. Ollas of chicha and masato were placed conveniently, and apparently all were taking advantage of this hospitable opportunity. Shuyani told Rand it was furnished by the Auca Ambi who always supplied abundance of liquid refreshments for this event. In fact it was sometimes with difficulty that some of the people were able to return home, while in some instances this task was left wholly to the favor of friends. Shuyani seemed anxious to tell Rand more, but could not since conversation had to be carried on in whispers in order not to attract attention to a strange dialect.

At about this time there sounded a pounding of a trocan at rear of the building. Some command was shouted and the crowd began to gather behind the two lines of musicians formed in front. Then the queña whistle took up a doleful wail and the drums were beaten in that same melancholy cadence. Matiyero advanced from the building garbed in a flaming robe with a large wicker basket, or container, suspended in front of him, like a cigarette girl's tray in a night club. Following Matiyero was a litter bearing the moon's consignment and carried by four sturdy Puracians, flanked on each side by three richly garbed members of the Auca Ambi.

All wore masks over their faces, as did Chinawa who followed directly behind the litter of treasures. It seemed Chinawa's task was to see the treasures well on their way back to the devil, and nothing further. Otherwise the procedure was entirely in the hands of the Auca Ambi.

The musicians followed directly behind Chinawa while the others fell in behind this. Everyone had now donned masks. Jitibi was quite perturbed at Rand's reckless folly of wanting to expose himself to the danger barefaced; so in order to appease Jitibi's anxiety Rand tied a cloth over his face just below his eyes in true bandit fashion. This served its purpose as far as Rand was concerned, and it complied with their custom. Though if the devil was anywhere nearly as adept at doing his stuff as he is reputed to be, Rand could not see how a mask would be a serious handicap.

Leaving Ubini, the procession passed through a rich agricultural tract where corn, rice, and other crops were grown in abundance. Although the houses were set some distance back, Rand could see here and there old building sites, the walls of which had almost disintegrated with time. These walls he could see had originally been of limestone and not the enduring granite of which most of the buildings of Purac were constructed. Later they came to an abrupt slope overlooking a mat of jungle where the rigid control of plant growth practiced on most of Purac was not in evidence. To the east, in the basin, was the same intense agriculture; but to the west lay the uncontrolled jungle.

"That's interesting," thought Rand to himself. "This addition to Purac did not sell like the other tracts. I wonder why?"

As they descended into the depression Rand saw they were leaving the granite plane behind and coming upon a limestone plane, a freak in geology. This explained the abrupt change in contour.

The procession followed along in the flat paralleling the elevation which was on the right. The wail of the queña increased with the excitement of the operators as the Uschu -- the hole -- was approached. The spirit of the occasion had begun to effect Rand. He could almost imagine himself in the presence of the super-natural. Again and again he would assure himself there was nothing in it, but all he could say was, "Bunk, pure bunk," which was a poor excuse as a logical argument.

Coming upon a small knoll overlooking the road ahead, he could see the advance column halt and begin to spread out. Jitibi pointed to this and whispered in an undertone, "Uschu." Shuyani and Maiboya refused to go farther. Near by was a large granite boulder weighing many tons that had fallen from the hill at the right. Rand told the three to climb upon this boulder and await his return. He then made his way through the crowd to the edge of the fissure in the earth called Uschu. It was in a line of drainage from the pampa behind. For years the water had percolated through this point and dissolved a passage through the limestone. The water had found another fissure farther back and was eating its way along some place below the surface, robbing Uschu of the medium that had eroded out its sides through eons of time. Rand dropped a small stone into the opening and heard it hit against a projecting side some place below then bump along with the depths, each bump becoming less audible until the sound was lost in the distance. The opening at the surface was about six by ten feet with hanging vines extending for some distance within.

Completing his inspection, Rand returned and climbed upon the rock and watched the procedure with the three others. Matiyero, standing at the brink of the hole, denounced Yushim -- the devil -- for sending gold to jeopardize the peace and security of Purac.

Then the five heavy rubber-lined sacks were emptied into the pit, after which the olla containing the diamonds was dropped in. At intervals during the ceremony, Matiyero would take from his basket small conical tubes of some powder rolled in banana leaves and would blow this into the air over the hole. This, Rand was told, was to keep down the evil spirits. Matiyero made some sort of public announcement in which, Shuyani said, he asked those who had implements possessed with evil spirits to rid themselves of them.

Someone cast in a chichica -- knife -- that had cut its owner; another a flecha -- arrow -- that had done some damage. Other articles followed.

Matiyero seemed to be waiting for something. No one could go until he concluded the ceremonies. There was a cry from beyond the pit. People fell back in horror as someone collapsed and fell to the ground. Not a sound was made by either man or instrument. Rand saw Matiyero standing rigid at the brink of the pit. One of the Auca Ambi strode toward the commotion. He looked at the prostrate form on the ground, then motioned towards the pit. The limp form was carried to the pit and tossed in. In horror Rand asked what had happened.

"The evil spirits have taken him," Shuyani whispered, barely able to articulate.

A surge of indignation swept over Rand. He did not know how it had happened, but he knew some cruel murder had been committed. The crowd stood in awed silence. Who would be the next victim?

Rand began to understand the danger he had urged Shuyani into. Suppose she or Maiboya were to be a victim, wouldn't he be directly to blame? He did not have long to wait, for while these thoughts were passing through his mind another victim collapsed within a few yards of where he himself was standing. He, like the first victim, was cast into Uschu without ceremony.

Rand was beside himself with the injustice and horror of the affair. He was on the verge of going and telling Matiyero that if another man went into that hell hole he would throw Matiyero himself headlong after the victim. But what could he prove? All Purac stood resigned to the fate. It had been going on for centuries and how could one unarmed man change it? Once more he was face to face with his old jinx, superstition.

There was a shout almost beneath the rock Rand was standing upon. Looking down he saw a log, on which several were standing, roll, and one fellow fell headlong into some vines. With a shout of pain the man jumped to his feet and the onlookers were horrified to see a large snake dragged into the open, its fang still imbedded in the victim's forearm.

With a bound Rand leaped upon the reptile with his high boots and stamped the life out of it before it could recover for another strike. With one slash of his knife he cut a hole back of the cuff of the man's sleeve, inserted a stick into this band and twisted it deep into the flesh of the arm, cutting off all circulation from the body. All this was done so quickly that only those standing near saw what had happened.

With a tourniquet on before the circulation of the blood could start to carry the venom through the system, Rand felt he was master of the situation. Looking at the reptile he saw that it was what he first suspected, a surucucu, or bushmaster, one of the most venomous and the worst feared snakes in all South America.

Calling Shuyani he told her to instruct Jitibi to hold the tourniquet in place while he lanced the wound. Only one fang had entered the forearm, a very superficial wound. With a swift stroke of his knife Rand had the wound laid open to the depth of the puncture made by the fang. The flow of blood flushed the wound. Rand asked Shuyani to have water brought to cleanse the cut. None seemed to be available, so a messenger was dispatched for water. Assured that most of the venom had been flushed from the wound, Rand had now nothing left to do but wait the arrival of water.

While waiting, his mask forgotten, Rand looked around and saw Matiyero standing near watching the proceedings. It was a plain case of snake bite and no room for superstition; so feeling himself on solid ground, so to speak, Rand pointed to the wound in the arm then to the dead snake he had stamped to death. Matiyero looked at the snake and threw up his hands in horror.

The water had arrived by this time and Rand forgot all about Matiyero as he cleaned the wound with a strong solution of potassium permanganate, crystals of which he always carried in the jungles, then bound it up. Shuyani was helping and they were both working desperately, oblivious of the fact that both masks were off and that they were the center of unsought interest.

When the arm was properly dressed, Rand released the tourniquet which Jitibi had been holding. The patient could not seem to realize that he was still alive. He stood dazed, but apparently he was not suffering any great pain.

"He's all right now," Rand said. "The only way he could die now would be from a weak heart, which isn't likely. All we have to do is to get him away from this place."

"Haurmi," -- "woman" -- Matiyero hissed, finding his voice at last, and Rand turned to find him starring at Shuyani. The conversation that followed was not understood by Rand other than that it grew animated as it progressed. It was apparent that Shuyani was telling Matiyero she had accompanied Rand to explain the procedure to him and that she was not intending to overstep the Puracian bonds of female ethics. Matiyero was appalled. The more he learned of the situation, the more horrified he became. The idea of trying to save a man's life who was bitten by a surucucu! Wasn't the surucucu the servant of the Yushim? The man must be cast into the Uschu at once. Nothing could save him and the longer he was kept from Uschu the more enraged the spirits would be.

The victim was pleading piteously. Matiyero glared from one to the other. The prophecy about the retribution one would instantly suffer who killed a snake was not being fulfilled. Nervously Matiyero dug into his basket and took

143

one of his tubes. This he placed to his mouth and blew the brown powder into the air, directly toward Rand and Shuyani.

"Do not inhale. Hold your breath," Rand said to her in Spanish. At the same time he removed his hat and while mopping his perspiring brow, began to fan vigorously with his hat. The current of air would diffuse the powder from in front of him and Shuyani. Rand thought he saw a look of chagrin sweep over Matiyero's face, and surmised he had thwarted the latter's designs.

Chinawa standing behind Matiyero was a silent observer of everything that took place, and although Shuyani could not help seeing him, she did not appeal to him for assistance in her discussion with Matiyero. Although Chinawa must have felt guilty in that he had permitted Shuyani to attend the ceremony masked as a man, he apparently was thankful that she was keeping his name out of it.

Unable to understand, Rand was an impatient onlooker and wanted to get an understanding of what it was all about. However, he did not dare turn his back upon Matiyero, and watched every move of the chief of Auca Ambi. The other members were standing around their chief awaiting his orders.

Matiyero was crafty enough to know that the longer the situation stood as it was now, the more his prestige would suffer. This stranger had not only stamped the life out of one of the reptile spirits, but had apparently saved the life of one bitten. Such a recovery had never been known before. Very well, he could deal with this treason in his own way. There would be plenty of means for chastising the headstrong in the future. He raised his hand above his head and declared the ceremony over.

Rand and Shuyani each took an arm of the victim of the snake bite and started to help him along.

"What was all the row about that snake?" Rand asked.

"No one is permitted to kill snakes near Uschu," Shuyani replied. "They are supposed to be spirits sent by Yushim to guard this region."

Rand stopped in his tracks. "That is the story, is it!" he exclaimed. "Very well. I'm not through with this yet."

He dropped the arm of the victim and returned hurriedly to where the snake lay. He cut off the head, wrapped it in some leaves, then tied the bundle to the end of a stick with a small vine. This completed he said, "Just as well be on our way now. I want this head for future use."

Several of the Puracians had watched Rand prepare the head to take with him. They were astonished, but this did not bother him. He wanted plenty of witnesses to what was being done. Jitibi and Maiboya were standing beside Shuyani. Now Jitibi pointed to a trail leading due north. By taking this they soon escaped the crowd, and following the narrow trail along a gentle slope, came to the level plane above.

No one had spoken since they left the scene of the near tragedy. Rand now turned his attention to his patient. The climb up the hill had started rapid blood circulation and a small portion of the venom had entered the blood stream and had made the native sick. Rand told him to sit quiet for a few moments until the nausea passed off. The patient, Rand learned was named Yanga and was a son of Pacha Bata whom Rand had enlisted in the mosquito control.

While they were resting, Rand looked back over the area surrounding Uschu. A matted jungle met his gaze. Elsewhere almost every foot of ground on this main pampa was growing useful plants or trees.

"Why is not that ground utilized?" Rand asked Shuyani, who in turn passed the question on to Jitibi.

"That," said Jitibi, "is infested with evil spirits. No one dares go near the place, only the Auca Ambi."

"And the runu -- snakes -- ?" Rand asked.

"No one dares try to kill them," Jitibi replied. "It would anger Yushim."

"Are there many runus near the Ushcu?" Rand asked.

"There are a great many. Many more than on all the rest of Purac and more than are found in the Zacha below. All the bad runu come out of Uschu."

Rand could now understand something of the conditions. The area near Uschu produced large quantities of grain -- food for rodents. In turn the rodents are the natural food of snakes. These snakes were not molested in their propagation ground in the jungle surrounding Uschu. Snakes increase with civilization owing to the absence of their predacious enemies found in the wilderness. The reptiles were protected by superstition -- as are cesspools of contamination the world over.

Yanga now felt able to travel and they started on towards Churic. At the first village reached the trio stopped to eat and Yanga demonstrated that his experience had not impaired his appetite. Shuyani and Maiboya had hurried on to Churic alone in order not to be seen returning from the forbidden ceremony. Of course everyone would soon learn of Shuyani's escapade, but Maiboya had not been recognized. Yanga stood the return trip to Churic very well. The news of his accident had preceded him, and his father, Pacha Bata, was one of the first to meet the party on their return. Yanga stood before his father and smiled broadly at the latter's astonished gaze.

After Pacha Bata had assured himself Yanga was really alive, he began to question Chinawa. Of course Chinawa had not seen the serpent bite Yanga, but Jitibi had. Jitibi described the incident. Wasn't he standing almost directly above and saw Yanga stagger back, dragging the snake fastened to his arm by the fangs? Then he pointed to the bunch of leaves in which Rand had wrapped the snake's head. When Rand saw interest centered on his package, he unwrapped the leaves and exposed the head to view. There was no doubt of the identity of the reptile. "Surucucu," they all pronounced in awe.

Interest having been turned to Rand and his trophy, an interpreter was necessary. They must have Rand explain his magic. Shuyani was sent for and when she arrived Chinawa told her to ask Rand how his magic had overcome that of the Yushan. Here Rand hesitated. How was he to explain the action of snake venom? That was what he had brought the head along for, but this explanation would take time. Besides, did he want to explain it to everyone? Matiyero was as much mystified as were the others and perhaps it would be advantageous to keep him mystified.

With this idea in view Rand simply told his listeners it was a serious matter. Then he told Shuyani to take Chinawa aside and explain to him that he, Rand, wanted just four, herself, Chinawa, Pacha Bata, and Jitibi, to go with him to a room where they could make a fire and he would explain the "magic".

The party entered a room next to where the gold had been stored. A fire was kindled on the rock floor and Rand split the snake's head neatly open along one of the fangs, back beyond the venom gland in the head, thus showing the connection of the fang with the poison gland. Then he split the head open along the other fang until he could pick the fang out. This he placed in a small olla in which he had previously placed some water, and put it on the fire. Soon the water was boiling. After this had continued for sometime, he dumped the water out and put in clean water. When this process had been repeated until Rand was sure the fang had lost all its venom in the process of boiling, he picked it up and taking from his pocket a low powered microscope, which he always carried, he showed them the hollow extending from the base of the fang throughout its length and to the needle-like point at the end.

They were all profoundly impressed by the small microscope and what it revealed. It was wonderful magic to them. Rand told them there were microscopes so powerful that objects too small to be seen with this one could be made visible. Pacha Bata remarked he could now understand how the people in Rand's country could be so wise, for they could see so much more than was revealed to the naked eye.

Rand had Shuyani explain the venom gland, how the compression on this poison gland produced in striking forced the venom through the hollow and out from the needle-like joint, deep into the flesh. They understood this. But how did Rand get the poison from the wound after the snake had deposited it?

Knowing he could not explain the circulating system, Rand merely said the tourniquet prevented the passage of the venom into the body and that the cut permitted the blood to wash it out, which was true of course, in a way.

"What would happen if one were bitten in a part of the body where no tourniquet could be used," Pacha Bata asked. This question pleased Rand for he could see his explanation had been understood.

"In that case," he replied, "there is nothing to do but cut quick and be sure all the area pierced by the fang is laid open for the blood to wash out as much as possible. The wound should then be sucked by the mouth and then the poison spit out. It is often impossible to save one so bitten."

After the demonstration was over Rand asked each person present to say nothing about his experiments for a few days as he did not want Matiyero to understand. This was approved. Jitibi was so enthusiastic over the information that he was almost ready to go out and get bitten by a surucucu just to show his knowledge; but Rand told him it was not always as simple as it looked, and to remember the boy who thought he could jump off the cliff with the parachute.

Going back to the patio they found Yanga the center of a curious throng who had come to see if he were still alive. Many of them had been at Uschu, while others who had heard of the incident had come to see one alive who had been bitten by a surucucu. Sometimes one had lived after a scratch, but never where the runu had such a hold that he was dragged by the one bitten. Even Matiyero had come, and perhaps he was the most puzzled individual in Purac just then. However, he did not make any inquiries as to the magic. It would never do for the chief of Auca Ambi to admit he had met with a magic he did not understand.

The approaching shower sent people towards their homes. Rand told Pacha Bata that he wanted Yanga to stay with him that night. Rand distrusted Matiyero and he did not want to risk any chances. He felt Matiyero would be pleased to see Yanga dead in the morning, and that catastrophe Rand was determined should not happen, if he could prevent it. Pacha Bata started for home, but turned back at the door. Looking around for Shuyani he motioned her to come, also Rand. When the three had reached a place that Pacha Bata considered absolutely safe from all ears, he had Shuyani ask Rand if runus really come out of Uschu.

"Certainly not," Rand replied. "All snakes come from eggs, just like chickens."

Yes, Pacha Bata knew some did. He had seen both snake eggs and baby snakes, but didn't the bad snakes come out of Uschu?"

Rand assured him they did not.

Pacha Bata considered this reply for a moment, then he turned and left abruptly, chuckling to himself as he went.

Rand looked after him in wonder. "What do you suppose he has on his mind now?" he asked Shuyani.

"Do not try to measure the Puracian mind by your own," she answered.

"I shall try to remember that," he replied. "Just look what a jam I got you into today. What killed those people?"

Shuyani shrugged her shoulders. "How should I know?"

"Are there always victims on each occasion?" Rand inquired.

"Yes, always,"

"But why do the people attend each time, if there are always some to be cast into the hole?"

"They go because they are required to by the Auca Ambi. Each village has a pro-ratio to supply. Each moon the curacas send their quota."

So that was it! It was compulsory service. Yet there was no weeping and wailing with the departure! But such is the primitive mind. It was the inevitable they had been trained to endure.

When they returned to the others, Rand noticed Chinawa seemed deeply impressed with the days events. He would look first at Rand then at Yanga. Finally he went to the latter and felt him over as though to assure himself Yanga was still normal.

Matiyero started for the Auca Ambi house. As the large raindrops, the forerunner of a tropical shower began to fall, a terrific crash of thunder, accompanied by a blinding flash of lightning, split a tall castaña tree standing in front of Matiyero's house. He stopped for an instant then hurried on as fast as he could run, whether from fear of a wetting or from superstition's terror, no one but himself knew. Chinawa gazed after him deep in meditation, then slowly shaking his head, he turned and went towards his room.

CHAPTER 13

The Stranger's Magic

Darkness was coming on with the rainfall. The evening meal among the men was without interest and immediately after it, Rand and Yanga retired to Rand's room.

Yanga was soon asleep in a corner of the room on some mats one of the servants had brought in for the purpose. Rand sat listening to the rainfall outside. He had about decided to retire when there came a timid knock on the door.

Upon opening the door, Rand saw Shuyani and Maiboya crouched in the shadows. Silently they slipped into the room and after the door was closed behind them, Shuyani, after hesitating for a moment, said:

"I had to see you. Perhaps you do not know -- do not understand. It's -- it's Matiyero. He says you are at league with the devil because you cured one bitten by the surucucu. No one but an evil spirit, he says, could do that."

"They can't believe that, the people can't! You know better, don't you, Shuyani?" Rand asked.

"Yes, I know better, but what difference does that make? Could I convince anyone? Besides, didn't you pledge those to whom you explained the action of a snake bite, to secrecy?"

Rand considered; would it be advisable to have Chinawa and the others explain his procedure, or keep Matiyero in the dark for a while? The more he could puzzle Matiyero the better it would be, he concluded.

"We can't do anything tonight, Shuyani," he said. "Thank you for telling me. We shall decide what to do tomorrow."

"You can't do anything tonight, that's true; but what can Matiyero do?" said Shuyani, glancing around the room.

"You mean? I see. Well, I'll look out for that. Yanga and I both being in this room alone, I can understand why the chief of Auca Ambi would be interested. But I shall be on my guard. No one can get in here unless I know it. I shall fix the door some way."

"How about the windows," asked Shuyani.

"No chance! I looked at those bars the first night I was here. It would take a sledge hammer to break them."

"Powders can be blown through them, can't they?" she asked.

"That's right, those powders! But I'll arrange that, don't worry. How did you get here?" he asked.

"It was a terrible chance. If the Auca Ambi haven't a spy watching this room, I don't know them. But I had to warn you."

"Poor friend, always getting into hot water on my account. You and Maiboya go now, and thanks. Just to show you that I appreciate what you have done for me, I promise to look out for the magic powders tonight. I'll be here in the morning, if that will be any compensation for the trouble you have taken."

"It will," she said and was gone like a spirit, she with Maiboya.

After they had gone, Rand took stock of the situation. First he examined the door. One of the heavy carved log seats he dragged to the door and blocked in such a manner that the door could not be forced without upsetting the heavy block. In case this was done, he would awaken. There were windows on both sides of the room, high small ones, but adequate for cross ventilation. The bars of the windows he examined again. No matter from what angle he looked at it, there were always those powders to consider. Rand knew the medicine men of the jungle knew many medicinal plants unknown to civilization. They studied plants for their toxic effect as well as curative powers. No doubt the medicine men of Purac had all the cunning of the jungle savage; even more, for they had been undisturbed on the pampa for centuries where knowledge could be developed and handed down with greater accuracy than among the harassed semi-nomadic tribes of the jungle.

Could it be possible that the drugs were so powerful that inhaling a few flakes of them might be fatal? If that was what killed the men at Uschu in the open air, there would be no chance with a handful of it tossed into a closed room.

He wished now he had watched the behavior of the men of the Auca Ambi today. Now he could not recall whether or not there was a medicine man near either of the poor fellows who collapsed. Perhaps he had better slip from the room and make his way to some place out in the park-like groves and sleep under a tree. But there was Yanga: he could not leave him to the danger -- if there were danger. Nor could he take him along, for how could he explain without an interpreter, what he wanted to do? Yanga was sleeping like a child in the security of the stranger's magic that was more powerful than that of the Auca Ambi.

Rand paced the floor trying to think what to do. He made a minute inspection of the door again. The rough door did not

154

fit very tightly, of course. There was an open space under it, and he noted a current of air flowing in through this crack.

"Now I have it, " he thought. "I'll sleep here. The air coming in here will be pure."

Arranging his bed he blew out the light and then took the bed clothing from the built-in bed and arranged it on the floor where his head would be near the crack where the current of air entered under the door. Feeling secure and tired, he soon fell into a fretful sleep.

Once he awoke, thinking he detected a strange odor coming under his door. He had never thought of this when he lay down, and now the possibility came to him so vividly while asleep.

However, nothing happened and he slept by naps until daylight. With the light of day came a feeling of security which made Rand really ashamed of the panic he had permitted himself to experience in the dark. When daylight comes how absurd appear our fears of the unknown which are experienced in the dark!

Yanga was fully recovered and had only the laceration in his arm to remind him of the deadly bushmaster's bite of yesterday.

He was unable to talk to Rand, of course; that is, he was unable to make himself understood, but he kept up a continuous monologue which Rand acknowledged by grunts of assent. He followed Rand into the garden and was right at his heels all the time. Of course it was difficult for the average Puracian to understand there were other languages besides his own.

Shuyani emerged and joined them soon after they entered the garden.

"Here I am, as I promised," was Rand's greeting to her. "I did not let the powders get me."

Shuyani looked at him with a wan smile, and he was at once ashamed of himself. If only she knew how he had behaved throughout the night, what would be her opinion! He had no right to the bold mood he affected now.

Chinawa came out and asked how Yanga was feeling. Chinawa seemed very jovial. Someone said something about Matiyero, and he laughed outright at the remark. Rand wondered what it was, but Shuyani did not enlighten him. Shuyani seemed to be the only one down-hearted, the rest were in gay spirits. Pacha Bata arrived and after one look at his son, went and patted Rand on the back.

Chinawa's larder supplied about half the neighbors with breakfast. However, most of the guests were interested in Yanga who seemed to be the stimulus for conversation. Rand was regarded with awe and he was sure some of the animated conversation was about himself.

Matiyero came later, and upon the latter's arrival there was a change in the assembly. Chinawa, Pacha Bata, and some of the others who had waxed eloquent in the talk before, had now nothing to say. All seemed to wait for Matiyero to take the initiative. But that gentleman had little to say. It was evident Matiyero's presence had produced a strained situation. They did not feel free to discuss matters as they had before.

At Rand's request, Shuyani told Pacha Bata to get his boys together in the afternoon in order that they might make an inspection trip to see how the eradication of mosquitoes was progressing. Then Rand and Jitibi went for a stroll towards the east of the pampa.

It was a relief to get out and stroll among the trees with Jitibi who had learned to respond to Rand's moods. If Rand wanted to talk in their limited way, Jitibi was always ready and anxious; while if on the contrary, he wanted to stroll along meditating in silence, Jitibi dropped a pace or two behind, always within reach but never forcing himself into cognizance.

In an environment favorable for meditation, Rand's mind naturally became occupied with Matiyero. Why did his coming throw such a damper upon the assembly in the patio? Before he came, Chinawa had been in a very agreeable mood, Rand had never seen him so care free. But with the coming of Matiyero, Chinawa closed up like a clam. Pacha Bata and others had done likewise. Somewhere there was a delicate adjustment in the Puracian life or custom that had been slightly out of balance. Of course Matiyero and his Auca Ambi were the wasp in the soothing lotion, but why? Wasn't the council supreme?

It was midday when Rand and Jitibi returned. The crowd had dispersed and the midday lull in action had settled over the village. Rand started to his room but saw Shuyani hurrying towards him.

"I have been watching for you," she began. "I was afraid you would go into your room before I could warn you. Matiyero has been in there."

"Matiyero? What did he go there for?"

"I don't know. After you left they talked for sometime. I wanted to hear what was said, but I could see they did not want me, so I left; but I kept Matiyero in sight. I saw him get up and yawn as if bored with the talk, then stroll leisurely about. Once or twice he passed the door of your room, but paid no attention to it. At last apparently thinking he was unobserved, he stepped quickly into the room. I was frightened, but what could I do? I did not dare tell anyone, although I was sure he was up to some mischief. In a few

157

moments he came out and strolled casually away, leaving for the Auca Ambi house soon afterwards. Whatever his purpose, I am sure it has been accomplished."

"Have you told anyone?" Rand asked.

"Not yet. I was awaiting your return. I wanted to tell you first."

"Where is Chinawa?" was Rand's next question.

"In his room. Pacha Bata and he are discussing something."

"Will you please ask them both to come here?"

"Certainly," she replied. She left on the errand at once and soon returned with the two men.

Rand asked her to tell them what she had seen. Chinawa and Pacha Bata both showed that they considered the situation serious. They looked at each other perplexed. Then Rand saw Chinawa's mouth set with a look of determination that Rand had seen before when Chinawa had been confronted with problems that taxed his primitive mind. Holding up his hand as a signal for the others to remain as they were, he strode into the room. Those outside listened with abated breath.

Not a sound came from within. At last Pacha Bata made some inquiries of Chinawa and the latter answered. Pacha Bata then went into the room followed by the others. The darkness prevented a clear view until their eyes had become accustomed to the subdued light. Not a thing was amiss, so far as could be seen. Chinawa shrugged his shoulders as if to turn the investigation over to the others.

The bag had not been molested. Rand was sure of that, for he always arranged it so that if it were disturbed it could be noted. Pacha Bata made a thorough inspection of Rand's bed. So far as evidence went, Matiyero had come and gone without touching anything. But Shuyani said she was certain from his actions that he had accomplished what he intended. Chinawa again appealed to Rand. Was there anything missing?

"Not a thing," Rand said touching his various pockets as one unconsciously will do when asked if he has lost anything. "Wait a minute," he said suddenly. The old thermometer case he always carried potassium permanganate crystals in was missing from the accustomed shirt pocket. Now he remembered, it had fallen from his pocket last night and he had laid it on the shelf by the lamp. Turning to the shelf he found the case was missing.

When he told the others of his discovery, Chinawa went to the shelf and looked outside. The shelf was visible through the window; anyone looking from the outside, could have seen the article placed there.

So Matiyero had stolen the stranger's magic. Rand had to laugh outright at the idea. Chinawa and Pacha Bata wanted to know what Rand would do now?

"I have plenty more in my bag." he replied.

"But can Matiyero work the stranger's magic?"

"Not much of a chance," Rand assured them. "Don't you remember I took all the venom from the wound before I applied the medicine?"

Rand felt an immense relief at what he had learned. That Matiyero was interested enough to steal the permanganate showed how much he was impressed with its powers.

After Rand had assured Chinawa and Pacha Bata that Matiyero could not perform wonders with crystals, they too began to enjoy the joke. Rand had Shuyani ask the three, including Jitibi, to say nothing about the affair. Chinawa and Pacha Bata returned once more to Chinawa's chamber. The others followed into the hallway.

"With those two on my side there can never be any trouble, Rand told Shuyani.

"Yes," Shuyani replied, "they are on your side, but don't feel so sure that will make you secure. Did you not see how they feared for your safety just now? Don't think you can learn more about the Auca Ambi in a few days than Chinawa knows who has been with them all his life. I can assure you Chinawa has a very good reason for fearing them. Perhaps it is because you know so little of the danger that you discount it."

"Very likely you are right, he replied soberly. Thank you, I shall remember."

They parted, Shuyani going to the girls' wing, Rand back into his room. Jitibi started for the patio, his objective probably being the garden beyond. However, he hesitated for a moment, as if in thought, then retraced his steps and went into the room with Rand. Jitibi considered it his duty as Rand's companion to remain near, even though he was likely to be forgotten by the former at times.

He found Rand pacing the floor in meditation. Seeing that this was one of the times he was not needed, Jitibi seated himself on the floor and took out his queña. The music was very distracting to Rand. He endured it as long as he could, then in despair he began looking through his kit for something to interest Jitibi and divert him from the musical mood.

An illustrated North American magazine suggested possibilities. Rand had placed this among his effects before starting because he had expected to use its pages in preserving butterflies. There would be no collection of butterflies; so why keep the book. Perhaps Jitibi would prefer pictures to music. The plan worked -- beyond expectation!

160

There was a typical cover on the magazine which Rand took care was not upside down when it reached Jitibi. The latter reached for the book just as the curious will examine anything. One glance at the cover and Jitibi saw it was no ordinary object he held. In astonishment he gazed at the picture then looked at Rand inquiringly. Rand nodded his head. What more could he say? Laughingly he added, in English, "Yes, some women look like that."

Jitibi jumped to his feet and walked to the window, -- he must have more light. He feasted his eyes upon the picture. Rand saw his lips move once or twice as if forming words to put to the picture. Then ever so lightly he blew his breath upon it. As this produced no results, he blew harder. Rand shook his head and laughed. Not able to blow a single thread of the garb, or a single one of the golden tresses, Jitibi was puzzled. Once or twice he started to touch the image with his hand, but stopped in embarrassment.

Rand assured him that it would be all right with the lady, so he touched his fingers to the smooth paper; but his face expressed disappointment. He turned the book over to get a rear view of the fair maid. A full page cigarette advertisement met his bewildered gaze.

Jitibi was stumped! He had never seen a picture before and the reflection of images which he had seen in water, or other mirror-like surfaces, had always represented objects in the neighborhood. Here he could see this girl before him as he had often seen himself in a basin of water, yet he could not lay his hands upon her.

Rand indicated that Jitibi open the book. An automobile advertisement appeared, but Jitibi had accidentally reversed the book. However, to a person who has never seen a wheeled vehicle, the wheels look as well on top as underneath. After

Rand had righted the book, Jitibi found a beach scene, with colored umbrellas, sand, and people -- everything but the water. Jitibi was unable to follow the lines of a tight-fitting bathing suit. He had seen red men and white men, but never all the colors of the rainbow in one crowd. He just must be informed about this picture.

"Shuyani," Rand said, and waved him outside. Jitibi's face brightened and he hurried out in search of her. Rand looked after his retreating figure and said to himself, "Volume one of Purac's circulating library starts on its rounds."

Later when Rand went into the patio from where the afternoon inspection trip was to start, he found Jitibi and Shuyani surrounded by an eager group of Puracians. Shuyani, it seemed had explained time and again about the various pictures, as far as she knew, but there seemed to be no end to the questions; therefore, she turned the magazine over to Maiboya to carry on while she took up her duties as interpreter.

Pacha Bata and his boys had arrived and the boys claimed to have eliminated all mosquito larva on this end of Purac. The cover design which won the prize for the best olla screen was a plain hoop covered with light cloth that fitted over the olla like a hoop over a barrel. It won approval by its simplicity. When they started out on the inspection trip Rand gave Shuyani a note book and pencil and asked her to keep the report.

This was the first inspection of the boys' work under Pacha Bata, and Rand was pleased with what he discovered. Some stagnant water was found in containers around houses, but as a rule everything was in promising shape. Invariably houses where water was found were houses where the people objected to the boys looking over the premises. How true was this to civilization!

When the party reached the Auca Ambi house they hesitated. The Auca Ambi was a large house, or series of houses, enclosing a big hollow square. No one had dared inspect the Auca Ambi. Rand asked Chinawa if they couldn't go in and look around and Chinawa gave his consent, though rather reluctantly, Rand thought. A servant who came to the door was dispatched to ask Matiyero for permission to enter. The latter appeared, after a long delay -- true to the trait common with autocrat officials who have power and no other idea of how to use it except to keep someone waiting their pleasure. When he did appear, however, he invited the party in, with the exception of Shuyani. Women could not visit Auca Ambi. Rand was keenly disappointed, for without Shuyani's help he could learn very little.

Matiyero was particular that the party should not get beyond the mere threshold of the Auca Ambi houses. A reception porch just within the enclosure overlooked the patio beyond, but plantings concealed everything beyond the patio. This reception gallery had elaborately carved furniture, the best Rand had seen in Purac. Richly carved cedar chairs fashioned from solid blocks of that material were common and proved to be very comfortable. There were racks of pecuñas -- blow guns -- on the wall. Also there were hard palm darts with the end smeared with curare, the vegetable poison used by many South American Indians for hunting.

Rand was not surprised to find these, for he knew the preparation of the poison was always left to the medicine men. He was not interested in the pecuñas, as he had seen them in use often and knew the Indians of the jungle seldom, if ever, used such weapons in warfare. The curare poison is too slow

163

for jungle warfare, the vicious arrow from the bow being far more effective. A body wound from this weapon always produces a septic wound that usually proves fatal, and no doubt is responsible for the prevailing erroneous impression that poisoned arrows are used promiscuously by South American savages.

Rand wanted to go through the buildings, but Matiyero afforded no such opportunity. So far as information about the Auca Ambi was concerned, the party gained nothing. Matiyero, Rand was told afterwards, assured Pacha Bata that he himself had attended the lectures, knew how to carry on the work, and would co-operate. Rand was convinced the medicine man was sincere, for he could see Matiyero, although crafty, as one necessarily must be in his position, nevertheless was intelligent.

Chicha was served without stint and Matiyero proved an agreeable host. Rand was wondering if his opinion of Matiyero had not been too prejudiced. He seemed not a bad sort. If the memory of yesterday at Ushcu had not been so vivid in Rand's memory! He half wished he could forget it all. He would like to be friends with Matiyero. If that individual would only work with him, Rand was sure everything would be congenial in Purac. Matiyero accompanied his guests to the outer door and there was formality in the parting, nothing of which Rand understood.

As soon as they were outside, Rand began looking for Shuyani who was nowhere in sight. Then he saw her come from behind a tree some distance away. She came rapidly towards the group. Rand saw she had his note book and pencil in her hand. This she gave to him when she came up saying, "Here is your notebook that you gave me when we started, Señor," and added something in Purac which was no doubt an explanation to the others of what she was doing.

"Oh, Shuyani," Rand burst out enthusiastically, "I wish you could go through that place with me. I am sure there are many interesting things in there. I wonder if we could get them to set aside the rules against women for once and let us go through together."

"There are women in Auca Ambi, many of them," Shuyani replied, "but I shall never be one of them," and Rand saw her shudder. Then she added, "Sometime when you have the leisure, look in your notebook Señor."

"I shall do that," Rand replied.

As they fell in with the rest of the group he walked beside her and continued.

"There will be no storm tonight, Shuyani, but a big moon, a big tropical moon," -- as if Shuyani knew any moons but tropical ones -- "and remember what one can have every day in the year at Purac? I have not had my daily jasmine yet. Don't forget it in the gloaming."

A stifled cry from Shuyani caused him to look at her quickly. But she seemed to be trying desperately to control herself, although it was plain she was very much agitated.

"I suppose I was never intended to understand women," he mused. "Mr. Kipling, I fear you have deceived me about the sex, for --

What have I learned from the brown and the red,
Has not helped me in the way that you said."

CHAPTER 14

The Face At the Window

Chinawa's daughters were giving a "tea party" in the patio, masato that fermented drink, being the beverage served. Rand was enjoying the novelty of his first matinee social event in Purac when he saw a look of horror suddenly sweep the crowd. Following their looks, he saw two men, evidently soldiers, dressed in white cuzmas and armed with chunta rapiers, marching directly toward the party.

From the hush that fell upon the assembly, Rand knew something of importance was taking place. The two guardsmen marched directly towards Chinawa with military bearing and, stopping in front of the chief councilor saluted and said something which of course Rand could not understand. Chinawa was obviously affected, but he straightened himself to his full height, and looking at the one who had acted as spokesman, he asked a question.

The guard, without a moment's hesitation replied, "Shuyani."

With a sharp cry of anguish, Shuyani turned towards Rand, then fell unconscious against him.

"That's all right, Shuyani," he found himself saying in English. "What's the matter? There is nothing going to hurt you."

Then, seeing that she had fainted, he began to call for someone to bring him some water -- to do something. At last it dawned upon him that his means of communicating with the Puracians was at that moment lying silent and limp in his arms. He would have to act alone. He started to place her on one of the carved logs that served as seats, when someone seeing what he had in mind motioned him towards the house. He carried her gently into the house and laid her upon a bed. Several women at once took charge and Rand, seeing there was nothing that he could do to help, returned to the assembly in the patio, to learn if possible the cause of all the trouble.

He noted the two guards were still standing rigid. Rand went directly to Chinawa and tried to inquire what it was all about, but of course he could make neither Chinawa nor Jitibi understand. Chinawa pointed to the two guards and then towards the Auca Ambi and said, "Shuyani."

"But what do they want with Shuyani?" Rand cried helplessly.

At the name, Chinawa nodded his head, but that was all. Then Rand recalled what Shuyani had said of Auca Ambi that there were many women in Auca Ambi but she hoped this would never be her fate. Just what was back of all this, he must find out, but he was helpless with Shuyani gone. If it had been a question of rudimentary exchange he would have been able to make himself understood in a matter of trade, but this matter required that he understand everything.

Then he thought of Nucui. "Nucui," he said to Chinawa, who was almost as distracted as Rand because he could not explain. A messenger was dispatched at once for Nucui. When she arrived, Rand demanded what the guards wanted that had caused so much disturbance.

Nucui spoke to Chinawa, ignoring Rand altogether. After what seemed to Rand a long time, she turned to him and said, "Shuyani has found another lover. She is wanted at Auca Ambi."

"But I do not understand. I do not think Shuyani wants to go to Auca Ambi," Rand said.

Nucui laughed, then turned to the guards and said something in the Purac dialect; the two guards turned and stared at Rand in surprise.

Nucui then said to Rand, "What Auca Ambi wants, it takes. You have lost your huarmigoc" --"sweetheart".

What on earth did this woman mean? "What Auca Ambi wants it takes!" Suddenly he thought of what Shuyani had said, "Look in your note book Señor."

He had forgotten all about that and now he recalled how disturbed Shuyani had been at the time. He must read that note at once, perhaps it would explain things. Taking Jitibi by the arm, Rand started for the garden. He held up his hand to Chinawa as he departed, to signify that he would return soon. Going to one of the secluded spots in the garden, he eagerly took out the note book and read, written in Spanish:

"Señor: The Auca Ambi has a tremendous power in Purac. The medicine men who live there take what they want. Woe unto any girl who pleases the fancy of one of the Auca Ambi for they take her, even should she be a daughter of a curaca. All those taken by Auca Ambi are dead to their people, for they never escape. The girls who are taken by the Auca Ambi are the servants of the high men until they tire of them, then they are passed on to the lackeys and guards.

"I saw someone staring at me from one of the windows as I waited for you to visit the Auca Ambi. It was for that reason that I left the place and I am now writing this while behind a

168

tree. I always feared the Auca Ambi and that is why I lived with my tarta -- father-in-law -- Huitoto, so I could be as far from Auca Ambi as possible. Now I fear I am lost, for I can never forget the look in those eyes staring at me from the window. I will see them in the dark and shall not sleep. God have mercy on my soul. Shuyani."

When Rand had finished reading the note, he placed the book in his pocket and started to return, determination on his face. Then he paused. Superstition which was at his throat a few days ago, was today crying for more than the life of the one who had saved him!

Looking at Jitibi, Rand placed his hand upon his shoulder. "Maci" -- friend --" he said in Quichua.

"Maci, maci," Jitibi repeated after him, with a concentrated effort, trying to recall its meaning. Then a look of understanding! Yes, he understood maci, it was one of the key words used by the Zachas --friends. Rand grasped his hand and squeezed it and they both repeated, "Maci." They returned to the assembly in the patio.

They found the group about as they were when they left. "How is Shuyani," were Rand's first words to Nucui. The latter shrugged her shoulders and said nothing. Chinawa wanted to know what Rand had said and when Nucui had told him he said he did not know. One of his daughters went to see and came back saying Shuyani was conscious but would not talk.

Rand asked if he could see her, but was told it was best for him not to as she had been requested by the Auca Ambi. The Auca Ambi must not be offended.

"Well, Shuyani is sick, she cannot go to Auca Ambi now," Rand said.

Chinawa nodded and began talking with the guards. But they were apparently reluctant to leave. Finally they agreed to go back to Auca Ambi for instructions.

Shortly after they had departed, they were seen returning with Matiyero. Matiyero was walking rapidly and it was evident he was not in the best of humor. When he reached the patio, he addressed Chinawa in no placid manner. It was plain he was telling Chinawa the Auca Ambi could not be trifled with. They had the fate of Purac in their hands and their wants must be respected.

While this argument was at its height Shuyani appeared, walking with difficulty, supported by Maiboya. Shuyani went directly to Chinawa and, taking his hand, patted it affectionately and spoke to him in a soothing voice. Then she turned to Matiyero and began some discussion with the Auca Ambi chief which continued for sometime. Matiyero seemed to be weighing something Shuyani said, and finally he nodded his head in assent. He then began to issue instructions to Chinawa. When Matiyero had concluded, he turned abruptly and went towards the Auca Ambi followed by the two guards.

After Matiyero had departed Chinawa told Nucui to go, also the other outsiders who were standing about. He then led the whole group into his private quarters. This was done in order to offer Rand and Shuyani all the privacy possible within the protecting circle of those they knew to be their friends.

When they were inside, Rand turned to Shuyani and said humbly, "I know it will be impossible for you to forget my frivolous, unpardonable behavior when I met you outside the Auca Ambi this afternoon. To think that I should be so thoughtless! I shall never forgive myself, the blundering cad that I know myself to be --"

Shuyani stopped him. "Never mind that. I know you did not know. When I saw those eyes devouring me through the window I knew I was lost. Although I hid behind the tree, I knew they were following and that I would never be able to escape." Then she paused. "Do you know -- did you read the note?"

"Yes, I read it, but too late. It was after they had come for you. I should have read it sooner."

"That would not have helped matters," she said. ""After I saw those eyes it was then too late. I knew the note was useless, I only wanted you to know -- to know --"

"To know what?" Rand asked.

"To know that I did not want to go to Auca Ambi."

"Why should I think you would want to go?"

She looked at him wearily. It had been a hard day and Shuyani was tired. Then she continued. "There are many things you do not yet understand about Purac. Perhaps -- with me gone -- you will find it difficult -- I --I did not want to leave you, but it won't be my fault, you understand," she said looking at him wistfully.

"What do you mean?" -- Then recalling the mood in which Matiyero departed, he asked, "What -- er -- will they come back?"

"There is no power on Purac that can save me from Auca Ambi. I would be there now only that my widowhood has not yet expired, and it is the custom that such widows cannot be taken to Auca Ambi. I have less than another moon. Matiyero has agreed to await that period, but when that time is up -- Well, you see it was Bacque, the son of Matiyero, who saw me through the window. They have sent for Huitoto to bring the records. Tomorrow we shall know what day I go to Auca Ambi after Huitoto arrives with the records."

"I can see you, can't I?" Rand inquired blindly, hardly knowing what to say.

"I fear not. Perhaps Matiyero will forbid it. Even now we must not prolong our talk lest we involve our friends."

"Shuyani," he said, "I want you to tell Jitibi that we, he and I, must always be friends. Tell him that no matter what he is told, I shall always be a friend to him and that I want him to work with me to save you.

Shuyani smiled as she joined their hands and said, "Friends, always."

They repeated the words, foreign to the tongue of each -- such an odd oath of friendship! When it was over Shuyani spoke to Jitibi for a few moments. Had Rand been able to understand he would have heard Shuyani consigning his destiny into the hands of the youth, since she was passing beyond where she could help.

Then Shuyani turned and walked into the room beyond. Chinawa had watched it all with keen interest. After Shuyani had asked Jitibi to look after Rand, and had left, Chinawa, trembling, approached Rand and grasped his hand, then pointed to himself. Had Shuyani been present she would have understood that she had left Rand with two protectors instead of one.

Rand went out to the patio, then into the garden beyond. He passed where the jasmines were growing, stopped arrested by their odor. That odor! Many times he had inhaled it, times when he was gay and carefree, but there had been other times when the odor spread from a wreath placed upon a new-made mound of earth. "Ah! Jasmine! You recall sorrow as well as joy -- in Dixieland, in Purac!"

Rand strode rapidly along the garden paths. How could he forgive himself? Wasn't he the cause of it all? It was on his account that she was in Churic. If it had not been for him she would now be happy with her friends. Happy with Huitoto who was now coming to Churic with the records that told the day when she must answer to the call of Auca Ambi. Hadn't he even been asked to be taken to Auca Ambi -- the trip which had been her doom? And then when he went to her after visiting Auca Ambi, he had jested!

That night always remained a blur in Rand's memory. He never even pretended to go to bed. All night long he paced the floor, devising scheme after scheme, none of which was at all practical, nor which he recalled afterwards. With the first rays of day, he was out and strolling around the village. He made a wide circle around Auca Ambi, though why he did not know. Coming back he passed near the house of records. Puca Uma was now almost forgotten. However, he felt better after the night of agony. There wasn't any use in walking the floor and wringing hands. He was going to fight.

Throwing his shoulders back, Rand walked towards his quarters and into the garden as though he owned the place. Selecting a choice bunch of jasmine buds he tied them together and strode back towards the house. Some of the Chinawa girls were in sight, but not the one he was looking for. Calling to one of the youngsters, he said, "Maiboya." The child disappeared into the house, returning soon with Maiboya. Rand handed the flowers to her and said, "Shuyani," pointing toward the house. Maiboya smiled and nodded, but as she started to go towards the house, Rand signaled her to wait a moment. Shaking his finger at the flowers he said, "You are not going to a funeral this time, do you understand?"

He then went to his room and lay down. He had slept only a few moments when a boy awoke him for breakfast. He now learned Huitoto had arrived with the records, having traveled all night, and that the calculating would begin right after breakfast.

There was elaborate calculating. The notched sticks and beans were juggled about until they found Shuyani must go to the Auca Ambi in seven days. A messenger was dispatched to Auca Ambi and Matiyero sent word that he would come in person to talk the matter over. He soon arrived, and Rand, unable to understand the talk, watched their actions. Matiyero kept his eyes steadily on Rand, at first, trying to stare the stranger out of countenance. He seemed surprised and certainly angered at not being able to do so.

There seemed to be a point that could not be settled. After some delay it was decided to go to the house of records to verify the count. Matiyero returned to the Auca Ambi saying he would send a man to open the building and the rest of the party went to the house of records. It was some time before the men came, then after the windows had been opened there was the usual delay to permit the spirits to retire before the door was opened. All were crowded around the door awaiting the next move.

Matiyero came out of the Auca Ambi and shouted something as he approached. When within a short distance of the party he stopped and began to make some sort of demand. At this instant the nest of sacred hornets -- the guards of the house of records -- fell among the throng. There was a wild scramble as hornets and Puracian profanity filled the air. Rand was toppled over by someone and they went down in a heap, Rand on the bottom. A howl of pain from the man on top of Rand told he had been stung. Rand noted a scar on the man's face as they arose.

In time all had reached a safe distance from which they could look back at the nest on the ground where the hornets were still angrily swarming about. Matiyero who had not reached the danger zone before the accident circled near with his tray of magic powders.

Jitibi and Rand were standing together watching the procedure. Matiyero came near and made some inquiry of Jitibi. Upon the latter's reply, he continued on his way, at the same time giving a command. Rand learned later this was a request for all who had been stung by the hornets to come forward. Three men answered the command, one being the fellow who had fallen on top of Rand. The victims of the stings were lined up and Matiyero began blowing the cones of powders into the air around them, none of it however, directly into their faces.

Rand watched the procedure, determined not to let a move of Matiyero's escape him. He must solve that magic powder secret if possible. Once Rand thought Matiyero blew powders against the air movement in such a manner that some of the particles would have proved very hazardous to Matiyero himself, if their toxic properties were what he had at first thought possible. Yet he was not sure his had been the case, and an instant later he saw Matiyero avoid just such a possibility when the cloud of particles in the air drifted his way.

Rand was so intensely interested in watching Matiyero's every move that he did not see one of the three victims fall to the ground. When he did notice, he saw it was the man who had fallen over him. Matiyero jumped quickly to where the man lay and began literally to fill the air with his spirit repellant powders, waving the other two victims away. Rand started to go to the victim's assistance, but Jitibi arrested the action and shook his head. It was evident Matiyero was to be given a clear field. He and he only dared combat the spirit which had struck the man down. The poor fellow would try to arouse himself, then apparently drop back to a semi-paralytic state.

Matiyero ceased blowing the powders, but he did not at once approach the victim. Rand was almost sure Matiyero was waiting for the air to clear, and apparently this supposition was true; for after a short wait, Matiyero approached the man who was now breathing with great difficulty and began to work over him, evidently looking for the hornet wound. He found it on the man's right shoulder. Down on his knees beside the man Matiyero massaged this point vigorously, then he got up, shook his head, threw his hands out with a gesture of hopelessness, and strolled away.

The people now approached the stricken man. Rand was one of the first to reach him. The poor fellow was in the throes of death. Rand had never seen a man die with such symptoms before; but he had seen monkeys act just that way many times when shot with the curare poison with blow gun darts. Hurriedly he looked for the sting on the right shoulder. When he found it, he found a crater-like bump with a hole in the center. The tell-tale hole was characteristic of the blow gun dart, but why the crater-like swelling? He had never seen that in curare wounds before. He must see the other men who had been stung, but how?

Shuyani, how he needed her now! Never before had he appreciated so much what she had been to him. Frantically he appealed to Jitibi. He wanted to see the other men. Holding up three fingers, Rand pointed to the victim, then turned down one finger and pointed to him again, then to the remaining two fingers. Jitibi did not understand. Rand was frantic. He did not recall any way he could identify the other victims. The people were collecting, thus making it more difficult to locate the wounded men.

Since he was accomplishing nothing, Rand stepped back and looked over the gathering. Finally he saw a group around a fellow. Making his way to the man in the center he found it was one of the men who had been stung. The wound was on the side of the neck. There was an enlarged flat swelling, not the crater-like form, and instead of a pin hole in the center there was a purple speck where the sting had entered. Rand was sure the dead man had not been stung at all.

Appalled at his discovery, he now went with Jitibi towards the house of records. At a safe distance the people stood back and watched the nest on the ground before the record house. The hornets had quieted down, but several were flying around ready to pounce upon anyone who came near. Everyone seemed helpless.

Matiyero walked up and down, but would not go near the nest. His powders evidently did not prevail against the sacred hornets. Rand made a motion as though he would crush them, but Jitibi shook his head vigorously. Looking at Chinawa, Rand said, "Nucui."

Nucui was some distance away and Chinawa called to her.

"Why do they not kill the hornets?" Rand asked when she came.

"No one dares to," she told him.

"Why not?"

Chinawa asked what Rand said.

"Can you kill them?" Chinawa wanted to know, when informed of Rand's inquiries.

"I will try," was Rand's answer.

"Go ahead," Chinawa said.

Rand picked up a bundle of dry palm leaves, which he saw near by. Fastening these in a bunch on the end of a stick he circled until he was in the rear of the building, then he ran to the building, watching the window until he was beyond the range of it. He then made his way along the walls where he could not be seen by anyone inside, should there be anyone in the southwest corner.

From this point, he could see the hornets still eagerly buzzing around the nest, which was lying on the ground in front. With his pocket microscope securely hidden from view in his hands, he focused the sun's rays upon the sheath of palm leaves. The flame that resulted was most mysterious to the gaping populace who stood with bated breath while Rand placed it beside the nest and the angered insects were consumed in the age-old game of "moth and flame".

Rand was scanning the sky for straggling enemies when a piercing pain struck him behind the ear. The surprise, together with the nervous tension he was already under, caused him to cry out sharply. A vicious slap, and he was rewarded at seeing the remains of a crushed hornet in his hand.

"Oh, Lord, what a relief," he ejaculated. "I thought at first I'd got in range of one of those windows."

Rand looked at Matiyero. He could see he was furious, but the die was cast, so there was no use in trying to get along with Matiyero now. Chinawa approached the building, others following shortly afterwards.

Nucui stared at Rand in wonder. Knowing there is no one more inflicted by superstition than the jungle Indians, Rand told her he had more magic in his pockets than Matiyero had in all the Auca Ambi house, and Nucui was ready to believe it.

Chinawa and Matiyero were having a heated conversation. Rand asked Nucui what they were talking about.

"Why do you have to ask me?" she inquired. "Don't you know everything that is said?"

Rand could see she was in earnest. "Yes, Nucui, of course I know everything that is said, but I think you would like to deceive me. I am just waiting to catch you in a falsehood."

"Chinawa wants him to have the men open the door, but Matiyero says it's not safe to do so yet."

Rand was on the verge of saying, "Tell Matiyero to open up, I'll go in," but he thought best not to do so. He decided it would be best not to show his contempt of the spirits just yet.

After Matiyero had delayed as long as possible the door was opened. Matiyero had the stone moved carefully and he was the first to enter.

Rand recalled that this was not the procedure on the first visit. In fact, Matiyero had not been here on that occasion. When Rand entered, his first act was to look up at the corner in the roof nearest where the hornets' nest had hung. He could see nothing suggestive there. He turned his attention to the count they were checking. In a few moments the verdict was rendered that both counts were the same. Somehow Rand was glad the records checked because the records of Purac was to be his discovery. He would never be able to go before the world and tell of how he discovered the mysterious civilization in the jungle, but he would carve the details on the granite ledge some place where in years to come it would be found. Perhaps posterity would call him Puca Uma the second. Then the absurdity of it all dawned upon him. He, thinking of the great things he was going to do when he could not even save Shuyani. At least, she had said he could not.

But he would see! Did he not tell those jasmines this morning he would fight for her?

It was past noon when they returned to Chinawa's house. After lunch Rand paced his room again, pondering the strange events. He was sure the man who had died was a victim of curare poison. If so, the dart was shot from one of the high open windows in the house of records. If it came from the house of records, there was some means of communication between the house of records and the Auca Ambi. An underground tunnel was the only explanation. That would be too much like -- Oh, bosh! Still how else could the matter be explained? It looked as if the hornets had been used to start the confusion during which the dart was easily used without discovery. Rand was almost sure Matiyero was looking for that dart and had removed it before he let others approach the man. Still a curare dart would not occasion pain like the sting of an insect; the pain of the former would be only in the lacerated tissue. Then what made the swelling? These were two factors that did not fit into the picture.

His theories must be proved, he decided. If there was connection between the house of records and Auca Ambi it must be found.

Rand startled Jitibi who was dozing on the bed, by his sudden decision to take a stroll. He had decided to survey the ground between the house of records and Auca Ambi. So they made their way in that direction.

But looking over the intervening ground offered no evidence of any possible connection. The ground was comparatively level with the exception of the gentle slope from the Auca Ambi downward to the other building. Since surface conditions offered no solution, Rand decided to scrutinize the land in that area.

The outcropping of the bare rock suggested only a few feet of soil at any place, covering the top of the Pampa where Churic was located. Measurements of the depth of soil beyond the building away from the escarpment showed that here, perhaps five feet would be the maximum depth of natural soil between the surface and the hard granite rock over the suspected area. It would be impossible for the Puracians to drive a tunnel through the granite this distance with the means at their disposal. The distance was at least a hundred meters. A tunnel above the rock would not stand up in that soil without props and lining to support the roof, and five feet of soil was not enough space for this construction without surface indications.

These Rand decided were the obvious factors. Now he must look for factors less obvious. Using a walking cane he thumped the ground and thought he detected a hollow area, but could not be sure. To continue the search would attract attention.

As he made his way back over the field of the morning tragedy, Rand noted the empty cones that had contained the magic powders Matiyero had blown over the area to control the evil spirits. He wanted some of the powders, but all of the cones were empty. They returned to Chinawa's house and at the doorway Rand said, "Pacha Bata," and motioned to Jitibi to go in search of that individual. Jitibi understood and hastened off on the errand. Rand then passed on to the patio beyond. Taking out his note book he wrote:

"Shuyani: I must have a talk with Chinawa. You are the only possible means of communication. Advise Chinawa. Rand."

He then asked one of the servants for Maiboya. When Maiboya came he gave her the note, together with a pencil and some sheets of paper, and said, "Shuyani," motioning her towards the house. Maiboya at once departed on the errand. With this much accomplished, nothing further remained to be done but await results.

Jitibi and Pacha Bata came first, the latter anxious to learn what Rand proposed. Pacha Bata had perhaps appreciated Rand's way more than any other Puracian. Shortly afterward Chinawa came to the door of his study and motioned them to join him there, which they did. When they were safe within the room, Chinawa produced the note Rand had sent Shuyani. Chinawa was clearly nonplussed.

First he seemed to be explaining some remarkable phenomena to Pacha Bata and Jitibi. Those two were all attention. Chinawa gave them the paper to look at, and their interest was equal to that of Chinawa's. The latter pointed to the note, then to Rand. Rand nodded his head, touched his hand to his lips, to signify conversation and said, "Shuyani," which instead of settling the dilemma, apparently increased it.

Jitibi who had seen Rand read his notebook, gave the other two some startling evidence. Still there was indecision. Pacha Bata made a suggestion, and all three left the room with a gesture to Rand to await their return. After a short delay they returned, bearing a sheet of paper and handed it to Rand who glanced at it and said, "Chinawa, Pacha Bata, and Jitibi."

The three stood dumbfounded. Accustomed as we are today to witnessing the progress of science, we perhaps forget the greatest step in our present civilization -- the art of writing. Perhaps if the primitive mind could witness the whole gamut of progress from the cave age to the present time, nothing would impress him more than a scrap of paper which could accurately convey a message from one person to another.

Chinawa handed the paper back to Rand and signified he should write one name only.

"Which one?" Rand pointed from one to the other.

Chinawa selected Pacha Bata. This name Rand wrote and handed the paper to Chinawa, The three departed as before, returning soon with another paper.

"Purac, Puca Uma, Matiyero, Maiboya," Rand read.

This test proved conclusive. There could be no doubt that Rand had no way of knowing the names suggested to Shuyani, yet this paper told him the names just as they had dictated them to her.

Although Rand did not know it at the time, these written messages had more influence with Chinawa than any argument he could have made. Had he been able to speak the Puracian dialect perfectly, he could never, by that means alone, have prevailed upon Chinawa to set aside the command of the feared Auca Ambi. He would not have dared to do so. But the paper carrying the message between Rand and Shuyani was greater "magic" to Chinawa than he had ever seen the Auca Ambi perform. Rand and Shuyani could communicate at will, so why try to keep them apart?

However, it seemed best to keep the Auca Ambi ignorant of the conference; therefore, Chinawa gave orders to allow no one to disturb their conference. Then he conducted Shuyani into the room.

The greeting between Rand and Shuyani was very formal. Rand at once began with the business in hand. The tragedy at the hall of records he did not mention, for he was sure all this was known to Shuyani.

"Ask Chinawa what killed the man today!" was his first request.

"The sacred hornets who guard the house of records," was the latter's reply as though he considered the inquiry a foolish question.

"Why did not the other stings also prove fatal?"

"There was nothing significant in that," Chinawa replied. "Men are often wounded, some die and others do not. The same may happen with the sting of the hornets."

"Are many people killed by the hornets?" Rand asked.

"It is not uncommon," Chinawa answered.

"Do they all act alike?"

"Yes, just like that. Matiyero knows the symptoms well. He says there is nothing that can be done about it."

"What are the powders for?"

"They are very powerful to keep off evil spirits. Always when death is around, the Auca Ambi blows the powders around to keep down evil spirits. Matiyero says that if it were not for the powders, all Purac would be at the mercy of evil spirits."

"Where do the powders come from?"

"They are made by the Auca Ambi and are so dangerous that only those high in the Auca Ambi are permitted to handle them."

"And are many men killed at Ushcu?" Rand asked.

"Often now," was Chinawa's response. "Years ago there were no men killed at Uschu, but the spirits were offended. Then they took revenge by coming out of Uschu each moon when the treasures were thrown in there. Since then it has continued."

"Who was the first victim of the spirits at Uschu?" Rand asked.

"It was Huahcuco. He was a curaca at a village near Uschu. He had a beautiful daughter who the Auca Ambi

184

wanted. Huahcuco objected to their taking his daughter. The spirits were offended and soon after he was stricken at Uschu. Then so many were stricken that the people would not go to Uschu for the ceremony; so the Auca Ambi had to force them to go.

"Long ago," Chinawa continued, "there were many women and few men because of wars. Now there are not enough women for the men. We do not like to see our women go to Auca Ambi."

Rand regarded these simple children of nature reflectively. Should he tell them what he was contemplating. Here were three of the best minds in Purac. He had been able to make them understand all his work so far, and without them he could not prevail against the Auca Ambi. He must have their help. Accordingly he plunged into the matter without further delay.

"You have seen monkeys die of curare poison?" he asked.

"Many times," Chinawa replied, "when working in the Zachas. We always supplied ourselves with food by use of the blowgun and the poison darts."

"You know how a monkey dies with curare poison. Very well, the man today died with curare and not from the sting of a hornet."

When Shuyani had translated this statement the Puracians stared at Rand in amazement. Chinawa's lips moved in an effort of speech, but there was no coherent mind behind to carry through constructive thought. Steeped in superstition handed down for centuries where the word of the medicine man is supreme, what chance had Chinawa to reason on occult problems that had always been taken for granted and never questioned. The three looked from one to another, then at Rand and Shuyani as though those two were demons threatening to destroy the very foundation of reason. Had Matiyero known what was going on and had come before them denouncing the blasphemy, Rand and Shuyani would have been executed without delay. Shuyani blanched with fear, although what she had endured the past few hours should have rendered her callous to all earthly feelings.

Rand began to wonder if he had not gone too far. Perhaps their minds should have been gradually prepared for his deductions. However, he could not recall his statement now. Success required that he go ahead, come what may. The best procedure, he decided, was to explain his theory to Shuyani and have her tell the Puracians in her own way, since he knew from experience she was far more capable of dealing with these people than he.

Accordingly he told Shuyani of what he had observed during the morning; that he did not consider it a mere coincidence that the hornet's nest fell just when it did; that someone within the building must have knocked it down; and that Matiyero knew what was going to happen and this was the reason he was attracting attention to himself by talking at the time. And since the man who had died and Rand were in the act of falling at the time the fatal wound took place, he suspected the dart had been aimed at himself and not at the other man.

The recital increased the strained tension, instead of relaxing it. The three Puracians could derive only suspicion from the conference between those two, no word of which they could understand. Twice Shuyani had to stop Rand in his recital and allay the impatience of the Puracians, assuring them the discussion was not to conceal what was being said, but to facilitate a clear understanding. When Rand had explained all his reasons for his stand, Shuyani then passed the story on to the Puracians.

Following every word she said, their reactions differed. Rand could see Chinawa was adamant, not a change in his features took place. Pacha Bata, he saw, was wavering between doubt and credence. Jitibi, his face swept with surges of color, indicated that he was converted and ready to go out and organize a crusade against Auca Ambi. In fact he once interrupted Shuyani's story to say that Matiyero had asked him, while he was standing by Rand, if he knew whether the stranger had been stung and seemed to be disappointed when he said he had not.

After Shuyani had completed telling what Rand had conveyed to her, the conference continued. Once Shuyani pointed to Rand and spoke the name Puca Uma. This statement brought Pacha Bata temporarily to her defense. Rand wondered what it was and learned later that Shuyani had compared him with Puca Uma, mentioning how Puca Uma had organized the Zachas while Rand had organized the boy scouts. How both would go down in history as organizers, bringing order out of chaos.

Thereupon Chinawa told Shuyani to ask Rand how he was going to prove the connection between Auca Ambi and house of records, even if it did exist.

This, Rand said, he proposed to do that night. He would go into the house of records, and if there was communication between the two buildings he would uncover it.

"But," objected Chinawa, "of course you could claim to find connections, but how shall we know what you find? We do not have magic powers and cannot see what the Auca Ambi can."

Now it was Rand's turn to be astonished. Did Chinawa think there could be a connection which was not visible to any but the Auca Ambi?

That was just what Chinawa believed.

Rand explained patiently that any connection between Auca Ambi and the house of records could be seen, not only by himself, but all the other people of Purac.

If Rand was sure of this, Chinawa was anxious to have him prove it. What did he propose to do? Rand explained that he would go into the record house that night and make a thorough search. "I am sure," he said "that I can prove my suspicions about the Auca Ambi, in time. If there is nothing to it, no one but myself will suffer. I do not ask anyone to go with me."

Here Jitibi eagerly volunteered to go. He wanted to accompany Rand, for he was confident Rand's magic was superior to that of the Auca Ambi. But Chinawa would permit nothing of the kind. Wasn't he chief councilor of Purac? If there was any skulduggery going on he was going to be in on the exposure. Still what could they accomplish in the dark, they could not find anything. To take a light inside would invite discovery.

Rand told him that he had a magic light which none outside could see because they would not light it until they were inside, a light, the likes of which no one in Purac had ever seen.

The agreement was that the three Puracians and Rand would go to the house of records after night. Pacha Bata and Jitibi were to open the door and let them in, then close the door and await outside until those inside asked to be let out. Shuyani of course could not go, she returned to her room. Rand and Jitibi went to the former's room, while Chinawa and

Pacha Bata remained to ponder over all the strange things that were taking place.

CHAPTER 15

The Deadly Powders

Rand took his flashlight out of his kit bag and after preparing Jitibi for what he was to see, he turned on the light. Jitibi was enthralled, but not greatly surprised. He was becoming sophisticated now. After Rand had instructed him in how it was operated, he had him take it in and show Chinawa and Pacha Bata how it worked. Once when Rand had thoughtlessly opened a flashlight into the face of a jungle savage, the latter instinctively struck out and almost knocked him down. Remembering this incident, Rand thought it best to have Chinawa prepared for what he would see when they were enclosed in the house of records. Jitibi was gone for sometime, the flashlight proving a fascinating toy for the others.

In spite of the bold front assumed by the Puracians during daylight, with the coming of nightfall, the power of the mystic all but overcame them. As the hour of departure for the mission approached, Rand was somewhat surprised to find Chinawa, who was to share the great danger, was the least panicky of the trio. As the four started for the field of their strange errand, Pacha Bata was very nervous. At the last moment, he insisted they go to Chinawa's room and send for Shuyani once more. When Shuyani came he instructed her to ask Rand what the signal would be when Rand and Chinawa completed their investigation and wanted the door opened to permit their exit. Chinawa said he would give the call of a frog, this would not be a suspicious noise coming from the building.

As they turned to go, Shuyani offered Rand her hand in farewell. "I know you will succeed," she said firmly.

"We shall," he replied as he felt something soft left in his hand, the fragrance telling him it was his favorite flower.

Chinawa, who was leading the party, stopped when the outline of the house of records became visible in the subdued light of a cloudy sky. He gave a signal for silence; they sat down and listened to make sure there was no one around. There was not much chance of any of the Puracians going near the house of records in the dark, not while the recent tragedy was so fresh in their minds. After a short wait Chinawa was satisfied the coast was clear. He got up and swiftly led the party to the door. Here they paused and listened again. Rand saw his three companions look at the roof above, from which had fallen the hornets' nest, one of the mysteries to be investigated.

After a nervous halt, Chinawa ordered the stone door removed. Rand assisted at this task which required but a moment. As soon as the door was removed, Rand crawled inside and reached back whispering, "Sanama," the word Shuyani had told him was "well" or "good" in Puracian.

Chinawa immediately followed Rand, reaching for his hand and holding it for moral support. Then Chinawa whispered, "Sanama," to those outside who silently replaced the stone door. The instant the door closed, shutting out the last vestige of light from the outside world, Rand felt a shiver shake the man whose hand he held.

Rand, born and bred in civilization, could not understand the willpower and nerve that were invoked by this pitifully superstitious man to defy the precepts of the only religion he had ever known and upon which the foundations of his universe rested.

Hesitating but an instant after the door was in place, Rand pressed the switch of his flashlight and threw the beam of light about the room. The single finger of light, shooting here and there, must have had the appearance of the eye of a demon. Again Chinawa shuddered and Rand was afraid he would become hysterical. He must get Chinawa's mind occupied with facts, not fancies. He threw the light to the roof in the corner just inside the spot whence the hornets' nest had dropped. From where they were, they could see nothing but the stonewall and roof, a tight joint between the two.

Rand began to search for means of getting up to this point. One of the blocks used for scaffolding he shifted against the wall directly underneath the area he wanted to inspect: by placing a shorter one beside this, he would be able to mount the higher block. Next blocking the light on with the switch, he handed the flashlight to Chinawa who was to hold the rays against the wall. He then climbed to the top of the higher block. The point was still several feet above his reach. The walls up to the eaves were smooth; the gables, however, were rough stones, and by using care, Rand was able to climb the rough stonewall gable to the desired point.

A casual inspection revealed nothing. Then Rand began to test the stones in the wall, one by one. Finally he found a small square stone loose. Carefully removing this, he could see the starlight outside by a clear passage about four inches square extending through the wall. He looked down towards

Chinawa with a smile of triumph, though of course he could not see Chinawa's face.

Replacing the stone, Rand slowly descended to the floor. Without a word, Chinawa handed Rand the light and then went rapidly up the wall. Chinawa in his bare feet climbed the rough stone gables with the ease of a carpenter on a ladder. When he reached the stone he removed it and peered out. Propping the stone against the wall with his body, Chinawa started to put his hand through the hole. His nerve failed him for an instant, then he peered through the opening once more. The friendly light must have given him courage, for Rand saw him thrust his arm full length into the hole. Having replaced the stone, he rapidly descended.

From now on Chinawa was a changed man. No longer was he a benighted savage, with every shadow an evil spirit ready to destroy him. Without a moment's hesitation he began to search for the passage Rand had had Shuyani explain he was sure existed. With his bare knuckles he was down on the floor knocking to sound the stones. His "Ah", told Rand of success.

Still Chinawa pounded upon the big flat stone which had sounded false. There was something strange about it, but he would soon see. Digging his fingers into the crack at the far side of the stone, he soon had it up. Then the puzzle was solved. Although the edges of the stone fitted accurately into a nice groove countersunk around its edge, it also rested on a heavy block of wood supported by under-pinnings from beneath, the whole arranged to deaden the hollow sound.

With the prop out of the way, they threw the light into the passage below and peered in. Back towards Auca Ambi led the passage. Rand climbed down, followed by Chinawa. Where the passage left the building, it entered a tunnel about five feet high coming together at the top at an acute angle instead of an arch, the roof construction being an inverted V, well curbed with masonry.

The first object to attract their attention was a stick about three feet long that had a sharp flat spade-like end. Picking this up, Chinawa examined the point near the light. He uttered an exclamation of satisfaction, then pointed to some flakes of wood fiber, of which hornets build their nests, adhering to the stick. There was no doubt that this stick had been used to shear the hornets' nest loose from its support.

The existence of the passage proven and evidence secured of the hornets' nest having been deliberately dropped into the crowd, Rand had accomplished his object and was ready to call it a day. But not so with Chinawa! Taking the flashlight from Rand he peered farther into the passage, took a few steps, listened attentively, then advanced a few paces further, Rand following. Chinawa was annoyed at the light the flashlight made and tried to darken part of its rays with his hand. Rand understood what he wanted and tied a handkerchief over the light to dim it. They started on, but again Chinawa stopped and motioned for Rand to remove his boots. When this was done, they continued on through the tunnel, its height necessitating a stooped position. They made long advances in the dark, using only flashes of the subdued light in looking for the other terminal.

At last they saw a dim light in the distance and by using this as a guide they were able to proceed without the aid of the flashlight. When they neared the light, they could see it was a reflection from the right where the tunnel made a right angle turn. When they arrived at this turn, they cautiously peered around the corner. Not two yards away was a curtain hanging over the mouth of this end of the tunnel through which filtered the light that had guided them. They made their way to this curtain and through its coarse weave could see the dim outline of a form moving about. He seemed to be boiling something in an olla over a charcoal furnace.

The room seemed to be a regular laboratory. There were half a dozen, such as the one being used, and there were piles of roots and plants lying around. Shortly after they arrived, the person inside threw some leaves into the pot, piled a handful of charcoal on the fire, picked up the lamp, and went out, shutting the heavy door behind him. Chinawa waited for a few moments, then stepped into the room, followed by Rand.

In one corner of the room were some short sticks which, upon examination Rand found to be small pecuñas -- blow guns. Rand appropriated one of these guns and a box of darts which lay on a shelf near by.

At the far end of the room was a series of rock shelves built into the wall. On one of these Rand found some of the cones containing the powders Matiyero had used. He picked one up and studied it. The large end of the cone was plugged with a cotton stopper, such as are used in test tubes. Carefully rolling the cone into a large section of banana leaf -- which in Purac served as paper -- Rand placed it in his pocket.

They thoroughly examined the room and the various articles it contained, most of which they did not understand. Chinawa gasped with astonishment as he peered into a crude rubberized bag. He picked up a large section of banana leaf, and taking a green leaf from the bag, wrapped it carefully in the banana leaf.

With a final glance around they proceeded to the curtain, climbed into the tunnel, and made their way back to the house of records. When they emerged from the tunnel they were astonished to find the door wide open, yet no one in sight! Hastily replacing the blocks and stones, they crawled through the door and closed it. Chinawa croaking all the while like a frog.

Not being able to find anyone, they hurried toward Chinawa's house. They had covered almost half the distance when Chinawa stopped. A moment later a flying figure rushed at them, hesitated a moment, then Rand found Shuyani in his arms.

"What's the matter, Shuyani?" he cried excitedly.

"Oh," she gasped faintly, then turning quickly to Chinawa she said something which made that gentleman bolt for the house in great haste.

"What's all the trouble?" Rand asked again, "and where are Pacha Bata and Jitibi?"

"Oh , you gave me such a scare," Shuyani panted. "Where have you been? Pacha Bata and Jitibi came back long ago. They waited so long for you that they became frightened; Pacha Bata gave the frog call and not getting an answer, they opened the door and called, but still no one answered. So they came running to ask me what to do. I was so excited I could not reason. Pacha Bata said you were both dead and he was going out and sound the trocan for the news to be sent all over Purac. I begged him to wait until I could come and see if I could find you, but he said there was no use to wait and I was expecting every moment to hear the trocan pounding out the alarm. That is why I told Chinawa to run and stop it, and I suppose he has done so since it isn't going."

Half and hour later Rand and Shuyani knocked on the door of Chinawa's apartment. When they were admitted Pacha Bata and Jitibi looked at them with sheepish grins.

196

"They were ready to sound the trocan for you, too," Chinawa said with a chuckle, "because you were so slow in getting here, but I told them they had created enough mischief for one night. I just got here in time to prevent the alarm."

Chinawa again chuckled at the thought. "It would have been a nice climax to have had Pacha Bata tell all Purac that we were dead in the house of records. Imagine the shock to Matiyero when he heard the trocan carrying such a message!"

Chinawa enjoyed the joke immensely. However had the trocan sounded the alarm, the situation would have shown a different aspect.

Shuyani, for Chinawa, now asked Rand how and when the passage between the two buildings had been constructed.

"How do you expect me to know?" asked Rand in astonishment.

Chinawa said Rand had known of its existence before it was discovered; therefore, he should know when and by whom it was built.

The question brought out the futility of expecting the natives to understand. Rand pulled at his short cropped hair in helplessness as he paced the room. It had taken time to build that tunnel. Evidently it had been excavated as an open ditch to bed rock, then the masonry built, the later the whole had been covered and the surrounding grade filled in, because there was not enough soil to conceal it otherwise. Besides some of the rocks, he recalled, were limestone which would have had to be transported for miles. Half the population of Purac must have been employed in its construction, yet its existence was now unknown.

Unable at the time to offer any suggestion, Rand told them that tomorrow he might be able to offer a theory. He must have time to think.

Then the trophies retrieved from the laboratory of Auca Ambi were examined. The plants Chinawa had found in the rubber-lined bag were, they said, muca. Shuyani told Rand it was a very deadly poison; that it grew around Ushcu but at no other place on Purac. At other places it was destroyed because animals would eat it and die. No one but the Auca Ambi dared touch it. Chinawa said that he had seen it in the hills far to the north of Purac, when he was in the Zacha. It had a thick succulent leaf and when crushed gave off but little odor.

The muca was then wrapped again in the banana leaves and placed in the corner of the room where it could be burned on the morrow.

The blow gun and darts which Rand had brought were next examined. The gun was about two feet long with a bore somewhat smaller than the lead in a pencil. The bore was accurate throughout its length. The mouthpiece was enlarged similar to the mouthpiece of a bugle. The darts were small, very similar to phonograph needles, each being incrusted with the dry black tar-like curare poison.

The pecuña, or blow gun generally used by the South American savage in hunting is ten or twelve feet long, the bore of which is the size of a lead pencil. The arrows or darts are the size of knitting needles, blunt behind where it is wound with a small tuft of cotton to fit the chamber. The front end is needle pointed. This point is covered with curare just back of which the dart is nicked, so that when it penetrates the flesh, the point will break off and cannot be pulled out, as would be the case when shot into a monkey. The blood must have time to absorb the poison; therefore, if the point of the dart does not remain in the victim it has no effect.

While looking at the darts, Jitibi dropped the container and they were scattered all over the floor. They were picked up hastily and replaced in their holder. While the miniature blow gun was a beautiful piece of workmanship, they all agreed it would be of no value in the woods as its range would be too short.

Rand decided he did not want to take a chance with the powders in the poor light. They must wait until tomorrow. Chinawa wanted Rand to sleep in his, Chinawa's, room that night. Chinawa's distrust of Matiyero had increased without any accompanying feeling of security against the medicine man's power.

Rand readily consented and went to his room for his bed clothing, taking the pecuña, darts, and powders with him. The latter he placed carefully on the back of the lamp niche, while the other articles he laid in the corner of the room behind his bag.

Jitibi had accompanied Rand, and when they returned to Chinawa's rooms, Chinawa wanted to know what was to be done about the night's discovery. Rand said it would be advisable to say nothing, for they could never convince all of Purac; the people would not want to believe. He had chosen these, his friends, because of their intelligence, and he asserted that from now on they, the four of them, would constitute the inner council of Purac. They would say nothing, but curb as far as possible any further injustice of the Auca Ambi.

After a pledge of fidelity, one to all, the party dispersed.

With the moral support he now had, Rand felt confident and slept securely in Chinawa's room. At the break of day he was up and off into the grove east of Churic, his favorite haunt.

He had not been able to account for that passage which existed unknown among these people who kept such an accurate knowledge of every event in the history of Purac. Or did they? Regardless of their wonderful advancement beyond the jungle savage in many ways, they were still primitive by a hundred customs. Their system of keeping dates, for instance: it was admirable, yet represented only by so many notches on a stick -- a simple matter.

Like a flash this thought answered his question. Notches, recorded dates, but the story itself had been handed down verbally. Wasn't that the only means of handing down history before the advent of writing? Had he not himself, after a hard day's travel in the jungle, watched his Indian carriers sit around and listen while one of their members recited the entire story of the day's events, although they, themselves had all been actors in those same events? Sometimes they would correct erroneous statements, but all would listen to the story as attentively as would a civilized audience to an interesting lecture. It was all they had to talk about.

The Puracians would narrate in the same fashion, of course. If the Auca Ambi forbade the discussion of an event, the knowledge of that event would be blotted out with the passing of that generation.

It was breakfast time when Rand returned. Going into the patio, he was somewhat surprised to find Matiyero in the midst of the assembly. The latter nodded to Rand in an affable manner, after which he departed as the others sat down to breakfast. Rand was very curious as to the object of Matiyero's presence, but there was no one to explain it, if such an explanation were known.

At the conclusion of the meal, Rand and Jitibi entered the former's room. Rand found the cone of powder on the lamp shelf just as he had left it. He would have a good look at those powders now by daylight. Taking the cone, he went to the window, then hesitated. He was not going to take any chances with those powders! He would go into the open to examine them. Beckoning Jitibi to follow, he went into the garden beyond the patio. Sitting on a seat he cautiously removed the cotton plug in the large end and peered in.

"Umpas," -- "water" -- he said to Jitibi in Purac. The latter disappeared and soon returned with a gourd of water. Saturating his handkerchief, Rand tied it over his face: the damp cloth would prevent his breathing any of the powders. With his pocket lens, he then examined the contents of the tube. It was a fine brown powder with a characteristic odor, the odor he had noticed when Matiyero had blown it into his face at Ushcu.

Equipping Jitibi with the wet handkerchief, he had him also examine the powders. After Jitibi had completed his study of them, Rand carefully replaced the plug in the end of the cone. They then returned to his room. The powders he put back on the shelf.

Then he went to the corner of the room to get the short blow gun from behind his bag, and was astonished to find it missing. Jitibi, who had seen Rand place the gun there the night before, rolled the bag around and looked in every possible place, but with no results. Both the pecuña and darts were gone.

Rand and Jitibi stared at each other. There was but one thing to do and that was to get the inner council together. They turned and walked out. Going directly to Chinawa's room, Rand sat down and watched the effect of the news upon Chinawa as Jitibi informed him of the loss. Pacha Bata was called in from the patio where he was in conference with his boy scouts.

After Pacha Bata had been told of the missing articles, Shuyani was sent for. When she learned the news she at once said Matiyero had taken them. They all seemed to be sure of this, but how did Matiyero happen to know they were there?

CHAPTER 16

The Runu's on the War Path

Had evidence of the visit to Auca Ambi been discovered and had Matiyero come direct to Rand's room in search of the missing pecuña, or had he gone into the room and stumbled upon the gun by accident and taken it? In either case, Matiyero must know that Rand had visited the Auca Ambi: whether or not he knew of the others involved in the affair, there was no way of knowing.

Rand wanted that blow gun. He was not particularly interested in the gun itself, but he wanted the darts. Someone recalled that the darts had been spilled on the floor the night before, and a more thorough search now revealed one of these poison darts which was missing in the night search.

Rand looked at the small short needles covered completely with the black curare poison. He explained to the others that he could not understand why the man who fell upon him in the scramble at the house of records had mistaken the puncture of this to be the sting of a hornet, and the swelling afterward.

Rand had previously investigated curare poison to the extent of carrying some to the United States and having a toxicologist of a well-known medical school expound its reaction. The action of curare had been explained as a paralytic, arresting respiratory action, the victim dying of asphyxiation. There should be no pain. Then why did this man cry out with pain? There was no way of answering this question except by making a test. Rand rolled up his sleeve and made a small superficial scratch on his forearm. He then took a dart and touched the exposed nerve tissue. There resulted a burning sensation which showed the dart to produce the stinging pain reported by the man who had been pierced. This, too, would explain the slight swelling of the tissue near the puncture.

Rand had Shuyani explain what he was trying to do and the results. As for the sting Rand could only suggest that of the many nettles; perhaps the Auca Ambi had succeeded in coating the darts with some of those toxic properties just as the curare is boiled out of the vines from which it is made.

The Puracians were interested in the experiment, but that over, their problem was, what about Matiyero? How much did he know?

Rand proposed that Chinawa go to Matiyero and request that the house of records be left open so that the light would give the spirits no dark hiding place. If Matiyero suspected the passage as the mode of entrance to the Auca Ambi, he would never consent to letting it remain open. He would, of course, not agree to its being open, anyway; but the more violently he objected to the suggestion, the more likely it would be that he suspected. A messenger was dispatched for Matiyero to secure his sanction.

While they were waiting, Pacha Bata wanted to know what about those magic powders. Rand admitted he did not feel safe with them around, but he would like to test them. A monkey would serve the purpose of a test if they would get one. That, they said would be no trouble. Pacha Bata had a monkey that had become so mischievous that he merited condemnation to the cooking pot, he had only been waiting an opportune time.

This monkey was sent for, but it was to be brought in a sack so as to not attract attention. Rand brought the powders from his room; Chinawa and Pacha Bata inspected them. They had seen nothing similar before. Rand showed them how to inspect the powders with the pocket lens for future identification should they find suspected material.

The boys had now returned with the monkey, a big hardy black one, ideal for the experiment since it would take more to affect him than the smaller monkeys commonly used as pets.

The gold room would be an ideal lethal chamber. It had only one window, the one in the rear. With the door in front closed, there would be no cross ventilation to diffuse the particles floating in the air.

The liberated monkey looked about the strange room and blinked at his surroundings. With the cotton plug removed Rand stood ready to make the test. The monkey was held until everyone got outside with just a crack of the door open. The monkey peered through this at the outdoors he wanted to enjoy. Nervously Rand placed the cone in front of the monkey and blew the full charge into his face, then jerked the door shut. Those outside heard the monkey sneeze once or twice. How long they waited, no one knew. They heard the monkey chatter but presumed it was because it wanted to get out.

After a period Rand shoved the door open and stepped back. From a distance they looked into the room for the monkey. There was something wrong for the monkey did not jump out when the door was opened. Finally they located him on the floor in a corner, rocking to and fro. Crowding to the door, but fearing to enter the room, the party watched the monkey dying with all the symptoms of curare poison.

Grabbing the damp handkerchief from his pocket and hastily tying this over his face, Rand rushed in and stooping over the monkey, tried to arouse it. The monkey toppled over after he reached it. Looking at it for a moment, he turned and hurriedly left the room. At the door he snatched the handkerchief from his face, and telling Shuyani to have them shut the door, he walked away muttering to himself. Rand was prepared to see the monkey effected by the powders, but to see it die as if by curare poison was a complete surprise.

Pulling himself together, he returned to the group standing silent at the now closed door. He must not let them see how surprised he was. His display of self-control would enable him to hold their confidence. Forcing a smile, he said, "The poor monkey did not have a chance in that closed room."

Shuyani advised the others of what Rand said, then they started towards the main part of the house. Arriving in the patio, they found Matiyero seated in the shade of the mango tree, a complaisant look upon his face. He told Chinawa he had come in response to the call regarding the house of records.

Shuyani went rapidly towards her quarters and Rand started for the garden in the rear. Jitibi made a move to accompany him, but Rand motioned him back towards the conference. He wanted Jitibi to add the moral strength of numbers to the inner council, for he feared the effect of the monkey's death had created a wavering in their ranks.

Rand strolled in the garden until almost noon and when he returned to the patio he found the bowl of good cheer, chicha, flowing profusely. If the Puracian members of the inner council had tried to drown their fear, the efforts had been highly successful. Pacha Bata, catching a glimpse of Rand, began calling to him excitedly, his manner plainly indicating that he wished Rand to join the celebration, though what the celebration signified Rand did not know and he rather doubted if Pacha Bata did either, in his present condition.

Rand accepted a gourd of chicha which he sipped occasionally, taking care the others could see his cup was not empty. Rand was consulted, questioned, and quoted, on many issues, without the least need of an interpreter. Of what those issues were, he had no idea. They were all too intoxicated to notice whether Rand had drank much or little. What they insisted upon was that his gourd must always be full.

He saw that Matiyero also was pretending to be one of the most reckless, yet he too was taking mere sips, while the others consumed chicha by the gourdful. Unheeded the noon hour passed, yet the drinking continued until the revelers were overcome. Chinawa's head began to droop and he stretched out on the seat to sleep. Servants carried him into the house. Matiyero started for home, but several insisted he remain; he did, for a while, but finally would no longer listen to their entreaties. As he started home at a brisk walk, Rand could see Matiyero was the only one among the Puracians who had remained sober. Moreover, Matiyero had stayed and promoted the dissipation until the crowd had reached a stage where action of any particular individual was ignored; then he left for home.

Rand went to his room and lay down. It was now long past midday and he was tired and disgusted. To have his co-workers enter on an orgy of drinking just when the situation was so critical, was discouraging. He had not seen Shuyani since she left him soon after the monkey had died.

The cool refreshing room in the stone house was very pleasant. Lying down on his bed, Rand tried to think what he would do next, but unable to get started on any definite line of thought, he dropped off to sleep. It was late in the afternoon when he awakened.

He made his way to the room where the monkey had been executed, but found the body gone. Rand was disappointed, for he wanted to examine the body. He proceeded into the garden and sat down in a shady nook. There was an unusual quiet over Churic. After some time Rand got up and began to walk about. He passed near the jasmine bushes, stopped and looked at them, plucked one flower and continued on his ramble. At intervals he would inhale its odor and wonder why it had such a strange influence upon him. Turning, he came face to face with Shuyani. They stared at each other in silence. At last Rand said, "Why don't you speak? I am not a ghost."

She came near and looked into his eyes for an instant, then inquired, "How do you feel?"

"What do you mean, are you, too, in league with Matiyero?" he demanded.

"Oh," she replied, "I thought -- "

"You thought what?" he asked.

"I thought you were -- well, I saw you with them drinking chicha, then they had to carry Chinawa to his room, and later several others. I watched you go to your room yourself, but when I stole to your door and looked in I saw you sleeping. So I thought you, too, were like the rest. But you are not?" she asked interrogatively.

Rand smiled at her. "No, I was not intoxicated, if that is what you thought. I don't think it would be advisable for me to celebrate with the gusto of the Puracians. In fact, I am not sure I have anything to celebrate."

"I am so glad," she replied. "You see I watched Matiyero all the time and I know he had some object in view. He only pretended to drink with the others."

"I, too, observed that," Rand answered. "I wonder what he wanted."

"I do not know, but I am uneasy about Chinawa. He has not yet roused up."

Rand considered a moment, then said, "Let me go see him." Together they went into the house.

Chinawa was lying on his bed, sound asleep. Rand felt his pulse: it was normal. To all appearances Chinawa was sleeping off a jag. Shuyani went out and left Rand at the bedside. Taking a seat near, Rand watched Chinawa's regular breathing. Members of the family looked in at intervals, but no effort was made to arouse the sleeper. As night drew near, Rand went into the patio to await the meal. He had eaten nothing since morning. One of the household servants brought the food and he ate alone, mechanically, unconscious of the food before him. Near the conclusion of the meal, Shuyani came towards him. He could see she was troubled.

"What is wrong, is Chinawa all right?"

"Chinawa is still asleep," she said. "It's Pacha Bata, -- he is very ill."

"That's to be expected," Rand laughed. "He has my sympathy, but he will soon get over that."

"But you do not understand; this is serious," she said. "It is not from the drinking, at least not all of it."

"How can you tell?" Rand asked.

"Because they have sent for Matiyero. They really fear he will die."

"Let us go and see him," Rand said. "We must get there before Matiyero."

Together they went to Pacha Bata's house. Pacha Bata was rolling with agony and holding his hand on his stomach. The look on his face indicated acute pain. Members of the family were standing around, but nothing was being done to relieve the man. Rand asked Shuyani to find out from the patient something of the attack he was having, but Pacha Bata was in too much pain to talk.

Some few moments later Matiyero came in. Without apparently seeing Rand or Shuyani, Matiyero went directly to Pacha Bata. Feeling the latter's stomach, Matiyero gave a grunt of satisfaction. He had located the trouble. Pouring into a gourd some liquid which he had brought with him, he made Pacha Bata drink it. Then he stooped and pretended to suck at the patient's stomach with his mouth. Matiyero pretended to be under tremendous strain. Once he stopped and looked around, slowly shaking his head. The wails of Pacha Bata's family caused him to renew the treatment. After much effort Matiyero gave signs of success, then he triumphantly stood up and took something from his mouth. He held it up to the light where all could see. It was a piece of glass from one of the small mirrors Rand carried in his kit. One had been broken and he had thrown away the pieces.

Those who were standing near Rand instinctively drew away from him, with the exception of Shuyani. Shuyani began talking to Matiyero but what about, Rand of course, did not know. He was puzzled at the behavior of those in the room. Matiyero's pose was one of surprise. Time and again he held up the piece of glass and regarded it sorrowfully. Then the discussion between him and Shuyani became heated and Rand heard, "Ushcu, Yanga, runu," therefore he surmised that the talk had something to do with the snake bite at Ushcu.

For the time being Pacha Bata was forgotten until Matiyero pointed to him triumphantly. Pacha Bata had ceased to writhe in pain and had dropped into a peaceful sleep.

Shuyani told Rand they had better go. Not a word was spoken until they passed into Chinawa's house into the garden behind the patio. When they were seated in their favorite nook, Shuyani began:

"Matiyero says you bewitched Pacha Bata and that had he not removed the glass from his stomach, which you placed there he would have soon died."

"How could he claim that?" Rand asked. "You know --"

"Yes, I know," she said in exasperation, "but what has that to do with it? Can't you -- won't you understand that what you and I think has nothing to do with the case? Oh, why can't you understand? You must not expect these people to reason as you do!"

"You are right, Shuyani. I have made serious mistakes, many of them. From now on I turn over all dealings with the Puracians to you and I appreciate what a mess I have already made of it, too. All I shall ask in the future is to live in peace. Let us go to the far end of the pampa and live, you and I. Live in peace in Huipuco's village."

"If only we could," she said, "but have you forgotten that in five days more I must go to Auca Ambi?"

No, he had not forgotten, but he had ignored the fact because he had been so sure his exposure of Auca Ambi would prove sufficiently embarrassing to cause them to abandon the demand. He thought he was freeing Purac from superstition, yet apparently he had accomplished nothing.

Shuyani told Rand something of her talk with Matiyero at Pacha Bata's bedside. Matiyero claimed to be very sorry to find proof that the stranger had tried to cause the death of

Pacha Bata. He was surprised because they seemed such good friends, Rand and Pacha Bata, but there was the glass, one piece of the stranger's magic in the stomach of Pacha Bata.

Then Shuyani had called attention to how Rand had saved Yanga, Pacha Bata's own son, from the runu when bitten at Uschu. Matiyero said that was nothing; that the Auca Ambi could do the same.

"No, they can not," Shuyani had told him hotly. "They do not dare handle the runus." But since she could neither convince Matiyero nor any of the others present, she had suggested they leave.

"Of course," Shuyani continued, "Matiyero came today and put some of his concoctions in Pacha Bata's chicha. He chose Pacha Bata because the latter is your strongest supporter on Purac. What he wanted and what, I fear, he has accomplished, is to make Pacha Bata your enemy instead of your friend. When he gave Pacha Bata that medicine just before he pretended to remove the glass I knew what was going to take place. The drink he gave him was coca leaves steeped in an alcoholic drink. The coca, you know, is the plant the Indians chew and from which cocaine is made. I have many times seen the medicine men pretend to remove objects from the bodies of those in pain."

"Isn't there any way the deception could be exposed?" Rand asked.

"That is our trouble now," she replied. "We have tried to expose too much."

Rand had to admit that seemed to be the case. Those powders, how could they be explained? He was now not so sure they, instead of the blow gun darts, had not caused the man's death yesterday, since the monkey's death was similar.

"Do you know what became of the monkey?" he asked. "I wanted to examine that body, but when I went back it was gone."

"Oh, the monkey, you had some of that for supper tonight," she answered. "Did you not know?"

"What? They ate a poisoned monkey?" he demanded.

"Why not? Don't we eat monkey killed with curare every day?"

"Yes, but that's different. Curare must be in the blood; it is too slow to be effective taken in the stomach."

"That I know nothing about," she replied.

Rand and Shuyani talked until late, but could arrive at no solution as to what was to be done. They parted as they came through the patio.

When in his room Rand felt the depression intensely. There was no welcome invitation tonight from the friendly Chinawa to share his room, nor had he any idea how Chinawa would feel toward him on the morrow. There was no one to light his lamp or to look to his comfort in other ways. He used his flashlight in preparing for the night, and when at last he lay down the quiet of the room almost smothered him. Then he thought of the monkey and the powders. Did he dare go to sleep? The more he thought it over, the less secure he felt. At last he got up, stepped from the room, and went into the grove where he spent the night under a tree.

It was after daylight when he made his way back into the village. He saw a child run at his approach. Once more he was suspected of evil occult powers. Chinawa greeted him very formally. Chinawa did not feel so well after his celebration of yesterday. They ate in silence. Jitibi was no where to be seen. There was a stir about the village and something out of the ordinary seemed to be going on, but what it was Rand did not know.

After breakfast, Rand sat on one of the seats in the patio. Maiboya came and handed him a slip of paper on which was written, "Matiyero has forbidden our meeting in the future. Shuyani."

Rand was not surprised, since he was prepared for anything. He got up and strolled through the village to the north rim of the cliff and looked off at the horizon beyond which lay the world outside Purac. Following the east scarp, he walked miles along the rim of his cage -- for caged he was on this pampa.

He came upon houses and gardens he had never seen before, for as yet he had not wandered far. It was almost noon when he started retracing his step toward Churic, and he had not gone far when he heard the boom of the trocan far off in the southwest. He stopped to listen, when the drumming was taken up by one nearer, then soon after the one at Churic also was booming. Rand listened for a moment then hurriedly continued on his way. Those trocans, he knew, were sending some important news. When he came in sight of Churic he could see people standing in groups talking excitedly; others were hurrying about.

Making his way towards Chinawa's house, Rand could see that he was being watched by all the people. However, without looking at anyone in particular, he made his way into the patio. The looks directed towards him were, no doubt, caused from the report of last night's affair at the house of Pacha Bata. But he felt there was no use trying to avoid the people. If something were about to happen, he wanted to get it over with. This suspense was unbearable. The patio was deserted, but he sat down and waited for whatever fate had in store.

His presence was evidently observed, for Chinawa soon came hurriedly towards him from within the house.

"Runu! Bacque!" Chinawa exclaimed, and added a lot of Purac words, which meant nothing to Rand.

"Runu; Bacque -- sanama," Rand said, intending to imply that he understood. Runu -- snakes. Bacque -- the name of Matiyero's son who wanted Shuyani. Sanama -- good. He understood the first two words, what next?

Chinawa stared at him.

"Shuyani," Rand said, to indicate she must come to interpret.

Without a word Chinawa turned and went into the plaza where Rand could see him talking to the people. A moment later the trocan was booming out a message. Rand was completely nonplussed, but he sat still and waited. The trocan continued to boom at intervals and people would pass in front of Chinawa's house trying to glimpse Rand through the hallway.

Chinawa returned with Nucui -- the command that Shuyani and Rand could not meet was being enforced.

"Chinawa says Matiyero asks you to please call off the runus," Nucui said to Rand.

"Call them off? What do you mean?" Rand demanded.

"You know," she replied, "the trocan says the runus are killing all the Puracians. Bacque is dead and the runus have not stopped, but are slaying everyone. You told them to do that. Now that Bacque is dead, please stop them."

That something out of the ordinary had taken place, there was no doubt, but just what it was Rand did not know. He must find out what it was before making any move.

215

"Nucui," he said, "you are doing better lately. You do not lie about me as you did when I first came. But I am not sure of you yet, so you get Chinawa to tell me of what has taken place today and, mind you don't try to deceive me," he cautioned.

Chinawa told Rand Matiyero was angered at Shuyani's accusation at Pacha Bata's bedside. When he returned to the Auca Ambi, he decided to prove to Purac that the magic the stranger had was no greater than his. Shuyani's statement before the people that it was not, would, he knew hurt his prestige among them. He had caught Rand trying to kill Pacha Bata, but the people were accustomed to such charges. If he could only prove that he could cure a snake bite, the same as Rand, confidence in him would be restored. He notified the people in Churic of his intentions. His son, Bacque, would go to Ushcu, let a surucucu bite him, and Matiyero would cure the wound on the spot just as the stranger had done. Not only Bacque, but Tupa, another member of the Auca Ambi would also get bitten and cured.

A large party, led by Matiyero, had gone to Uschu early that morning with this purpose in view. Matiyero had given orders for none to wear masks as he would see that no demons molested them.

Shortly before noon the trocan had sent a message that a runu had killed Bacque and was destroying people right and left.

"What have I got to do with it?" Rand asked.

"You told the runus what to do," Nucui answered. "Chinawa came and told you of it and you said it was good, that you had them bite Bacque because he wanted Shuyani. When Chinawa sent your answer to Matiyero by the trocan, Matiyero asked you to please make them stop."

Rand's attempt to talk the Puracian dialect with Chinawa had thus only made matters worse. Of course he had no intention of saying it was good that the snake had bitten Bacque, but evidently that was the way it had been understood, and adding the name of Shuyani had been taken as his reason.

"Tell Chinawa that I shall instruct the runus not to molest other Puracians," he said. "Matiyero can come home in peace."

Rand knew of course the snakes were not starting out in battle array. If several of the party had been bitten, the remainder would take particular pains to keep at a distance. It would be safe to promise the day's casualties from snake bites were checked.

Chinawa hurried out to file the message with the trocan operator and Rand, after going into the garden, wrote the following note to Shuyani:

"I have just learned something of Matiyero's escapade at Uschu. When they get back find out all that took place and send me the information at once. Rand."

With this done he went to the left wing and called for Maiboya to whom he gave the note to be passed on to Shuyani. Early in the afternoon some of those who had gone to Uschu in the morning began to arrive in Churic. They were eagerly questioned by the people of the village, but none of their accounts reached Rand.

About mid-afternoon Jitibi arrived. He approached Rand hesitatingly. Rand ignored him for some time until the latter began to grow nervous, then Rand said, "Shuyani," and motioned for him to go towards the girls' quarters.

Jitibi was gone for over an hour. Then he returned with a long note from Shuyani. Rand opened it and read:

"As we suspected the other day, Matiyero stole your snake bite medicine. This morning he promised a big demonstration at Uschu. Bacque and Tupa would let the runus bite them in front of all who wanted to go and Matiyero would cure them just as the stranger had.

Many of the men of Churic went, also many from other villages. Arriving at Uschu, they began to look for surucucus. Matiyero said they must be large ones. Two were found at about the same time, and Bacque went to one, Tupa to the other. Bacque let his bite him in his hand; Tupa's was very big and lazy, and was slow to anger. Tupa was teasing it with a stick to get it to strike. He must have been nervous, for his foot caught in a vine and he fell sidewise in front of the snake, which struck out and bit him in the side of the neck. He died at once.

In the meantime Matiyero was lancing Bacque's bite. Bacque did not have to be held for treatment like Yanga. Bacque was brave. The medicine was applied, but the pain caused Bacque to cry out in agony. The cry that the runu had killed Tupa swept the crowd into a panic and they fled, taking Bacque with them to Ubini. Bacque became delirious and Matiyero sent a message by the trocan for the stranger to come and cure Bacque. The reply came that you had told the runu to kill Bacque because he wanted me. Shuyani."

When Rand read the note through he realized at once what had happened. It was plain that Matiyero, carried away by his success of yesterday, had decided to complete the discredit of Rand by using the permanganate. He went to Uschu with a large crowd. The snake which had bitten Tupa had no doubt struck the jugular vein. Death in a few moments was inevitable with the venom from the bite of the Bushmaster placed in the blood stream. With Bacque, the fangs had very likely placed the venom between the bones of the hands where the cut would not reach. Matiyero had mistaken the use of the tourniquet for a device to hold the victim while the cut was being made. His son was brave and did not need to be held. Now both were dead.

CHAPTER 17

Uschu is Sealed Forever

Late in the day there was a stir among the people. In the distance could be heard the doleful wail of the queña. People crowded into the open or at windows as the procession came into view. Rand from within his room watched through the barred window as the line passed to the Auca Ambi, led by Matiyero who walked with downcast eyes. Behind Matiyero was a crude stretcher borne by four men on which was the still form of Bacque; behind this was another bearing the body of Tupa. The Auca Ambi in the falling darkness received its tragic mementos of the day.

All night long there were shrill wails carried into the darkness of the tropical night from the Auca Ambi house. If one had been near Auca Ambi, he would have heard a low mumbling chant which increased in volume and pitch until it reached the high notes that carried into the distance. A steady rain beating against the buildings added dreariness to the mournful rites.

With the coming of dawn all was quiet. Auca Ambi was as quiet as were the forms borne into its gateways the night before. Rand did not care to leave the protecting walls of Chinawa's grounds.

After breakfast the village resumed the routine that had been in vogue for centuries. Plantains were brought in on the backs of carriers. Girls with baskets of yucca and other things were bringing in the daily food supply. The day was well advanced when Nucui came to Rand where he apathetically sat on the patio. He looked up as she approached and asked, "What is it, Nucui?"

"Matiyero says you can never have Shuyani," was her answer. "He sent me to tell you."

"Well, what does he propose to do now?" Rand asked.

"He will do something terrible to Shuyani. I don't know what."

Rand jumped up, his anger overcoming his discretion. "You tell Matiyero that if he dares touch Shuyani he will be the next one to go," he said glaring at her as he spoke.

Nucui backed off, cowed at the look she saw in his eyes. She turned and left hastily while Rand paced the patio unable to sit still. Half an hour later there was a cry of, "Runu! runu!" Everything else was forgotten as people rushed to see what was going on. Nucui came running to Rand and said, "Matiyero says stop them, he will never molest you any more if you will stop them."

"Stop what?" Rand asked.

The runus are going into the Auca Ambi to kill everyone," she exclaimed. "Matiyero wants you to stop them."

"Where are they?" Rand asked at the same time starting towards the Auca Ambi, Nucui following.

As they neared the building, they could see people looking at something on the ground near the doorway of the Auca Ambi. Rand drew near and Nucui, following close behind him, pointed to a spot near the wall. There, stretched out in the grass, its head in the direction of the Auca Ambi door, was a Jararaca --fer de lanc -- that vicious, active snake of the South American jungle. Confused in its wanderings by the excitement it had created. it had stopped and its beady eyes were watching the scene before it. Its mottled dark green color blended with the grass on which it rested.

Rand knew there was nothing strange in the reptile's presence where it was. It would be an ordinary incident at other times. However, now its discovery, with its head towards the door of Auca Ambi could have but one meaning to the inmates thereof. It was bent upon their destruction.

Matiyero called from within to Nucui to promise Rand anything he asked, if he would call it off. If he would stop the snakes he, Matiyero would never bother Rand or Shuyani again.

After Rand had listened to these entreaties in silence for a while he promised to call the snakes off if they would summon a meeting and come to some sort of agreement as to the future. Matiyero agreed to this with alacrity.

Seeing the advantage chance had thrown his way, Rand had decided to make full use of it. If superstition was all they could understand, he, too, would use that.

He sent for a bag, then with a pole he pinned the reptile's head down and forced it into the bag, which he tied securely. This he carried to the gold room and placed there for safe keeping. While awaiting the conference, which was to be in the afternoon, Rand thought of a possible explanation for the queer action of the blow gun darts.

Accordingly, when Matiyero came, he had Nucui tell Chinawa that he wanted some of the regular large sized darts and a blow gun. He also asked for Shuyani as interpreter. When the messenger came with the darts Rand brought out the snake. Next he removed the back from his watch case and gave it to Shuyani to hold for him. Then he let the snake out of the bag, assuring the people he would not let it hurt anyone. Pinning the snake's head to the ground, he grasped it around the neck with his thumb and forefinger pressed against its jaws; he pried open the mouth with the disk of his watch case and placed the fangs within the disk. He then squeezed the head and tiny streams of the greenish yellow venom poured into the disk. When a few drops had been extracted in this manner, Rand replaced the snake in the bag which he again placed in the gold room. Then he took the blow gun darts and placed their tips in this venom until he secured a good coating all over the black curare poison. Rand now laid the darts in the sun to dry. This done, he dumped the poison out and cleaned the back of the watch case.

Matiyero had been a close observer of everything that had taken place; also the councilors had watched. Rand now asked for another monkey and one was sent for. When it arrived, he placed one of the envenomed darts in the gun and asked Chinawa to shoot it into the monkey.

When the dart hit the monkey, the point broke off in the body. Of course the poor monkey chattered with pain; but soon however the blood began to absorb the poison and in a few moments the monkey was dead. Picking up the limp form Rand looked for the dart. When it was found and removed, there was swollen tissue around the puncture. "That is the way the sacred hornets kill," Rand remarked.

He watched Matiyero, but that gentleman's reaction to the procedure was masked by the blank expression on the primitive face.

"Poor monkey," Rand mused, "your sacrifice to the advancement of criminology was in vain. Poker is the game Matiyero should take up."

Unable to solve the mystery of the poison darts, Rand turned to the subject at hand. He asked to be given charge of Ushcu and the surrounding jungle. He would plug up Uschu so no more runus and bad spirits could come out of it. He would then clean the surrounding jungle, kill all the runus and plant crops. He was to be furnished one hundred men for the work each day. Where would they put the curi and other things of Yushin?

"There is no need to bring the gold to Purac," Rand told them. "It can be left in the woods where it is found. There cannot be much free gold in the streams now while the deposits under the ground will be safe there. As for knives and flechas that hurt people, as well as other articles possessed of evil spirits, those can be burned.

There was a discussion over Rand's plan. While they were talking it over he went to the bag that contained the snake and began to talk to it in an affectionate tone. Shuyani reported that the proposition had been accepted.

Rand wanted an understanding about Shuyani's future, but she objected. It would be much better not to violate too much the Puracian tradition just now until the sorrow and bitterness had been forgotten.

Rand was to go to Uschu on the morrow. Each curaca was to be notified how many men his village was to furnish to make up the week's quota of one hundred men. Each week the men were to be changed. Twenty-five men only were to report at Uschu tomorrow and those were to construct cooking sheds to take care of the workmen.

Ignoring the momentary desertion of Jitibi, Rand notified him he was to be chief of staff. Then he told Pacha Bata he wanted him to select three of his most intelligent boy scouts and bring them over to take charge of sanitation. These last statements seemed to relieve the strained feeling and the Puracians began to converse freely among themselves.

Rand told Chinawa to decide what crops were most needed in Purac, as he proposed to have the rich soil of Ushcu produce food instead of runus. He then carried the bag containing the snake to his room and began preparing for his move to Ushcu. The note book he sent to Shuyani with an extra pencil. "These," he wrote inside the book, "are our only means of communication. Keep me posted and I shall do the same by you."

Chinawa had about recovered from his celebration and the shock of the preceding days. At supper Rand got him to send for Nucui, and when she came Rand told her that it would be necessary for her, too, to go to Ushcu for a few days until they were organized, then she could return to Churic. Nucui was willing to go.

After supper Rand went into the garden to stroll in the evening twilight. But the garden was void of interest; even the odor of the flowers depressed him. He could think of nothing but Shuyani and her dark, troubled eyes. Slowly it came over him that he loved this strange, shy girl of the jungle. He wanted Shuyani -- wanted her more than he had ever wanted anything before. Trembling with emotion, he hurried to his room, set the lamp on the the bed where he could see, and wrote:

"Dear Shuyani: I love you more than anything else in the world. Trust me and everything will come out all right. Write me often and be sure to let me know if you are in danger for your safety means everything to me. Rand."

When he had finished, he gave a final glance about the room. The bag containing the Jararaca in the corner caught his attention. "Old timer, I am going to see that you get a big juicy rat for happening along at such an opportune time. Maybe several rats, for that matter, for I feel sure you and I are going to reform Churic. He satisfied himself that the sack was tied securely, then retired for the night. There was no need to fear the powders as long as he had the snake near him.

In the morning he awoke after a refreshing sleep, the best he had enjoyed in several nights. And what a different prospect the day offered. There would be work, a definite objective in view. What a relief. He went whistling into the garden. A bunch of flowers were shoved into his face and he saw Maiboya for an instant, as he took the flowers from her, then she went flying through the plantings. Rand gave chase and caught a glimpse of two girls as they ran laughingly into the house. There was no need to wonder who the other girl was.

After breakfast the delegation going to Ushcu began to collect. Jitibi was busy giving orders. Chinawa assigned tools and other paraphernalia to carriers. Most of the food would be supplied from nearby chacars. In addition to Rand and Jitibi, nine men were Churic's quota for the day. There were also three women going to do the cooking in addition to Nucui. A carrier took Rand's kit, while he suspended the bag containing the Jararaca on a pole which he carried over his own shoulder. The women, of course carried most of the cooking utensils.

All Churic turned out to see the expedition leave, but there was a feeling of apprehension rather than confidence. Only two days before, they had watched another expedition bound for the same place set out with all the assurance of the Auca Ambi that it would be a success, and yet had it not proved disastrous? Chinawa insisted on bidding Rand good-bye, regardless of the latter's assurance that he would be back.

With a wave of his hand, Rand was off and the others followed close behind. Rand told Nucui she could stay with the other women, he would call her when he wanted her. He must become independent.

Arriving at Ubini, Rand prepared to take possession. The party was not expecting him to take charge of one of the Auca Ambi houses. Someone wanted to send the news by trocan, but Rand would not permit it. He was through getting permission. He told Nucui to tell the people that since he was assigned to clean up Ushcu, that region was under his control.

Selecting a camp-site on the cliff above a spring, Rand instructed the men to begin the construction of a tambo for the cooking department, also sleeping quarters. In front of Ubini he set three men to excavating a hole. It must be three feet around and four feet deep and the walls smooth, with no sharp corners. Then he and Jitibi, with one man, went to Ushcu. Rand had planned to bridge Ushcu over with timber and cover it with several feet of earth.

He made his way along the granite ledge parallel to the basin. When he reached the point even with Ushcu, he looked over the ground below him. There was the perpendicular cliff several feet down, then a rather steep slope to Ushcu which lay in a funnel-like depression. If he only had a big charge of explosives! A charge would dislodge tons of rock which would roll into the mouth of Ushcu. But explosives were not to be had.

Some few feet from the edge of the cliff was a crack extending down, showing where a section of the cliff was breaking off. In years to come disintegration would dump that section of rock into the valley below, but disintegration was as remote as explosives. Why think of either? But he

227

could use the methods of the Incas and send that section of the ledge trembling into Ushcu.

This he did, in time, driving heavy dry hardwood wedges into the crack and wetting them. This expanding process was continued for a few days, and spread the crack until tons of rock gave way and rolled into the hole below, blocking it completely. After leveling it off with small stones, he had the place covered with soil. Ushcu was now sealed forever!

CHAPTER 18

The Peaceful Reign of Bunco

When Rand had returned to camp after his first inspection of Ushcu, he had found the hole in front of Ubini completed. He brought out the bag that contained the snake and dumped the reptile into the hole. The Puracians watched from a safe distance until Rand motioned them to come up and look in, which they did. He pulled some leaves and grass and threw them in the hole, saying, "There, you can hide in that."

The Puracians were impressed with his talking to the snake. Nucui asked what the leaves were for. "They are a bed, of course," Rand replied. "Do you think I want him to lie on the damp ground?"

Jitibi asked its name.

"I shall call him, 'Bunco', Rand replied, adding to himself, "I should call it, "Ace in the hole', in this freeze-out game."

Rand had a substantial cover placed over the hole so no one would fall into it in the dark. He also had Nucui announce that anyone who caught a rat or other small rodent should bring it to Rand alive. Rand slept alone in the Ubini house, Jitibi preferring to sleep under the new shed with the men.

The next morning before going to work, Rand called all together and had Nucui explain that perhaps the runus would be angry at having their homes destroyed; therefore it would

229

be necessary for all to be on their guard. Every man was to carry a heavy string around his waist, and if one was bitten, he was to tie the bitten limb with this string back of the bite. He was to call those near him to help, then Rand was to be sent for at once. No one was permitted to go without these strings for tourniquets. The men then went at the task of clearing the jungle.

That evening with the full quota of one hundred men in camp Rand organized them into two teams and showed them how to have tugs of war, races, and other team contests. These teams were maintained throughout the duration of the work at Ushcu. One team took the name of uturunco -- tiger, the other the name of ahua -- tapir. The growl of the tiger or the whistling snort of the tapir was the rallying cry in many a friendly contest.

Nucui remained with them for a week, at the end of which time several of the men wanted to serve in the next week's quota. This express desire Rand was glad to see, for of course those offering their services were the most intelligent and were able to assist in the work, relieving Rand and Jitibi of much detail.

Pacha Bata came, after three days, but instead of bringing three of his sanitary squads, he had six, and reported that more wanted to come. Evidently the rumors spreading over Purac as to the project, were favorable.

Rand was glad to have the six scouts, for south of the camp there was a swamp in which anopheles and culex mosquitoes bred in numbers. The former were malaria carriers, the latter -- Rand did not know what disease they carried, but it was sufficient that they carried ravenous appetites. A small ditch drained the swamp water, and with the hunt on for hollow trees, pitcher plants, and other breeding places, the days of the mosquitoes were numbered.

The workmen made good progress with the clearing. The procedure was to cut all small brush first, then the large trees, from which all branches were cut -- the jungle system of clearing. When the brush had dried out, a fire was started; and as soon as the ashes cooled, the planters went over the area with sharp sticks and punched holes into which were dropped grains of corn. Later banana shoots and other permanent plants were set in.

Rand made a trip to the Jichis, the point where the men were lifted up and let off the pampa. Here he constructed windlasses where two men could lift up a man from below, where formerly half a dozen had been required.

Rand was elated with his progress and his notes to Shuyani were enthusiastic. Bunco thrived in his home in front of the building. He did not have to lie awake nights to waylay rats, for once a week one was dropped beside him; and although he took his meals regularly, he never welcomed visitors. The moment a shadow appeared above his hole, he would draw back his head, his tongue playing like flashes of lightening, while he regarded the disturber with shiny eyes.

Shuyani sent Rand a note almost every day and sometimes she sent flowers. Once he opened a package which he supposed was from her for there was the odor of jasmines. With the opening a crude wooden spring threw brown powder, but fortunately not into his face. However, he took precaution after that. How did Matiyero know of the jasmines? Perhaps Nucui had told him, Rand concluded.

Rand puzzled over the powders more than any other factor. Unable to secure another sample, he had not been able to conduct further experiments as to its lethal power or to identify its source. Once he thought he had perhaps found its origin in the pollen grains of the muca plant, but it did not have the characteristic odor. Nor could the Auca Ambi secure the quantity used from this source. Whatever the powders were, there must be abundance of raw material.

He also had Jitibi examine some of the pollen grains under the microscope and the latter pronounced them different from the mystic powders.

The muca plant Rand experimented with time and again. Its tea placed in food or drink always produced death within a short time. There were rats in abundance to experiment upon. It was a powerful alkaloid and Rand was now certain it had been placed in some of the chicha the men drank at Ubini the day the gold was cast into the pit.

The irritant incorporated in the curare darts was not snake venom, Rand felt quite sure of that. The Puracians, like all South American savages, regarded snakes as possessed with supernatural powers and let them severely alone. The snake charmer of the Orient does not exist among them, This was a fortunate circumstance for otherwise Bunco would not have enjoyed the prestige he now had.

Jitibi, who had mastered his fear of the Auca Ambi, moved into the building with Rand and assisted in the experiments. Rand also instructed Jitibi in the care of wounds and other sanitary measures, until the latter's skill in protecting the health of the colony became more famous over the pampa than was that of the Auca Ambi.

The workmen came upon some old ruins in the center of the jungle; no one had ever known they existed, therefore, Rand decided their building was contemporary with the arrival of Puca Uma.

One morning Jitibi called to Rand excitedly. Going to the door he saw Jitibi staring into the hole in which Bunco had lived. He ran quickly to Jitibi's side and to his surprise saw instead of the green mottled Bunco, a grayish black snake lying contentedly on the leaves with the appearance of being well fed.

Sometime during the night a Mussurama, the big harmless snake that preys upon smaller ones, poisonous or non-poisonous, had wandered into Bunco's quarters and Bunco had gone the way of life in the jungle. Rand lifted the big fellow out of the hole and let him go his way. The news of Bunco's finish was carried to Churic.

CHAPTER 19

Puca Uma The Second

The clearing of Ushcu was complete and only a few men were now employed. Rand had begun laying out a village for a permanent settlement.

One morning a few days later Rand was busy overseeing the landscape plantings of the new townsite of Ubini, when a runner brought a message from Chinawa for Rand and all his helpers to come to Churic at once. He told his boy to pack his belongings and follow, while Rand, himself, started at once at the head of his faithful workers. He wondered at the time why the trocan had not been used to send the summons.

Arriving at the outskirts of Churic, Rand could see he was once more the center of interest, as the people rushed to the roadside to see him pass. The male population was armed and in military dress, as on the occasion of Rand's first reception at Churic. This martial dress Rand had almost forgotten in the peaceful days of the last few weeks. Apparently some crisis was at hand.

Rand hurried towards Chinawa's house. The latter, in his official garb was standing in front of the house, impatiently waiting for him. Without a word he took Rand by the arm and led him inside the building. Whether the action was authoritative or otherwise, Rand could not decide. A military guard stood at the doorway. There was no doubt the procedure was to be legal.

Most of the councilors were within the patio. Rand wondered why he was not conducted to the official council building where he was first received by the council instead of within the grounds of Chinawa's house, since the occasion seemed to be official. Chinawa, however, conducted him into his own private quarters. They were followed by Pacha Bata and Jitibi only.

Rand experienced a feeling of relief as he observed it was to be a meeting of the inner council. When within Chinawa's rooms Rand greeted his friends with sincere affection. What a relief was their friendly attitude after the threatening looks from the crowd outside. He was disappointed, however, at not finding Shuyani awaiting him in the chamber. He turned to the door leading to the family wing. He was happy with the anticipation of seeing her appear in the doorway, smiling at him in her timid manner. He had never seen her since he had written her of his love. But her daily notes, though characteristically modest, told him his love was reciprocated.

When she did not appear as he had expected, he turned to his companions for an explanation. He spoke her name inquiringly. The agony in Chinawa's face told of tragedy. Then he waved his hand toward Auca Ambi and said, "Matiyero."

The world turned dark and Rand felt himself falling. Chinawa's friendly pat on the shoulder roused him out of the abyss of hopelessness into which he had momentarily dropped. His dejection touched the hearts of his three companions.

Chinawa made Rand understand that soon after the report of Bunco's death had reached Churic, Matiyero had demanded that Rand be put to death. The council had objected, then Shuyani had been seized and taken to Auca Ambi. Purac was now on the verge of civil war. Rand asked impatiently why he had not been summoned by the trocan, but was told that neither faction dared use the trocan since they did not dare let the enemy know what was going on. Chinawa had sent a messenger south and the trocan and runners would spread the news from there.

"When did the Auca Ambi take Shuyani," Rand asked, "and why?" He was told that she was taken the evening before and that the reason given by Matiyero was that Shuyani was a dangerous individual because of her repeated intrusion into masculine affairs, such conduct was not to be tolerated by the Auca Ambi. Women, he said, were supposed to till the soil and attend to the wants of man, but nothing more.

At this time there was a pounding on the door and Chinawa called that he did not want to be disturbed. However, the messenger shouted that Matiyero had ordered the Guaquamayo regiment inside the Auca Ambi and the commander wanted to know if he should comply with this demand. Rand saw the look on Chinawa's face that he had learned meant determination.

"Tzama," --No," -- thundered Chinawa as he bolted from the room, almost knocking Pacha Bata down, and throwing the door wide open as he rushed into the open.

Pacha Bata followed Chinawa, and Rand and Jitibi were left alone. The two friends stared into each others eyes for a fleeting moment. There was no need of words. Intimate association for the past few weeks had taught them to know each other. As if by instinct, they both turned and started after Chinawa and Pacha Bata. A slight sound caused them to turn. Maiboya was standing in the doorway; she handed Rand a small section of palm leaf torn from one of the common floor mats, on this was written "coraje" -- courage." There was no need of a signature.

When Rand and Jitibi arrived on the plaza everything was in confusion. The varied military units were present, but there was little semblance of order. Apparently no authorized commander was in charge, most of the crowd was in front of the Auca Ambi.

Rand could see Chinawa making his way through the throng. He mounted the steps of the Auca Ambi, said something to Matiyero, then turned and addressed the gathering in front, in a dictatorial manner. He waved his arms as a signal for them to disperse which they did, then Chinawa hurried back to the plaza where he ordered the commanders to form the various units into military order. These instructions the commanders endeavored to carry out, but the soldiers would not stay in line, each being more interested in argument than military formation. No sooner would a line be formed than they would be broken up in the endeavor to listen to some argument between supporters of the two sides.

The council ceased to function as a unit -- in fact it ceased to function at all. Chinawa assumed all responsibility and asked for advice from no one.

A messenger came running to Chinawa who hurried to the work shop where bows and arrows were made. Several carriers from the Auca Ambi had their arms full of these weapons and were starting back to the Auca Ambi. Chinawa commanded the weapons returned to the arsenal. The fact that Matiyero had ordered Guaquamayo regiment which was armed with bows into the Auca Ambi, then his attempt to secure bows and arrows from the work shop showed that Matiyero expected war and wanted bows inside the Auca

Ambi, since the guards in Auca Ambi were armed only with lances which are good weapons for close fighting, but useless against attackers outside the building.

Off to the south could be heard a trocan pounding out a message -- the first to be heard, regardless of all the excitement. Soon after the trocan in the south had started, the one in the Auca Ambi began sounding. But almost instantly there was the booming of some half a dozen of the Churic stations and the interference drowned out the Auca Ambi message while the one in the south carried on.

Matiyero was unable to get a message on the air. If the trocan within the Auca Ambi stopped the other did the same, but the moment the Auca Ambi instrument started to spread Matiyero's propaganda, the others began again.

Matiyero appeared in front of the Auca Ambi and again ordered the Guaquamayos inside. Many of the soldiers began slowly to go in that direction. Chinawa and Rand confronted Matiyero. Matiyero ordered the soldiers inside while Chinawa commanded them to stay out. There was a tense moment as the soldiers hesitated, unable to decide whom to obey. At this moment a cry was heard and Rand recognized the battle cry of the Uturunco and the Ahuas -- the Tigers and the Tapirs -- of Ubini. The Tigers and Tapirs, led by Jitibi, pushed their way through the crowd and lined up on each side of the Auca Ambi doorway.

Jitibi said anyone could go inside who wanted to, but they must leave their arms outside. Then he turned to Matiyero and advised him not to try using any blow gun darts on any of his, Jitibi's men; that the days of the sacred hornets were past.

Matiyero glared at Jitibi then turned to go inside. Rand wanted to storm the place, but Matiyero informed him that if a single man crossed the threshold of the Auca Ambi Shuyani would be put to death instantly. This was why they had taken Shuyani into the Auca Ambi.

"If Shuyani is molested not an inmate of Auca Ambi will be spared," Rand shouted after Matiyero who only laughed and disappeared inside.

Chinawa again ordered those in front of the Auca Ambi to depart and they did so. There were many wild rumors and when Chinawa asked the council to assist him in maintaining discipline the council again refused to do so.

Some were openly in favor of making peace with the Auca Ambi even to delivering Rand into the hands of Matiyero. Chinawa stood alone before them and, with eyes blazing, told them that never would he, Chinawa concede a single point to the Auca Ambi. That if the council wanted to make peace with Matiyero the first act must be the removal of himself as chief of the council. This demand was given in such a dramatic fashion that not a councilman had the courage to suggest they do so.

About this time someone came from the Auca Ambi and said Matiyero had promised his constituency within the building that he would send evil spirits among the populace of Churic and the rebellious would be slain right and left, that all Churic would be wiped out if they did not abandon open rebellion against the Auca Ambi.

Consternation swept Churic with the spread of the threat. Many of the older people implored Chinawa to spare them the wrath of the spirits. Let them live in peace with the Auca Ambi as was the custom.

Jitibi still held his guard at the doorway of Auca Ambi and permitted no one with arms to enter. When Rand heard Matiyero's threat he made his way alone to Jitibi and they held a whispered conversation. If Matiyero planned wholesale death Rand felt sure he knew how he would attempt it, for he had observed that water carriers were busy carrying water inside the Auca Ambi as if preparing for a siege.

After Rand had departed, Jitibi maintained his guard on the steps and observed everyone that passed. The water carriers came and went as before. After half an hour's vigilance Jitibi left his guards in charge of one of the members and followed two water carriers. When they passed in front of Chinawa's house Jitibi commanded them to go inside. With a glance at Jitibi's lance they obeyed.

The two carriers were taken before Chinawa who examined the contents of their water ollas. Each olla contained a cloth bag which was full of mashed muca leaves, also a weight to sink the bags, when cast into the spring. Rand had instructed Jitibi to watch for water carriers who had ollas loaded, instead of empty ones, when going to the spring. There was not much chance to kill all those rebellious towards the Auca Ambi, but had the contents of those ollas been dumped into the spring there would have been enough casualties to start a stampede in Matiyero's favor.

The ollas of poison were stored in the gold room and the carriers given similar ollas which contained only water, and were told to go on their way and that Matiyero would not be told of their being detained. The carriers, of course, did not know what they were doing. Matiyero had told them they were to empty the ollas into the spring when no one was looking, then to fill their vessels and return as usual, but to report to him without fail upon their return.

The poor water carriers never knew of the substitution in their cargoes. They were surprised when they returned to Auca Ambi to have Matiyero take the ollas, pour the water out and destroy the ollas. There had been no more water carriers sent out of the Auca Ambi after those two departed.

Immediately after this Matiyero began the mysterious rites that were to send the evil spirits to slay the rebellious. The tragic suspense that had held the crowd that day at Ushcu now hovered over all Churic. Chinawa realized that something must be done to stem the crisis, but what could he do? Without knowing what to do or say, he began to address the crowds. He told them there had been no evil spirits at Ushcu, but that the Auca Ambi had cast men into the pit for no reason other than because the people had rebelled at giving their daughters to the medicine men. Rand could see Chinawa was floundering along, hoping against hope. He could not prevail long. If death should come to a single Puracian now, all would be lost. Very likely Matiyero had other sources of poisoning out, too, which had not been intercepted.

Rushing to his room Rand hastily tore open his bag and emptied the permanganate crystals into his handkerchief. As he made his way to the spring he tied a small rock with the crystals and threw the package into the spring. Hurriedly he returned to where Chinawa was still holding the crowd against the panic.

Then Rand addressed the crowd. He told them that he, Rand, was the greatest medicine man in the world. That it was true their people had been cast into Ushcu without cause and that they, the victims, had appealed to him to save their brethren from the cruel fate and to prove it their blood would darken the waters of the spring as long as Matiyero defied Chinawa and the supreme council.

"If you don't believe me go look at the water," he finished.

The crowd surged toward the spring and almost immediately there was a cry of , "Monamai Ico! Monamai Ico!"

-- "He speaks true." Then there was a general stampede, everybody trying to reach the spring to see the water. Even Rand accompanied Chinawa with members of the council to look. Rand was almost ready to laugh at the dramatic effect, but his heart sank again at the thought of Shuyani. How empty was the victory as long as she was in the hands of that inhuman monster.

The sun was sinking low and Rand could not help but regard the nightfall with apprehension. Matiyero had supplied his garrison with all the intoxicating beverage they wanted and there were wild orgies within the quarters. He had sent out his spies to report on conditions in the village, for as yet not a death had been reported to confirm the Auca Ambi's predictions. Matiyero was still ignorant of the failure of the water carriers to execute his orders, and he had no doubt there would be many victims within the village shortly and that his position would again be secure.

With the spring darkened by the blood of victims cast into the earth charged against the Auca Ambi, Chinawa considered the time opportune for a parley to save Shuyani. Accordingly he went to the Auca Ambi and demanded a conference with Matiyero. The latter met him at the entrance and conducted him to the reception porch just within the enclosure. Matiyero refused to recede from the original demands, other than that he would exchange Shuyani for Rand.

Chinawa, seeing there was no chance of success, was leaving the Auca Ambi. In the hallway he paused and in a loud voice, for the benefit of all the Auca Ambi garrison, announced that anyone who wished a pardon for treason against the supreme council would be forgiven if they would leave the building and cease to identify themselves with the Auca Ambi.

Of course Matiyero was furious and demanded the Auca Ambi guards to slay Chinawa. Jitibi and his sentinels at the doorway were forced to protect Chinawa with their lances.

Shaking with rage, Matiyero grabbed something from a nearby shelf and hurled it at Chinawa. The latter threw up his arm to guard off the object and it hit the arm that was shielding the body, then fell to the floor. Chinawa picked up the object and passed out the doorway where he met Rand.

Chinawa's arm was bleeding from half a dozen lacerations while inspection revealed eight or ten dark thorns imbedded in the flesh. The object Matiyero had used was about the size of an orange having a hard center with a wax surface. There were dozens of short palm thorns set into the wax, the points projecting in all directions. These palm thorns have needle-like points, but are brittle, and the points always break off when they stick into the flesh. A small short vine was attached to use when handling the weapon. Each of the thorns were coated with a black dry tar-like substance which both Rand and Chinawa recognized as curare poison.

Chinawa's face bleached when he understood what had happened. He was punctured in several places with the curare, blow gun poison, thorns and they were broken off in the flesh with no chance of removal before the blood had taken up the poison.

Rand called for Jitibi to help and together they carried Chinawa to his house as quickly as possible. Walking would have excited blood movement and this Rand wanted to avoid. They laid him carefully on a seat in the patio. Rand began frantically to split the flesh near each thorn and to remove it with his tweezers. It was too late, he realized, for the warm blood had softened the poison and each thorn came out clean, the friction of removal causing the poison to be left in the wound. Chinawa looked at the first thorn removed and shook his head.

"It's no use now," he said, "It is too late."

However, Rand continued to remove the thorns in a frantic hope of removing some of the poison. Chinawa began giving final instructions to his family. Rand had the thorns all out before the poison had begun to arrest Chinawa's breathing. When this started Rand stretched the victim out and started artificial respiration. Chinawa objected to being annoyed and asked to be left to die in peace, but Rand continued the work.

Pacha Bata came and stroked his friend and co-worker affectionately and bade him good-by. Rand worked desperately with Chinawa and had Jitibi order warm wraps to keep up the body temperature. The work was tiring and Rand asked some of the onlookers to assist and when they had acquired the movements Rand devoted his time to checking on Chinawa's reactions to the treatment. The latter's pulse became weak, but later grew stronger. When assured of this Rand announced that the victim would soon be out of danger. An incredible stare from his helpers was the only response to this information. Nevertheless, in a few moments Chinawa said he felt better and although the improvement was gradual, it was sure.

Rand had insisted Chinawa drink enormous quantities of water. As the sun sank in the west, Chinawa was able to walk again. The stranger's magic had triumphed over the Auca Ambi. But the victory was a sad one for Rand. He instructed his helpers to watch Chinawa, to keep him in the open air, and to call if there was any indication of a relapse. Then with a vacant stare he stumbled into the garden.

"Shuyani!" I can save them all but you," he moaned.

A moment later another crushing report was brought to Rand. Pacha Bata, he was told, had deserted and gone to the enemy. The vigilance of Jitibi's guards had been relaxed while they were working with Chinawa and Pacha Bata and twelve men, all armed, had passed inside and joined the Auca Ambi. And what made the information even more cruel was that most of those who went with Pacha Bata were staunch supporters of Rand, some who voluntarily served the entire period at Ushcu with him.

Pacha Bata had been acting queer all day, Rand remembered. Since their first meeting early in the day, he had avoided Rand, going here and there talking with first one then another, but always going elsewhere at Rand's approach. No doubt the sight of Chinawa being stricken had been too much for Pacha Bata. He would make his peace with the Auca Ambi while he could.

The darkness of the tropical night coming on was no deeper than Rand's remorse. He had thoughtlessly promised that the spring water would remain red with the blood of Matiyero's past victims until retribution was paid by the Auca Ambi. How foolish that promise. Even now the water would be clearing, tomorrow not a trace of the stain would remain. Now that it was too late, he realized he had staked all on the day's events, and had lost. Night with its eerie shadows would cow the superstitious natives into quiescence until morning came with its stimulating light.

How woefully he had failed! Even if he could stimulate the native courage into attack upon the Auca Ambi at daylight, the very first move would be Shuyani's death knell. With Shuyani gone, what had he to fight for? Nothing, but a bleak life among these people. Every nook on Purac was associated with their friendship.

Ah, friendship! This platonic term had long ceased to express his feelings toward Shuyani. She represented the warm glow of love that had transformed this jungle retreat into a garden of Eden. She and she alone was all that remained to him in common with the world outside. Together they would be confined physically in their jungle prison while mentally they could wander afar. True Shuyani had not seen the world as he had, yet she was educated and had a yardstick by which she could measure his descriptions. She was of that adventurous stock who are the vanguard in frontier movements, be it in the jungle or on the plains. In prosperity their children are sent back to civilization for education, in adversity they adjust their lives to environments.

He returned to where Chinawa was reclining in the patio, but the latter's look of gratitude could not alleviate his dejection. Then someone hurried in and thrust a piece of paper into his hand. Mechanically he unfolded it and read:

"Pacha Bata and his brave band are with me. I am safe. Shuyani."

Rand read the message over twice before its meaning dawned upon him. Crushing the paper into his clenched fists he jumped up and shouted the glad tidings. "Shuyani is safe. Pacha Bata is with her."

But the news did not surprise Chinawa. "All day," he told Rand, "Pacha Bata has been selecting volunteers whom he could trust and who were willing to defy the Auca Ambi for this purpose. They will be barricaded in a room with Shuyani. Now we can storm the Auca Ambi."

Investigation, however, disclosed the fact that the only entrance to Auca Ambi was being blocked. The heavy doors which swung in were being reinforced by big timbers and rocks piled inside.

"A ram will do the work," Rand decided. "I must have three long, heavy poles for a tripod, heavy poles like the ones in the roof."

Almost instantly men were on the roof of the council shed ripping loose three of the heavy poles about twenty feet long, which Rand had designated. Other men Rand sent in search of a small log which would take at least fifteen men to carry. Never had his instructions been carried out faster.

The three poles he had tied together at one end for the tripod, a rope hanging down from this supported the heavy log which was to serve as a ram. The window of Shuyani's room was pointed out to him as they moved toward the Auca Ambi. Rand called to Shuyani and she answered, confirming her location.

"Stand away from the wall," he advised, "and we shall soon have you out."

For sometime past the trocans had been sending messages. There were shouts now from the south. They were calls of the Tiger and Tapirs, the co-workers of Ushcu. From the outlying villages, like the flood of a mountain's stream, the Puracians poured in from the south. There was a cry in the distance:

"Yamapain Puca Uma Rabue." -- To the help of Puca Uma the Second."

Others took up the cry. Soon Huipuco stood beside Rand. Rand smiled a welcome, then continued with his work. The tripod was set up beneath Shuyani's window. The heavy log was suspended near its center about breast high to a man. A cry from the far side of the buildings was followed by a glow, as a dozen arrows, the shaft of each carrying a fire brand pierced the thatched roof of the north wing.

At the same time men were swinging the heavy log back and forth, bringing its end against the stone wall directly under Shuyani's window. Almost with the first blow the wall began to give and a few strokes caved it in.

Before the men could be stopped a hole as large as a doorway was broken into the wall, then frenzied hands tore at the loose stones. When Rand at last got his excited workers to desist he reached into the breach and Shuyani joyfully seized his hand.

No one knew what followed. Rand embraced Pacha Bata, he never knew how many times. He wanted to embrace everyone he saw but Shuyani was in his arms and he carried her all the way to Chinawa's house where the entire household was standing out in front watching the conflagration, and waiting for Shuyani.

In the meantime the fire lit up the whole village as the roof of the Auca Ambi was consumed. Outside of Auca Ambi all was joy and rejoicing, but inside was tragedy. The inmates were told of all that had taken place outside. Not a man had fallen victim to the evil spirits as Matiyero had promised. The stranger had even cured Chinawa of the curare poison. Then had come the hoards of Puracians from the south and the cry, "Yamapain Puca Uma Rabue."

Drunk as were those inside, they knew the magic of Matiyero had failed. Yet magic was everything to them. Now it was the stranger's magic that reigned.

No one ever knew, or was asked, who was responsible for Matiyero's death. He had lived by superstition and by the same means he died. His body was found in one of the few rooms that had combustible material enough for the fire to follow down from the roof above. But his death was not from fire. There were a score of lance wounds in his body.

The end had come with a suddenness that had stunned the villagers of Churic. Only the group at Chinawa's patio understood in full what had occurred. Shuyani told of how two Auca Ambi guards had been stationed at the door of her prison room with lances ready to slay her in retaliation for any attack upon the building. Of how late in the day she had heard Pacha Bata's voice and soon after heard a thump at her door as Pacha Bata overpowered the guards there; then Pacha Bata and his band had rushed into her room, shut the door and defied the Auca Ambi inmates to attempt entrance. Of the commotion that followed as those in the Auca Ambi made frantic efforts to block the front doorway against the assault they knew was inevitable.

Rand tried to apologize to Pacha Bata for suspecting treachery in the latter's acts which subsequent events had proven the most loyal, courageous and devoted.

"That is nothing," Pacha Bata assured him. "I, too, talked of you in a shameful manner today."

"When?" inquired Rand.

"All day," Pacha Bata replied, "I took your Ushcu friends aside and told them what a cheat and fraud you were. If they said nothing, I had no use for them, but if they told me I was an old fogie and an ungrateful liar, I knew they would be useful. And they were," he added with a sly smile.

"What did Matiyero have to say to you?" Rand asked.

"He wanted to know if the spring was really dark with blood and if the people could drink the water. I could see his chagrin when I told him no one would think of drinking the water," answered Pacha Bata.

"Then I asked him what he had done with Shuyani and he pointed out the guards at her door and said, "Just wait until I get my hands on that stranger and then I shall attend to both of them."

249

"One of my men then gave a signal to Jitibi's door guards who created a commotion. Those inside the Auca Ambi were attracted to the door, so we went into Shuyani's room without any trouble.

"Matiyero threatened to destroy all of us with the magic powders if we did not come out, but we each had a damp cloth to go over our faces, also one for Shuyani. We donned these, but we saw nothing of the powder. I wonder why?"

Rand could offer no explanation as to why the powders were not used.

"Was that all?" Rand asked.

"No, I told Matiyero that if he wanted us he could place his mouth on the door and draw us out like he removed pain from the body," Pacha Bata concluded with a chuckle.

CHAPTER 20

Facts, Fables, or Rumors

An Englishman, Mr. Charles Stanfield, who had designed an airplane motor, was out to show the world what he could do. He crossed the Atlantic by easy stages and reached Para, Brazil. From here he proposed to cross the world's greatest jungle, the Amazon basin.

Leaving Para at daybreak, he planned to make the Massisea landing field on the Ucayali river in Peru within that same day. This feat he accomplished but he surprised the official at the Massisea field by asking what landing field was some distance east.

He was assured there was no landing field east of Massisea. However, Mr. Stanfield was just as sure there was one. He had seen it to his left, had swung around and flown directly over it and would have landed, but the facilities looked rather crude; so he had pushed on to his destination. The airport was there, for he had read upon it, "AIRPORT", in box car letters.

No one took Mr. Stanfield seriously. The various governments on whose land the lettering could have been located pointed out that their official language was either Spanish or Portuguese, and landings within their domains would be marked in the official language, until some international system had been adopted.

The newspapers throughout the world contained pointed paragraphs in the joke columns. Some English paper wanted to know if Mr. Stanfield had seen any golf course where one could stop off and get a bit of practice. Argentine, whose polo team was like that ancient warrior looking for other worlds to conquer, wanted to know if by any chance any polo fields had been seen. Papers in the United States pined for the Brazilian hospitality that must have preceded Mr. Stanfield's take-off.

In a few days the incident was forgotten by everyone, except Augusto Delgado, one of the young pilots on the Iquitos Massisea hydroplane end. Augusto was in Massisea when Mr. Stanfield arrived and knew the latter had been sincere as to what he had seen.

Some two weeks later, Augusto was lying over at Massisea. He had worked on his engine all forenoon, and in the afternoon he decided to try it out.

Up the river he went. The engine was running perfectly. Over to the east he swung, and after flying in this direction for sometime, he saw the escarpment of Pampa Diablo standing out. Toward this he flew. And there, indeed, glaring upon a green field below, were the white letters, "AIRPORT."

Augusto circled low. There was a long narrow opening where a plane could alight, but it must have wheels, while Augusto's ship was equipped with pontoons. He circled the place time and again. He could see people below and real houses, not the jungle shacks.

On a slip of paper he wrote, "I shall return tomorrow and visit you. Delgado." Flying low he dropped this in the plaza, then back he went to Massisea. He was elated at his discovery.

He asked for a land plane for the next day, and was almost heartbroken when told there was none available. There was a party of tourists passing over the line for Iquitos and this party

252

had to get the Amazon river boat the next week. It would tax the line to capacity to handle the passengers.

After the excitement of her rescue had subsided, Shuyani and Rand were seated in the garden where she was telling her story, as she snuggled contentedly in his arms.

"You see it was like this," she began. "You told me that if some trees were cut on the athletic field, an airplane could land there; so I got Chinawa to order the trees cut. I had seen airplanes in the book you had. There was the word, 'AIRPORT' on one of the buildings. I made those letters by using bolts of new cloth. For days nothing happened, then one day a plane passed over. It circled once and went on. I had begun to lose heart. Then yesterday another plane came. It came very low and dropped this note. Chinawa got it, but Maiboya slipped it to me. But he did not return. Do you think he will come tomorrow?" she asked hopefully.

"I presume he will," Rand replied, carefully suppressing any appearance of excitement.

"Matiyero was very angry," Shuyani continued, "and told Chinawa the cloth was the cause of the planes coming. He gave orders that no more clothes be spread on the ground as it caused planes to come. Could it have been your friend who brought you here?" she asked.

"No, I fear not," Rand replied. "His name is not Delgado. However, if anybody comes here with a plane, we shall go away with him, you and I, out into the world of happiness. Would you like that?" he asked.

She was too happy to reply, but he needed no answer.

The M. L. A. personnel at Baña were at dinner. A messenger came in. "Here is the official inquiry to the

253

Commandante, "Ask pilots at Baña if any of them have ever flown over Pampa Diablo region?"

Alberto Vargas dropped his fork at the question, but hurriedly picked it up and continued the meal in silence. What should he do and why the inquiry? Alberto had only returned that afternoon from a hunting trip in the jungle and had not heard of Mr. Stanfield's report. The messenger was gone before he had reached any conclusion.

An hour later Alberto and two others were sitting in the club house. The radio was tuned in on a Lima station. News flashes were coming in.

"Pilot Augusto Delgado of the Iquitos San Ramon line flew east from Massisea yesterday in the Pampa Diablo region. He confirmed the report of Mr. Stanfield some two weeks ago as to the existence of a landing field in that region. Pilot Delgado flew over the site several times and would have lighted, but he was flying a hydroplane. He reports the word, "AIRPORT" just as did Mr. Stanfield. The officials will investigate the matter soon."

Alberto stared at the radio. Other news came in, but he did not hear it. The others told him of the Stanfield report.

Going to his plane, he began preparing it for the morrow. He had it turned and headed out of the hangar, all ready to go. "The facilities looked rather crude," Alberto mused, "I suspect they are. I shall take a couple of cases of gas along." These he ordered placed in the plane. At three A.M. Bana was startled by the roar of a plane as Alberto took off.

He was over Pampa Diablo at daylight. Back and forth he flew, but could see nothing of the airfield reported there. When the sun came up, he passed over the northern rim. There were a village and people.

He flew low and saw one person in the crowd who wore trousers. He could even recognize Rand. After this discovery, Alberto did not look for any more airports, he was looking for a place to land. The lane between the trees was the only place, and here he landed.

The plane came down and skipped along to almost in front of Chinawa's house before it came to rest, not twenty yards from where Rand stood. In fact Rand, knowing how the plane would have to land, had kept the pathway clear of people. The propellor was still turning over as the crowd gathered around, wide eyed with wonder.

One look at the Puracians and then Alberto was on the ground and the two friends were greeting each other as though it had been years since they had parted. When Alberto had had time to observe the Puracians, he turned to Rand inquiringly.

Rand looked at his friends startled expression and said, "Yes, this is Pampa Diablo."

Then he conducted him before Chinawa who's curiosity at the plane's visit had caused the latter to forget executive dignity and to come forward with the eagerness of a boy.

"This is my friend who brought me to Purac," Rand said, addressing Chinawa in Puracian language. The latter welcomed Alberto cordially, regardless of the law of Puca Uma in reference to visitors.

Then Alberto was introduced to Shuyani. Rand did not know her last name.

"Torres," she said.

"I had an uncle by that name," Alberto said, as he looked at her wonderingly. "Santiago Torres. He lived on the Apurimac, then went to the Urubamba some years ago; I have heard nothing from him since."

"He is dead now," Shuyani said slowly. "He was my father." She looked at Alberto, a look of expectation in her face.

"Of course," Alberto exclaimed, grasping her hand, "now I can see it is you Shuyani. Rand, you have found my lost cousin."

As the natives crowded around the plane, Rand took a stick and drew a circular line on the ground around the plane. "This line," he told them, "must not be passed."

Alberto was skeptical as to this protective measure, but it proved its worth for not a Puracian passed its boundary.

While at breakfast Rand gave Alberto a brief sketch of Puca Uma's history as handed down by the Puracians, ending the narrative with a description of the house of records and its contents. At the mention of records actually existing, Alberto's interest increased immensely. He had listened to many legends somewhat similar, none of which could be proven, but here was apparently a story with substantial evidence.

When breakfast was over, the two friends, accompanied by a group of Puracians, went at once to the house of records. When Alberto had verified the fact that the history went back 551 years, he turned to Rand with sparkling eyes, said, "This actually establishes the coming of Puca Uma before Columbus. Have you thought what a sensation this will create in the outside world?"

Rand could not repress a smile. Had he ever thought!

"Yes, I have," he said with emphasis. "But my problem was not, 'What did it mean?' but 'How to make it known.'"

From the house of records, the party proceeded to the Auca Ambi. The burning of the thatched roof off the Auca Ambi buildings had done but little damage. Matiyero had been the only one lost, the others having gone to various houses in the village after the conflict was over.

The adult population of Churic had remained at a distance, but not so with the youngsters who were finding many strange toys among the abandoned buildings. The party went to the laboratory, but the boys had depleted its stock. All the miniature blow guns were gone. Chinawa at once forbade the children using them since the darts were dangerous.

Next to the laboratory was a room that had not been opened. Some members of the Auca Ambi who had returned said it was Matiyero's secret room. No one was permitted to enter it. Forcing the door Rand cautiously entered. The roof gone, the light from above flooded the floor which was covered with ashes.

On a table were piles of cones containing the mysterious powder. An olla filled with the powder stood on a table while a screen over a pot, loaded with the same material, was set over a charcoal furnace. In a corner on the floor was a pile of what Rand knew was the material from which the magic powders were made. He looked at this for a moment then laughed outright. The material was common puff ball fungi.

The pot the spores were steamed over contained a plant with a pungent odor, this was what had given the powder its characteristic odor, and was, no doubt, used to prevent identification. The lens proved the fungi spores and the mysterious powder to be identical.

The Puracians laughed and enjoyed the joke with Rand. At this time Shuyani and Maiboya appeared and Rand explained the discovery to them.

"Oh," Shuyani exclaimed, "Matiyero, too, had bunco!"

Then Pacha Bata became serious and said, "But it killed the monkey."

"That's true," admitted Rand. "I wonder if we laughed too soon."

"I think not," said Shuyani, "for Maiboya's little brother just showed us one of the guns and said he had had one once before that he had found in the stranger's room. He said he used it to shoot a monkey that he saw in the window of the gold room, but Matiyero saw him and took the gun away from him."

There was one fire swept room that evidently contained several articles of a combustible nature. Among the debris someone dug up a rust eaten sword, damaged beyond hope of identification.

"That," Rand announced "was the sharp stick with which Puca Uma could sever a head at one blow."

This was the first positive evidence connecting Puca Uma with the outside world. Chinawa took charge of the weapon and promised it would be given the care it deserved. As the group turned to go, Jitibi observed some of the Puracians looking at a small section of burned cloth. "There is nothing artistic about the design," they said. Jitibi gave the cloth a casual glance, then a startled exclamation escaped him. Hastily he took the cloth to Rand who became electrified with interest for the faded characters on the charred cloth were English script.

"Where did it come from?" Rand demanded.

Someone, it seemed, had fond an old charred bamboo cylinder and inside was this cloth folded and rolled. The fire had consumed most of it. A small section had the following fragmentary message in English:

"secretly by Sir Walter Raleigh
on the Orinoko to prepare for colonization

of that paradise of birds and beasts, the
Indians to protect themselves from
treasure seekers the scourge of

to Purac far from the accursed Manoa.
But I fear Sir Walter will never
find me here after all these
miles of hostile jungles."

Nothing more was legible. Rand translated what he read for Alberto and Shuyani.

"What do you make of it?" Alberto asked.

"Puca Uma was an Englishman and came to the Orinoca with Sir Walter Raleigh in 1595," Rand answered.

Then why do the records go back before the time of Columbus," Shuyani inquired.

"That," Rand answered, "can be charged to the Auca Ambi. Why they falsified the records, I cannot say other than that it was for some means to create confusion. Possibly to confine information to their keeping. It was easy to falsify the records by filing another notch, while one once cut could not be erased.

"Which would explain a lot if jackknives were invented about the time vital statistics was busy with Methusela" Alberto added.

Shuyani was shocked at her cousin's sacrilegious flippancy. "But the Orinoca is far from here," she said.

"Quite true," Rand admitted, "but the fearless pioneers of those days went every place. Their bones repose in every valley on this continent, while their descendants very likely are the foundations of rumored white Indians found in remote regions."

En-route to the patio Rand's thoughts were on the strange message which had cleared up, in a way, the origin of Puca Uma.

"Paradise of birds and beasts --" This phrase was from Sir Walter Raleigh's journal of his first visit to the Orinoca which proved the authenticity of the document.

"Manoa, the accursed and scourge of treasure seekers --" Why should a follower of Sir Walter Raleigh have a grudge against the seekers of treasures in the New World? Perhaps after all Sir Walter's enthusiasm about El Dorado was camouflage. Did he not feign leprosy in order to gain time in adjusting his affairs?

Out of the hazy past the true history of affairs began to stand out. Sir Walter Raleigh was by circumstance a soldier, but by choice a kind-hearted husbandman to whom a useful plant was more valuable than gold. Never did he exploit the helpless natives and the cruelty practiced upon them by the Conquistadores touched his heart. English colonization and freedom of the poor Indian was Sir Walter's goal. "English artificers might teach the Indian," was Sir Walter's contention. Puca Uma was this type. Sir Walter had secretly selected an intelligent youthful associate who had a kindred disposition and had been secretly left on the Orinoca. This would account for Sir Walter's persistent faith in the country for some place he had a trusty ally working to bring about his colonization plans.

Puca Uma had done wonders at Puric, a Darwin in the jungle. Undoubtedly he had left complete records that would clear up everything, but those documents were destroyed either deliberately or otherwise.

Puca Uma assuredly would leave his story and this message accounted for the absence of any rock carving that would be more endurable. That centuries, instead of years, would pass before his message would be seen he did not foresee. The stick records he had established for the Puracians was a simple method they could understand.

Rand dug into his pocket and brought forth the cloth scraps that connected this genius of the past with history. Dismayed he found a crumbled mass, not a legible word of the message remained. He stopped, hand extended, palm upward. "Look," he exclaimed.

Shuyani grasped the extended hand and made a futile effort to restore the fragments into readable order.

"What a pity," she said sympathetically.

"Pity," Rand cried, "pity does not begin to describe the loss. Do you realize that this is all that is left of what was the most valuable document that ever fell into my hands? Now how am I to prove the history of Puca Uma?"

"That's strange," said Alberto, rolling the decayed mass between his thumb and finger. "Cotton cloth found in the graves on the coast of Peru is in perfect state of preservation, some of it perhaps a thousand years old."

"Which proves that an arid desert's climate has the decided advantage over a tropical rain forest when it comes to preserving historical data," Rand answered. "This country," indicating the Amazon basin with a wide sweep of his hand, "every dale of which has witnessed human drama, but will never its history be known for the tropical jungle smothers the footsteps of man, leaving no more trace than the wake of a passing vessel over an uncharted sea.

"Chance gave us the priceless document which I have carelessly destroyed by cramming it in my pocket as I would a worthless paper."

Rand's dejection touched his companions. Even the Puracians who knew nought of the document's importance could tell he was sorely distressed. Something had gone wrong with "leaves that talk" as they had termed writing.

"Never mind," Shuyani said in a consoling manner, "we know what it said."

"Yes we know," Rand replied sadly, "but how are we to convince the world of what we saw? No one will believe a word of it. You have to prove things in these days. Do you know that publicity men are inventing stories like this every day? No one will believe a word of this tale."

"No one?" her words were almost inaudible.

Rand looked into her eyes for a moment then smiled. "No one except -- those who count," he answered with finality. "I was never able to convince the world at large on any question, so now I don't give a whoop. We know and shall not care what others think."

When the party returned the younger set passed into the garden while Chinawa and a few of his intimates stopped in the patio. Jitibi and Maiboya were showing Alberto about. Rand and Shuyani took up the question which confronted them.

"Shall we declare the Auca Ambi abolished forever?" he asked.

"No, indeed," she answered. "The Auca Ambi has too strong a hold upon the people. You can't expect people to abandon the belief of a lifetime over night. Matiyero is gone, but someone will take his place, rest assured of that."

"You are right, Shuyani," he answered. Then after a moment's reflection he continued. "I shall be head of the Auca Ambi myself. Am I not Puca Uma the Second?"

"You?" Shuyani ejaculated in alarm. "You stay here now, since we can go?"

"No, we shall go, but I shall remain head of the Auca Ambi with a threat to return if my orders are not carried out."

"But have you forgotten the law of Puca Uma?"

"No, I have not forgotten, but remember I am Puca Uma the Second."

Rand called a meeting of the council in the presence of all the people.

"You have rightfully called me Puca Uma the Second," he said, "and so I am. The law of Puca Uma, that no one shall leave Purac, was wise when given. If Zara Pacha were to tell you to water your gardens in the dry season it would be good advice, but nothing would be so foolish as to continue to carry water after the rains had begun to fall. Now people travel by air and all the Zachas in the world cannot prevent it. Shortly I shall leave, but I shall come again, if you need me. I have, as you have seen, greater magic than had Matiyero. The Auca Ambi must obey me. This I demand as its head. As Puca Uma the Second I give you a new law: In all things the council is supreme."

"Arise, Council," he commanded, "and stand in the midst of the crowd."

When the council had collected he commanded all to extend their right hand toward the council and repeat:

"In all things the council is supreme."

This he had them say slowly three times.

"Each of you remember this, the law of Puca Uma the Second, and repeat it at all councils, for in protecting the council you protect yourselves."

The people were profoundly impressed with the fetish ceremony and stood in silent veneration until Rand told them to celebrate a feast for this memorable event.

It was with conflicting emotions that Rand and Shuyani prepared for their departure.

"What an ideal life," Alberto remarked as he looked at the happy and contented Puracians.

"Yes indeed," Rand replied. "What shall we do with them?"

"Do with them?" interposed Shuyani. "Is it necessary to do anything with them?'

"That's just it," Rand replied, "with our vaunted civilization we pity the poor savage, but look what civilization did to the South Sea Islanders. Purac is our secret and we shall preserve and protect it. Let them live on in their contented simplicity."